Deathspell

MORE BY CONNOR PETERSON

Books in this Series
Deathspell
Shadowcast

Novellas
Temptation in Neon
Red Ink (2019)

Short Stories
Lost Highway
(Nocturnal Embers, an Anthology)

Writing as P.W. Davies
Follow Him Home
Make Him Tremble
Heart Shaped Fire

Writing as Peter Dawes: Short Stories
All Fall Down
Turn About is Fair Play
(Red Phone Box, a story cycle)

Deathspell

USA TODAY BESTSELLING AUTHOR

CONNOR PETERSON

This book is a work of fiction. Names, characters, places and incidents are products of the author's imagination or are used fictitiously. Any resemblance to actual events or locales or persons, living or dead, is entirely coincidental.

A Crimson Melodies Book

www.crimsonmelodies.com

www.writerofstuff.com

Front Cover Design © 2015 by Crimson Melodies Publishing

Front Cover Image iStock.com/Choreograph

Sign Up for the Author's Mailing List

There's an easy way to get more stories like Deathspell.
Go online and sign up for Connor Peterson's email list to receive the
latest book news, exclusive content,
invitations to author appearances, and more.

writerofstuff.com/mailinglist/

"The one certainty in tiger tracks is:
follow them long enough
and you will eventually arrive at a tiger,
unless the tiger arrives at you first."
- *John Vaillan*

PROLOGUE

The cold had been enough to force men indoors when night fell, but did not yet bear the chill of winter. I recall drifting out of the room we occupied, listless from the tedium of watching my father unpack. Wood creaked beneath my feet, well-worn from the hundreds of travelers who had come and gone from this establishment. My eyes cast downward, I mused on how many of the impressions had been left by us through the years, thoughtful for a boy of fourteen years, or perhaps, too idle to entertain more frivolous notions.

A frown tugged at the corners of my mouth. My hand slid down the bannister, the sound of Father's cough still echoing in my ears after being a constant presence for the last week. The toll of travel had been harder on him as of late, and while his suggestion I fetch us food had been an obvious distraction, I knew better than to argue against it even if we had plenty of trail rations left from our trip. The main hall beneath came into view the further I descended the stairs, until I found myself immersed in a lively crowd.

Fire crackled in the hearth. Men gathered at tables conducted private conversations, sparing me the occasional glance when I meandered past. Oil lamps flickered, casting shadows on the wall and giving the area added warmth. I allowed my gaze to drift from one thing to the next while bypassing the main collection of benches and customers in favor of heading toward a long counter, made from the same wood apparent elsewhere. As the innkeeper looked up, he gave me a polite smile.

Old John is what the regulars called him, and if he possessed any other names I was not aware of them. While he bore less in the way of height than some men, he made up for it in sheer girth, not all of which could be attributed to the size of his belly. In contrast to the lithe young man I had begun growing into, Old John was arguably three times my weight, with arms larger than the size of my waist, or such is how it appeared to me. I exchanged his smile, a request for food dancing across my tongue and about to be birthed if not for the sound of the front doors opening.

I had reached the counter and slid up onto one of the stools as they walked in —two men, both similarly dressed, donned in cloaks dyed crimson with hoods they lowered while lingering by the door. Both men dark-haired and lean, the taller of the two leaned over to whisper in his cohort's ear, garnering a nod in response before he strode toward the back of the building. His shorter compatriot headed in my direction, parting ways in a manner that made me think more of the constables than idle travelers. It only made me more curious, the onset of hunger dismissed as something more interesting stole my attention.

I remained silent as the stranger settled in beside me, falling into that ritual boys observe when adults overshadow them with their more pressing concerns. "Can I help ye with anythin'?" Old John asked, both palms resting on the polished wood, while my eyes fell from the sight of the men out of respect. I folded my hands on my lap to keep them still.

"We're looking for a man. He might've just come into town," he said. I remember thinking this hooded man spoke proper English, just like my father had taught me. It stuck out, as I had become accustomed to the people we met being anything but eloquent, and caused me to take another glance at the crimson cloak. I furrowed my brow at the emblem embroidered on it – a flame within a circle, as though the man bore some stake in nobility. I didn't care for the air that surrounded him, however. Father had told me to avoid men who bore any hint of danger, and rarely did business with them himself.

Which made what passed through his lips next all the more bizarre to hear.

"Richard Hardi," the stranger said, raising an eyebrow at Old John. "Does the name sound familiar?"

At first, I failed to register it. Something told me I should look up and so I did, but it wasn't until Father's name echoed in my mind that I glanced at Old John with a wide-eyed expression. My gaze shot to the stranger when I felt the weight of his stare, and as our eyes met, my throat turned dry, speech stopped up in my throat. Taking a longer, deeper look at the man, I felt the rest of the room melt away, even if only for a moment.

There I sat, all of fourteen years to this man's twenty-four? Twenty-five? It was hard to gage solely by regarding him. He still bore the benefit of youth, but the gravity of his gaze suggested someone much older than he appeared. Father often had people calling after him, especially in the towns we frequented, but his warning replayed in my mind as our stalemate continued. *'Men who make your blood run cold are often doing the devil's work.'* The fact that this man had me frozen with shock, desperate to run away, seemed to add credence to my father's superstition.

"Lad?" The innkeeper cleared his throat, knocking me out of my trance. My sights jumped to the innkeeper in time to see him frown, his expression attempting to admonish while conveying something else. I couldn't quite tell what. "Do you have manners, or do I need to tell your Pa to remind ye of 'em?"

"I..." My voice sounded odd as it passed through my lips. I forced myself to stop and attempt speech again. "I'm s-sorry, sir," I said, fighting the compulsion to glance back at the stranger.

"Aye, as ye should be." John nodded, his eyes narrowing while he reached for a cup. Pouring it full of ale, he thrust it at me and waved me away. "Now, take this up to him and be gone so I can finish business with my other customers."

"Yes, sir," I said on automatic, taking the drink and motioning away with it. My movements all seemed to be directed by a force outside myself, including the compulsion to lower from the stool and walk back in the direction of the stairs. I felt an issuance of protest within the recesses of my mind – I had come downstairs for food, it said, not for ale

– and yet pressed forward on instinct. Both hands clutched onto the cup, as a lifeline and out of fear that I might drop it any moment. Halfway across the room, I chose that moment to turn my head and glance over my shoulder. What I saw defied all understanding.

Old John and the stranger stared at each other, but something was wrong about the expression on the innkeeper's face. His eyes looked panicked, his face turning red like something had lodged in his throat. The cloaked man's lips curled in a twisted grin, his gloved palm pointed upward. He closed his fingers and the invisible assault against John intensified, forcing a gasp from his mouth until a sickening crunch preceded him toppling to the ground.

The mug fell from my hands, its contents splashing across the floor.

My feet scampered for the stairs, hand gripping onto the banister while I raced toward the second floor. In my periphery, I saw the man walk away from the counter and paled when his voice echoed through the dining hall. "He's here," he shouted. "And he's got his whelp with him."

Clenching my eyes shut through the final stairs, I opened them only while rounding the corner and sprinting down the long corridor before me. As I reached the end of the hall, I held out a hand and pushed against the door, slamming it open and forcing it shut just as quickly. Air passed through my lips and into my lungs in gulps, taken and expelled fast enough for me to feel lightheaded.

"Christian?"

The tall, slender man to whom I bore a striking resemblance furrowed his brow at me. Whatever bewildered look must have been on my face, it was enough for Richard Hardi to sober instantly. "Christian, what is it?" he asked. "What's wrong?"

My hands shook as I pushed away from the door and pointed at it. "Father, there's men here. One of them killed Old John," I said. Swallowing down a rush of fear, I tried to compose myself enough to explain. "T-they have red cloaks and the one who killed Old John said your name. I don't know who they are, but they... he... he just killed him. Just by looking at him."

His gaze shot from my face to the door while a short coughing fit assailed him. I watched him process my words, his expression paling.

"God, not now," he said. "Not again." The sound of footfalls in the hallway spurred him into action. He composed himself enough to hobble to the other side of the room, reaching for a chair and sliding it back to barricade the door.

I blinked, bewildered. "Father, what are you doing?"

"We haven't the time for me to explain, Christian. We need to get you out of here."

"I don't understand."

My father ignored me, shuffling to the trunk yet half unpacked. He plucked a linen bag out from inside before he started tossing the remainder of its contents onto the bed. "I want you to get to your brother's house. Do you hear me? Run as fast as you can and tell him what happened. He'll keep you safe."

"What about you?"

My question went unanswered. A change of clothing, length of rope, and my good cloak found their way into the bag before he moved onto the next trunk. I furrowed my brow as he swung it open – it was my father's personal belongings and while he always demanded to keep the trunk with him, he very rarely unpacked it. I fumbled for words while he pulled out a cylindrical case made of bronze, encrusted with gemstones.

He slid it into the sack and tightened the strings to shut it. "Take this," he said.

"Take –" I jumped as the sound of an adjacent door being kicked in sounded down the hall. My father tossed the bag at me and reached back into the trunk, pulling out a sheathed sword. Another banging noise echoed, this one making even my father startle. He closed the distance between us and reached around my waist, securing the sword into place. I shook my head the moment he pulled away. "Father, please tell me what's happening."

"I can't, son." The noises were coming closer. The look in my father's eyes turned deadly serious. He clutched me by my shoulders, leaning close to place a kiss on my forehead before pulling away. "Run. Hide. Sleep in the trees and tie yourself to a branch if you have to. Find your brother, but make sure you're not followed."

Tears stung at my eyes. "Father, please, I don't understand. Some man hurt Old John and now you're —"

"Yes, I know. I'm not making any sense. We all have a past, my son. One day you'll understand this." Our eyes met and in the two beats which passed, an expression crossed my father's face I'd never seen before. His hand drifted to a simple gold chain he'd worn around his neck for as long as I could remember, a medallion hanging from it which bore an interlinking series of triangles engraved on a small oval. Before another thought could be spared, he lifted it over his head and secured it around my neck. "Don't ever take this off. It'll keep you safe."

I shook my head, fighting a losing battle against the urge to shed more tears. "Please, don't make me leave you."

A final banging noise directed both of our attentions away. The footsteps sounded close to the room and then stopped, forcing a moment of tense silence my father finally broke. His Adam's apple bobbed when he swallowed and a wheeze accompanied the next breath he exhaled. "Out the window with you right now. I demand it," he said, twisting me around by my shoulder. I faced the window, still clutching dumbly onto the bag given to me by my father and stumbling forward once he gave me a push.

My fingers fumbled with the latch for the window shutters. They kicked open once their tether was loosened, a strong gust of wind entering the room and extinguishing two of the candles which had kept the area lit only seconds before. The night looked pitch black with neither a star, nor the moon visible in the horizon and yet, he expected me to be able to find my way out of the village. I glanced back at him, pleading with my eyes.

His mouth opened, but a loud bang at the door interrupted him. We both jumped, and Father coughed with vigor as the chair flew forward and the taller of the cloaked men emerged into the room. His lips curled in the unholiest of grins when his eyes and my father's met, his voice bearing an accent I didn't recognize. "There you are," he said. "You've been a hard man to find, *Richard*."

"You would've done well not to try," my father said as the strange man closed the distance between them. The light which Father's recent illness had stolen returned to his eyes briefly, one hand reaching inside his cloak and emerging with a blade. He lunged forward and plunged the knife into the man's chest in one swift motion, forcing the other man to stumble backward. This seemed to be all the reassurance my father needed to turn his back on our attacker. "Now, Christian. Out the window!"

I climbed onto the ledge, following the instruction on instinct as another cough assailed him. He struggled to regroup, doubled over, a thin strand of red-tinged spit hanging from his mouth that he wiped with his sleeve as his breaths came in wheezes. I motioned to jump back into the room, but froze when the man my father had stabbed recovered, pulling the dagger out and dropping it to the ground. Pain racked his expression, but didn't prevent him from drawing his sword.

The events which followed played in slow motion.

My mind cried out, a scream of warning stuck in my throat I struggled to produce while knowing it was too late. The armed man thrust his weapon forward, running my father through until the blade protruded from his chest, coated in blood. "You missed," he said, whispering harshly into my father's ear.

A whine escaped my lips and the tears already stinging at my eyes spilled onto my cheeks when the man pulled his blade out. Richard Hardi fell to his knees, looking up at me with his final plea latent in his gaze. *Get out of here. Run. Hide. Find your brother swiftly.* My father collapsed onto the floor and stilled, the action one of alarming finality.

Finally, the sound stopped up in my throat sprang forth as an agonized wail.

The armed man grimaced as our eyes met, my vision blurred until I lifted my sleeve to wipe the moisture from my face. I watched his gaze flick to the sack, confused and distraught when he charged forward and swiped at me with his free hand. The precarious position I maintained worked to my advantage when I flailed back at him and lost my balance in the process. He hit me hard enough for me to sail back and out the window, unable to grab hold of anything to stop my hasty decent.

The sensation of flight became the feel of falling too fast for me to regroup. My body twisted into an upright position, legs kicking and arms reaching out, but failing to claim purchase on anything but thin air. I toppled around once and hit the ground below in a painful thud, my knees unable to bear the brunt of impact and sending me flat onto my backside. The first dizzying sight my eyes took hold of was my father's killer, leaning out the window to look down at me.

"The urchin's escaped!" he called out. "Someone get out there and get him."

I scrambled to a stand and limped until my legs could support my weight again. The world around me spun so violently, I couldn't figure out whether to find somewhere to hide or huddle into a corner and throw up until someone or something came to put me out of my misery. "Get to Jeffrey," I managed, more tears falling and my face contorting as I tried to hold back the torrent which wanted to follow. It had not yet registered why I was crying or what in the hell was going on. For all I knew, I would wake to discover the entire thing a bad dream.

The nightmare demanded I run. So, I ran.

I didn't look back. Not even when I heard the pounding of footsteps on the dirt path behind me. Not even when I heard the whinny of horses and cut into the woods by the road, barreling through branches and feeling a few of them cut into me along the way. I emerged by a stream and waded across it, into deeper woods. A protruding tree root tripped me up on the other side. My knees stung anew and I bit my lip against more weeping, clamoring further until I reached the edge of the forest. I came upon a country road and jumped into the cart of a passing wagon, not even of the mind to thank some higher power for the stroke of serendipity. All I knew was that somehow, I had made it away.

Days later – dirty, hungry, and bloodied from the excursion – I found my way to my brother Jeffrey's farm. He accepted me without hesitation and, in time, put me to work, but my mind was always elsewhere, chasing a shadow I couldn't catch. The experience had shattered something within my psyche, leaving me to mend the pieces.

The adult I became carried that fourteen year old boy with him wherever he went. I might have grown into fruition as a man, but there had been a scar inflicted upon my soul, an imprint left that no time could ever heal. Within my dreams, I would replay Richard Hardi's last moments, and in my thoughts I would muse on the emblem those two strange men wore on their cloaks.

A flame within a circle. The sigil of my father's killers.

CHAPTER ONE

Nine years later.
18 September, in the Year of Our Lord, 1465
North Devon, England

I t had been planned for several days, down to its last detail, and had I an ear to bend, I might have bragged for both of our sakes while watching it unfold. The night bore the pitch black of a new moon, the air pleasantly crisp and a vantage point provided to me by nature itself so I could enjoy the show. Poised in a tree branch, I picked at the dirt beneath my fingernails with the tip of my dagger while resisting the urge to hum a tune that had started to dance through my mind. Everything seemed to be playing out exactly as we had intended.

Had I more faith in the Almighty, I might have been inspired toward a prayer of thanks. As it stood, not even the absence of a captain to watch over our unwitting victims could move me toward such a gesture. My adult years had taught me that God had little time for anyone without a bag full of coins or a parcel of land to his boast, and a few pence went further in the hand of a whore than a priest's coffer. The day churches provided prostitutes would be the day I graced them with my presence.

The irony of my name was far from lost on me.

Instead, I simply shook my head at the guards stationed in front of Lord Bertrand's residence. It took only a few minutes after my co-conspirator departed for them to crack open the cask of ale delivered to them. *'With the lord's compliments.'* It took every measure of my scant self-restraint not chuckle at the comment when it had been issued and sure enough, within a short period of time their constitution had proven just as weak as their wits. They went from jolly to raucous and had taken a turn toward incoherent, stripping off pieces of armor the warmer the alcohol made them. This meant it was my turn to play.

Lowering the dagger, I wiped the blade across the fabric of my pants. As I slid it back into its sheath, one of the guards slumped against his comrade, provoking the latter to shove his cohort aside. I tsked under my breath, lifting to the balls of my feet and crouching. "Don't be too quick to turn away such ready advances," I whispered to no one but the night. "You might find yourself enjoying it."

I grasped hold of the branch with one hand and used it to swing to a soundless landing. The years had been kind to me in more manners than one, gifting me with a light frame and nimble fingers all too willing to do the Devil's work. The leaves collecting on the ground crunched softly when I took my first step, but the guards were none-the-wiser to my presence. As they erupted into another fit of laughter, I crept closer and paused, fingers brushing across the hilt of my sword.

One of them turned away, hearing the rustle my movements created and squinting into the area where I had taken refuge. I huffed with derision, a light burst of steam rising from my nostrils and mingling with the air before anyone else could take notice. Still, the man glanced toward his friends again and cocked a thumb in the direction where I was crouched. "Rabbits're running all over the place again," he managed, the actual words sounding much more slurred.

The guard who had been slumped righted himself and spat on the ground. "So? Killit an' make us somethin' to eat," he said.

"Do I look like a bloody cook?"

"Ain't gonna say what you do look like."

The third man burst into cacophonous laughter, his friend readily joining in. The one whose attention I had garnered bristled, his gaze flicking back toward me while my hand shifted from sword's hilt back to the dagger. An opening gambit played out inside my mind, a slow grin creeping across my lips when he took his first step forward and confirmed the course of action. I held my breath, stilling my thoughts as had become ritual for me. The last moment of silence before the storm was always the sweetest.

When he took another step forward, I sprang into action. The dagger I clutched sailed between us and plunged into the guard's chest. Dashing from the shadows, I slid my sword from its sheath and swung as the two other guards charged to engage me. The leaning guard came first, taking a slash across the throat and falling backward. His compatriot balked, lifting his sword a moment too late and watching in horror as I knocked it to the ground and thrust mine forward. The blade ran through his stomach with little effort. When I had dislodged him, I delivered a final, killing blow through his chest and stepped back to admire my handiwork as he dropped to the ground.

I paused first to catch my breath. Then, I whistled toward the edge of Lord Bertrand's property.

A horse whinnied in the distance. The sound of hooves advancing at a cantor followed, a cloaked rider steering the horse in my direction while towing another behind him. I collected my weapons and produced a piece of cloth from a pouch on my belt. Without looking up, I addressed my accomplice with a smirk. "A flawless execution, as always," I said. "Go on and gloat. I know you want to."

He laughed as he alighted from his horse.

We made eye contact once my blades were cleaned and I was able to slip them back into their sheaths. If scoundrels could be said to have best friends, he was that to me, and more. My partner in crime, I always called him, but *Paolo Bellini di Verona* is how he would have introduced himself, with a smarmy grin and flourished bow. He stood three inches shorter and weighed at least one stone more than I, with dark, wavy locks of hair and a perpetual beard he kept trimmed as close to his face as possible.

Both of us wore the same dark clothes, with leather armor and matching swords. The emblem on his cloak mirrored mine; a thorny black rose, embroidered so that it would hover over one's heart if they had the fabric gathered close to their chest. Taking a deep breath inward, Paolo exhaled it with a loud sigh. *"Che bella sera,"* he said, extending his arms with two sets of reins still in his grip. His accent was thick, even when he switched to English. "Three dead guards and an empty house. You are welcome."

He bent at the waist, gesturing as if tipping an imaginary hat at me. As he handed me the reins to my horse, I chuckled. "Oh, *I'm* welcome? They didn't just fall on their own swords, you know."

"I made it easy for you." Paolo dismissed my objection with a wave of his hand, grinning at me as I shook my head. Together, we led the horses to a hitching post and secured their reins into place. Both of us turned to regard the front door, he and I taking a deep breath almost in unison. Paolo exhaled his to speak. "What are we looking for?"

"Roland said you're to find a locked box in a library. There's a bundle of letters containing some vital correspondence the Yorkists want us to obtain." Glancing toward where I knew there to be cottages, I ensured the peasants had wisely decided to stay abed before leading us forward, into the house itself. We maintained a comfortable silence until we stepped fully inside and paused to evaluate it. A pensive frown tugged at my lips as I reached into a pocket for my tinderbox. "I, on the other hand, am keeping watch. The servants might be away, but one of the vassals is bound to notice the guards got suddenly quiet."

My companion nodded, his brown eyes following the action of my hand. I opened the small container without so much as looking at it, pulling out its contents while scanning the room for something to light. "Be a dear and fetch me that candle, would you?" I asked, nodding in the direction of the mantle.

Paolo affected an air of offense, but even with his back turned, I sensed the moment a grin danced across his lips. He marched over to the hearth as I mirrored the expression which had painted itself in my thoughts. "You'll have to give me more encouragement before I want to 'be a dear', *amico mio*," he said.

"Then be spiteful and fetch it just the same."

He laughed softly, shaking his head as he brought over what appeared to be beeswax, half depleted with a blackened wick. I shifted items around in my hands, pressing the flint against the charcloth and sighed as I examined the opulence of nobility on display. "Can you imagine how much he spent on that measly thing alone?" I asked.

"He has a candle and we killed his guards." Paolo's eyes shifted from me to the piece of steel I struck across the flint. I caught a hint of amusement in his gaze. "After this, we steal from him and get paid."

"Such sweets words which ring so pleasantly to my ears." I struck the flint twice more and grinned with approval once the cloth caught and summoned enough of a spark for me to light the wick. "There you are, pretty flame. Catch hold of that so we can have some light."

"I don't know what I fear more. How good you are at that, or how many times you talk to the fire."

"Well, it would be ill-mannered of me to ignore her considering how many times she behaves for me." My eyes remained set on the task of not burning myself, until the candle came to life and allowed for me to extinguish the cloth. I tossed its remnant into the hearth and pointed at one of the oil lamps. "Light one of those for me so I might shut the door."

"*Fai come vuoi.*" Paolo carefully walked the candle over and lit the lamp before nodding at me. I exchanged the gesture, hurrying to the door and pushing it shut, immersing us in nothing but the glow of the two vessels. My gaze shifted around the room, so focused on the play of the shadows that I jumped when I felt Paolo kiss my cheek.

"Keep watch, then," he said. "I'll be right back."

I raised an eyebrow and he laughed, headed toward the hallway and disappearing around the corner. Once he had departed, I lowered the hood from my cloak and tousled locks of deep brown which had gotten longer than I might have liked. My mind stole to a brief memory, recalling an eighteen-year-old man with his legs propped up on a table, hands meticulously cleaning one of his daggers after returning from a job. The foreigner seated across from him had demonstrated a few sleight-of-hand tricks mastered as a petty thief in Verona, making coins disappear with a deft maneuver of his fingers.

"Do you intend to do that to the nobles?" I had asked, glancing up at him with a smirk.

He had grinned, a sparkle of mischief in his eyes as he pledged to double his pay within a month. When he managed that and more, I asked when he planned to return home with his riches. "There is no going home, *amico mio*," he had said, the laugh lines on his face still present despite the heaviness which had settled on his soul. "We are both orphans – you without parents, and me without a country."

Ever since then, we had been nearly inseparable.

Pacing closer to the fireplace, I ran my fingertips along the mantle, disrupting a thin layer of dust in the effort to appear nonchalant. Paolo would be swift about his work, but still, I rarely enjoyed keeping still. The hearth had been cold for some time, further proof that Roland's client knew what he was talking about. Lord Bertrand had been called away, one of the few noble supporters of House Lancaster remaining after a disastrous battle had unseated most of their power in the area. It had been four years and yet, the bickering taking place over the English throne seemed only to have gotten more pointed, evidenced by an empty house with not even a servant present inside it. Truth be told, I cared very little for the affairs of nobles, outside the possessions in their homes.

That, and the chance to investigate a matter of personal concern.

My eyes scanned the mantle in more than mere idle curiosity. When I failed to see anything of any direct importance, I shifted to the darker side of the room and worked on lighting one of the lamps poised by the far wall. The small flame grew in stature until the immediate area became consumed by a warm, pleasant glow. Drawing a deep breath inward, I breathed in the scent of burning oil and began a much closer examination of the entryway.

I was craning my neck to get a better glimpse of a tapestry hanging from the wall when the sound of footfalls echoed down the hall. Paolo emerged from around the corner, prompting me to spare him a quick glance. Yet again, the man's fingers had done too good of a job at picking locks, and as I gradually relaxed my demeanor, he studied me with an impassive expression. "You're looking again aren't you?" he asked, setting the lit candle back down on the mantle.

I fought the urge to frown. "Did you find the letters?" I countered, in an effort to avoid the question.

Paolo pushed away folds of his cloak and produced the bundle, holding it up to view. "These were the only ones locked away. You'll have to read them to know for sure." He hesitated for a moment, hiding the collection out of sight again before walking a few paces closer. "*Amico mio?*"

A grumble passed through my lips, my gaze drifting away, caught up in scanning the woodwork for any special carvings or drawings. "Yes, I was looking, but considering how few times we find ourselves in the actual residence of a nobleman, I figured I'd seize the opportunity. You have no obligation to help me."

"I know I don't." He sighed and I swore I heard him mutter something in Italian under his breath. "I'll gather the bodies and prepare the pyre. You look around in here or whatever it is you need to do, but I'm leaving after the guards are started to burning."

My grin broadened despite myself. I heard him open the front door, my eyes still fixed upward. "You always say that, and yet you always wait."

"This might be the time. Don't tempt me."

"Just a few moments to scour the library, I promise." I glanced back at him.

"*Grazie.*" Paolo gave me a much shorter bow, his eyes expressing both concern and understanding as they regarded me one final time. He turned to depart, leaving me to watch until the front door shut behind him. As it did, I exhaled a tense breath and resumed my search of the main room. Once I was satisfied it contained nothing of note, I decided to continue elsewhere.

I fetched the candle from the mantle and disappeared in the same direction Paolo had headed earlier. Encountering what must have been a servant's quarters, I poked my head in to evaluate the room before abandoning it in favor of walking upstairs. High ceilings and ornamental wood carvings made up the duration of my ascent, with more of the same forms of art hanging from the walls. A portrait of the lord of the manor himself had been affixed near the very top, provoking the thought once more over how men of nobility chose to spend their money.

Somebody's bedroom opened up to me next, with more lavish furnishings than had been present in the servant's quarters, including a chest of drawers and an armoire. Another area adorned in much the same manner followed shortly thereafter. In the next room, I spied the presence of shelves with books arranged on them and followed the compulsion at once to enter it. If a house bore anything of consequence, it did always seem to be found in the library.

I smirked as I saw the box Paolo had broken into. Beside it lay a quill and vat of ink, which I gave only a cursory glance in the effort to hurry myself along. None of the books captured my attention and nothing else on the walls carried even a hint of intrigue to it, bringing my gaze back to the writing desk. As I paced closer to it, something caught my eye, forcing me to pause.

Briefly, I was fourteen years old again, in the tavern while watching an armed man strangle Old John without so much as laying a finger on him. A shaky breath passed through my lips while my heart raced, the sting of tears fresh in my eyes as I picked up a wax stamp and turned it over. It hadn't been the first time in nine years I'd seen the symbol, but I would have known it had I been blind and forced to trace the impression with my fingertips. As I admired the circle and flame, I wondered if enough years would ever pass for the pain to dull. Something told me if it had not in nearly a decade, it never would at all.

Using the candle, I stole a blank piece of parchment and poured wax from the candle onto it. As it cooled, I pressed the stamp into the congealing puddle, lifting the paper once I was finished to ensure I had made enough of a mark for comparison's sake. "Just to verify, Lord Bertrand," I muttered to nobody but myself. "Perhaps I might be back to pay you a visit."

"Christian!" Paolo shouted, from outside the house.

"Coming!" I called back, hastily folding the parchment and stuffing it in my pocket. Taking the candle downstairs, I extinguished the oil lamps, but protected the flame long enough to emerge from inside the manor.

I freed a hand to pull my hood back over my head. The sound of horses whinnying prompted me toward where Paolo stood, holding their reins while regarding a mound of bodies and brush dry enough to catch fire. When I reached it, I knelt before the makeshift pyre and lowered the candle's flame to light some of the kindling.

It went up quickly, flourishing without any wind to stop it from igniting. Once I was certain it had caught, I blew out the candle and licked my fingers to snuff out the wick. Paolo remained silent, only casting occasional glances at me, a small head shake indicating he saw when I slipped the candle into the satchel which hung from my mare, Tempest's, saddle. "I thought I was the thief," he finally said.

"Can't let you have all the fun," I quipped back. We exchanged a glance before both of us regarded the burgeoning conflagration before us, quickly becoming transfixed. Its warmth cut through the chill in the air, and not for the first time I mused on how accustomed I had become to the smell of burning flesh. The notion quickly left my thoughts, given over to the sight of the flames.

Paolo cleared his throat. "Did you find anything?" he asked, handing me the lead for my horse

I took it in hand. "He had a wax stamp with the symbol," I said. "A friend of theirs at the very least if not a full ally."

"Does this mean you're going to see your brother?"

"I'm going off to think. Seeing my brother is an unfortunate necessity."

Paolo and I glanced at each other at the same time. He took a deep breath and exhaled it slowly. "What do you want me to tell Roland?"

I shrugged. "That Christian was being Christian. He knows better than most what that means."

"He also threatens to give your money to the village whores when you do this."

"Oh good. That means I'll be paid up with them."

Paolo succumbed to a laugh and walked to his horse's side, sliding his foot into the stirrup and mounting the beast's saddle with one fluid motion. I settled myself onto mine, only with less finesse, provoking her to rear back a half pace before a tug on the reins settled her again. "I will ride with you to the normal place then?" Paolo asked.

"*Grazie, amico mio*," I said, in a much less authentic accent. Extending a hand toward him, I motioned toward his back. "Hand me the letters. I'll check them while we have a little light."

He nodded and tossed them to me once he had freed them. I gave their contents a casual glance before handing them back, certain our work here had been completed. The night bore enough quiet to it that our exodus from Lord Bertrand's manor bore all the leisure of being unencumbered. We made it to the crossroads several kilometers out well before the rays of dawn threatened to crest over the horizon.

I winked at Paolo and he loosely saluted me before directing his horse toward town. As his figure faded in the distance, I stole a deep breath and glanced heavenward. A symphony of stars played across the obsidian sky above me, disrupted by the occasional barrage of clouds. Tempest began a slow trot down a path I first traversed long ago and had been on ever since.

Jeffrey's farm would be half a day's journey, but I knew for a fact I would not feel a second of it.

CHAPTER TWO

The tree remained standing after all these years, guarded by some force of nature that demanded my sole place of sanctuary in this world remained intact. While Paolo knew of its purpose, there was only one other person who knew of its existence. As it rested on his landowner's property, I could hardly prevent him from making the discovery. I crested the hill leading up to the forest's edge, spying my brother standing near the place I had called home for two short years.

Whether or not Jeffrey anticipated my arrival, he had placed himself in a prime location to witness it.

I rode to the base of the tree and alighted from my mount. Picking up one of the apples that had fallen from the branches, I pocketed it for my horse and waited, brushing her mane with my hand and positioning myself so that my back would be to Jeffrey when he approached. Within moments, I heard the familiar footfalls stride up to me and pause. A bitter smile tugged at the corner of my mouth when his shadow eclipsed me. "I thought for once I might escape one of our little visits," I said.

Jeffrey remained silent until I turned to face him. Slightly taller than me, he wore our lankiness in a less emaciated manner, his cheekbones sharp, but his arms much stronger. Eyes the same color blue as mine regarded me with what I could only interpret as solemnness. "I'd be offended if I didn't know better," he said. "You always complain at me, but then you get chatty after being a brat." Jeffrey cocked a thumb toward the house. "Why don't we skip the formalities and go back to the house? Anne baked bread before heading to the market and the girls have been asking after you."

"Someday, I am going to tell them how ill-mannered it is that they make me less vexed with you."

"I'm sure they'll listen with rapt attention."

Shooting him a look of annoyance, I tugged on Tempest's reins and pulled her along. The sooner we could get this visit out of the way, I told myself, the sooner I could return to my affairs. We walked in silence, toward a small peasant's residence tucked away near one of the barns, pausing briefly so I might secure my horse inside first. I freed Tempest of her bit and bridle and finally fed her the apple I had pocketed for her, garnering a snort from the animal before she accepted it.

"She's just as temperamental as her owner," Jeffrey remarked.

"Or just as ill at ease around you," I said. Turning to face my brother, I took a deep breath to settle my nerves into a more amiable disposition. Jeffrey granted me the mercy of holding his tongue in favor of leading me back outside. The sound of laughter resonated out from the open doorway as we approached his home. Two small girls emerged from inside, making a mad dash for where I stood.

I succumbed to a smile despite myself. Five and three years old respectively, Ivette and Ida wore simple dresses and had flowers in their hair they'd undoubtedly picked from the fields. In unison, both called out, one more articulate than the other, "Uncle Chris! Uncle Chris!"

Crouching down, I scooped them both into my arms and hefted them up in unison. They erupted into squeals of mirth, kissing my cheeks and causing me to laugh. "Now, if you maul your Uncle Christian, there won't be anything left of him afterward," I said.

Ivette shook her head at me. "Silly Uncle Chris, we aren't wolves," she said.

"Ah, but you look ferocious like one." My face scrunched when she touched noses with me. "Let me hear you growl."

She pulled away, raising both hands to simulate claws. Her sister watched, mimicking the action, including when she attempted to snarl at me. My eyes widened, the grin barely suppressed as they giggled once more. "My word. *That* is a scary growl," I said.

"Scarier than a wolf!" Ida exclaimed.

"Much more so." Ignoring the way my brother smiled in the periphery, I set them both down, tousling their hair as I straightened to a stand. "Down with you beasts. Uncle Christian has been riding all night and needs something to eat."

"Okay! Okay!" They each took one of my hands and tugged me along. Jeffrey chuckled, following close behind and shutting the door once we were all inside. The windows were open and the scent of fresh bread still lingered in the air, reminding me of the gnawing that had started in my stomach hours ago. Both girls released their hold on me when I approached a bench, allowing me to settle into place with a relieved sigh.

Jeffrey nodded at them. "Run along, you two," he said. "Uncle Chris and I have things we want to talk about."

The girls looked crestfallen at the thought of having to leave us alone. I bent enough to look Ivette in the eyes as she summoned a pout. "Talk with your sister about what games you'd like to play with me later," I said, punctuating the comment by touching the tip of her nose with my finger.

She giggled, scrunching her nose and nodding. Placated enough for the time being, the girls bounded off, disappearing out the front door and undoubtedly into the fields. I sat back as the door slammed shut once more, tempted to frown when I caught Jeffrey glancing at the embroidered emblem on my chest. Out of implied duty, I removed my cloak and placed it beside me.

Still, the way he held himself even once he looked away caused me a moment's hesitation. I raised an eyebrow, clearing my throat as he produced a knife and cut into one of the loaves of bread. "You know, I allow the girls to call me Uncle Chris, but I really wish you wouldn't validate that," I said, knowing how petulant I sounded and not apt to care.

Jeffrey huffed. "Are we going into this again?" he asked.

"My name is Christian. I'd think you'd be more mindful of that given the fact that mother named me."

A derisive laugh sauntered past Jeffrey's lips. He fished in a cupboard for a plate and produced what looked to be dried bits of beef. "You hold onto that excuse as though you even remember her." Two pieces of bread made their way onto the plate, with a sizable portion of meat. "Tell me, Christian, what have you done for the Lord lately?"

"Given him many a soul to judge." When Jeffrey set the plate onto the table in front of me, our gazes met with equal amounts of frustration evident in the exchange. I frowned, picking up a piece of the bread and tearing at the crust. "I know my profession leaves a poor taste in your mouth."

"That's one way of putting it." He mirrored my frown as he sat across from me, watching me begin to eat. "I know neither mother, nor father, would've wanted you to exist like this."

I shrugged, chewing first and swallowing before speaking. "Both of them are dead, Jeffrey."

"It doesn't change that they wanted what was best for you." He rested an elbow on the table, pointing in the direction the girls had disappeared. "Every time I see you with those girls, it breaks my heart. You should have a family. You would make a good father, but not with this life you live."

"Ah, the well-worn paths we tread when we speak."

"Ones we will continue treading until you learn better. You lived a different life under this roof. I like to try to remind you of that."

"And it suited me poorly." I popped a piece of beef into my mouth and scowled at my brother. "Shall I counter as I normally do? You don't know anything about the life Father and I lived after you ran off?"

He laughed, glancing heavenward with the action. "Oh, right, the waking up in a different town every few days and never having any comfort or stability. Is that why you live the life of a rogue, Christian? Is it the part of you that resented the universe for taking Father away from us, or is it the part of you that resented me for trying to teach you something different?"

"Both. Naturally." I flashed the most sarcastic grin I could fashion, finishing the bite in my mouth. "Are we finished with this part of the discussion now? If so, I would like to finish my meal in peace."

"By all means." Jeffrey extended a hand out toward me, prompting me onward. With a nod, I continued to eat despite how uncomfortable the room had become. We settled into this posture for what felt like hours, even after I finished off my food and Jeffrey rose to take the plate away. He leaned against the wall, watching me produce my dagger and start to pick at my nails. Finally, he broke the quiet. "So, out with it," he said. "You were headed to the tree again. What brought you home this time?"

I fought the urge to tell him I hardly considered his place home. "Do you really want anything to do with this?" I asked, my gaze flicking up to meet his.

He rolled his eyes. "You end up telling me something anyway. I'm learning not to fight it."

"Fair enough." Stealing a glance into the other room, I ensured we were alone before reaching into my pocket with my free hand and producing the parchment I had taken from Lord Bertrand's house. I held it up so Jeffrey could see the wax seal on the front. "Recognize the emblem?"

His disposition sobered. Walking to close the distance between us, he snatched the page in hand and unfolded it. "The flame within the circle. Father's killers." He looked up at me. "Where did you find this?"

"Inside a noble's house. It would probably be best if you didn't know whose."

"It would've been better if you hadn't gone looking in the first place." He flipped it around, glancing at the back before handing it to me once more. "If his family finds out you and your band of... hired hands... were in his manor, you'll suffer the loss of your head."

"I doubt he'll work out who slipped into his house anytime soon."

"So, he wasn't one of those souls you sent to be judged?" Jeffrey arched an eyebrow at me. "This does nothing to make me less concerned for your welfare."

"You behave like this is the first time I have killed and stolen." Sighing, I slipped my knife back into its sheath and secured it back into place before pocketing the parchment as well. "He's away on house affairs, Jeffrey. He'll eventually hear his guards deserted their post. Perhaps even discover that some letters are missing, but what does that matter? You're missing the relevant point."

"And what would that be?"

"I found another man of power associated with these mercenaries."

My brother narrowed his eyes, the weight of his stare unrelenting and forcing my gaze away. "You're playing a dangerous game," he finally said. "And I don't think it's worth it. What will you do if you ever stare Father's killer in the eyes? Drive a sword through him and be on your merry way?"

A huff passed through my lips as Jeffrey sat back down. My eyes met his briefly, a form of fatigue threatening to settle on me I had learned not to indulge. "You never take any of this seriously."

"No, I don't, and for good reason. We've been over this a hundred times. We even opened that scroll Father gave you and studied the parchment inside. It made no sense to me the first time you showed it to me and it hasn't made sense any other time since."

"I think because you continue to doubt what made it important. I swear to you, there was witchcraft behind what happened to Father. I have *told you* as such countless times."

"And you sound no less mad, Christian, than you had when you first presented this foolish idea to me."

"It is not foolish!" I pounded my first on his table and quickly retracted my hand. My gaze shifted to him, then to the far wall, my frown deepening. "You know, for such a religious man, you are very quick to dismiss the supernatural."

"I simply refuse the idea that Father was killed by a practitioner of the dark arts." Jeffrey paused, the volume of his words turning softer, as though that would make them any more winsome. "I think he was killed because he upset the wrong man and it finally caught up to him. The same way it'll catch up to you if you're not careful."

My voice, in turn, became fraught with agitation. "I don't know what to make of you sometimes. You pretend that you care, and prod me to share my thoughts, but then you mock them the moment I speak them." Regarding my brother again, I felt tears escape my eyes, my spirit shaken by a profound amount of melancholy. "You really make me wonder if you ever cared about Father."

Jeffrey sighed. He reached forward, a hand settling on my shoulder and giving it a gentle squeeze. "Christian, please..." His gaze turned genuinely contrite. "You have to understand there're certain things in this world that I believe and some things I think are foolish stories and myths."

"Then tell me why he was killed. Why did those mercenaries come after *him*?"

"I don't know, brother. I really, honestly don't."

With a nod, I felt more like brushing the matter aside than pursuing it any further. I took another piece of bread and left the room to engage my nieces in some light-hearted play, waiting until my back was to Jeffrey before wiping away the moisture on my face. When Jeffrey's wife returned home, she greeted me with the same look of displeasure she always did, which only underscored how I felt about being there. As it stood, I didn't have an actual home. I hadn't in years.

Jeffrey begged me to stay, but in the middle of the night, I snuck from his house with a lit candle and wandered to my tree again. Rolling up my sleeves, I placed the small source of light aside, hoping its glow would be enough to do what I normally did by day. The wind kicked the flame around, but it held steady. Once I was certain it would not extinguish, I bent low and felt under an adjacent bush for the hand shovel I kept hidden there. Pulling it out, I then drove it into the ground to displace the first spadeful of earth.

Several followed in their stead, each push further into the dirt just as determined as the last. When I heard the clunk of metal against metal, I stopped, placing the shovel aside in favor of reaching in and unearthing the box with my hands. Dirt covered my arms up to my elbows by the time I finished – some smeared across my forehead when I wiped away sweat – but within a short period of time, I settled onto my backside with the container in hand. My chest rose and fell in slowly diminishing breaths.

Finally, I unlatched the lock and lifted the lid. The contents inside had only been added upon through the years, with the cylinder Father had given to me the first thing my eyes always found. Beside it rested a carving of the killers' sigil I had made shortly after his death, and a crystal I had taken from the body of one of my more recent targets. As I produced the parchment with the wax seal from my pocket, I held it up one final time and placed it with the other treasures. They joined a vault of lies, misdirections, and half-truths as the spoils I had collected as a member of the Brotherhood of the Black Rose.

Shutting the metal box, I sighed and returned it to its grave. Dirt quickly filled the hole again, smoothed out and concealed by the rock I had removed in order to unearth it, before I slid the hand shovel back into place. A breeze caught the candle's flame and whipped it around while the air around me fell silent. The ride back into town would be long, and while I had no desire to return indoors, I knew I was too tired to leave just yet. "A short rest it is, then," I murmured, with only the night to bear witness to my words.

My fingers slid beneath my shirt as I reclined against the tree and settled into place. Despite layers of callouses, I could still feel the engravings on my father's medallion and brought it to my lips, kissing it before hiding it beneath layers of fabric once more. I held onto it until my lids grew heavy and my body lapsed into light sleep. It wasn't until dawn crested over the horizon that I woke, curled on the ground beside the now-extinguished candle.

After drawing water to clean the dirt from my hands and face, I dressed again by the light of the sun and trudged back toward Jeffrey's house. My brother was already awake as I approached, pausing on his way to the barn with his wife standing in the doorway. I nodded at her and she glanced away while Jeffrey dusted off his hands and closed the distance between us. "If not for the fact that your mare is still stabled, I might have suspected you gone already," he said.

"I considered it, but I thought that might be rude," I countered. As I glanced toward Anne, I spied the girls gather at her sides and summoned the first genuine smile I had managed since waking. "Besides, it would be poor of me not to give my nieces a proper sending off."

As I spread my arms, they raced into them and gripped on tight. I made promises of bringing treats for them and waved off Anne as she asked if I wanted anything to eat before I left. As the girls wriggled out of my grip, I shot another look at Jeffrey, which was enough prompting for him to follow me away from the house. "I've imposed enough," I said in passing, turning my back the moment my brother assumed a place by my side.

I waited for the door to shut behind us before leading the way toward the barn. Not making eye contact with Jeffrey, I still managed to be aware of the frown tugging at the corners of his mouth. "Your visits aren't an imposition," he said.

"Calling your brother a fool is hardly endearing enough to make him want to stay."

"Damn you, Christian." Jeffrey walked in front of me, stopping me in my tracks. He frowned. "I pray constantly for you. Whether or not you choose to believe it, I do love you."

I huffed dismissively, side stepping him to continue walking into the barn. Freeing my horse, I secured her bridle into place and lifted myself into her saddle once I had finished. My hands gripped tightly onto the reins while she took a half step back and breathed a grunt. "Please continue to pray for my wayward soul," I said, nudging Tempest with the heels of my boots. "Maybe salvation might find me despite myself."

The mare trotted forward, picking up to a full gallop once we had cleared the barn's entrance. Jeffrey remained a shadow on my back, the echo of his parting words lingering in my ears, even after we spirited past the edge of his lord's property and well on our way to town. Once again, the temptation to breathe vows I could not keep surfaced, laced with the desire I had to depart and never return again. Somehow, I always found my way back there, though, and each time, I left a great deal heavier than I had been when I had arrived. Such is how it had been since I was a young man, I reminded myself, lapsing into ancient memories throughout the duration of my ride.

And such is how it seemed it would always be.

CHAPTER THREE

The fact remains consistent for both wild animals and adolescent boys; the more you attempt to tame one, the more it will resist.

I remember the first day it became clearest to me that my time at Jeffrey's farm had come to an end. Wiping the sweat from my brow, I squinted against the harsh sun and saw nothing before me but unadulterated horizon, stretching out into infinity. The crops surrounding me formed a prison, the sickle in my hand a shackle I had held onto faithfully since my father's death. My own demons had been in pursuit and, after two years, had finally claimed me.

My brother stilled the oxen and called to me when I continued my statuesque pose in the middle of broad daylight. The sound of my name echoed in my ears, eyes shutting with the third invocation as I wondered how a soul could feel so tired after only sixteen years on this mortal coil. I didn't know what needed to change, but had reached a time of reckoning and threw the sickle down the fourth time Jeffrey summoned my name. "Christian, you get back here or don't bother returning!" he said when I sprinted in the direction of the house.

When I departed, I vowed to take his words to heart.

Pausing first to bury a few belongings near one of the trees, I hitched a ride with a passing cart and traveled the rest of the way on foot, not knowing where I was headed, but bound to settle somewhere eventually. Within a few days, the city gates of Exeter opened up before me, accepting an orphan boy with no employable skills and nothing else to his credit, save but the sword at my side. I didn't know what to expect and simply wished for a place to rest my head and a way to fill my stomach by the day's end. At first, the awe of it was enough to distract me.

The stench of the city burned my nostrils and spires loomed over me, containing the heads of prosecuted criminals as a warning to the rest of its citizens. The times Father had taken us through similar towns flashed through my thoughts while I stared wide-eyed at the macabre wonders before settling on more ordinary affairs. The roads which made up the main thoroughfare were abuzz with activity, young children racing past while crowds gathered around storefronts and friars preaching salvation. I used a few pence stolen from my brother to purchase a meal and slept out by the horses when one innkeeper took pity on me enough to allow it.

The next day brought with it a reckoning, however. If I was going to make it on my own, I had to figure out how. At first, begging for scraps and foraging whatever I could from the piles of refuse and troughs of animals kept me fed. I slept each night with the horses and washed myself in the creek far outside town. By a week into my newly acquired emancipation, I began to wonder if any of the local tradesmen would take on an apprentice while knowing I was far too old to count on receiving that sort of favor. Hunger tempted me toward stealing while the sight of men who had been caught doing so warded me away from it.

The solution to my problem found its way to me on accident.

A group of men had been sitting near the back door of a tavern, drunk from ale and wasting time as the sun began to dip in the horizon. I polished the blade of my sword, taking refuge from the bustle of activity happening indoors while also attempting to ignore the gnawing in my stomach. Buildings loomed on either side of me, the scant glow from their windows providing the light from which I worked. I would've been content being left to my thoughts if one of the inebriated men had not chosen that moment to rise to his feet.

"Hey, lad," he called out, toward where I sat, further up the scant space alley and nearer to the main road. His voice bore such a grating tone to it that my task came to an immediate halt. He laughed, but I fought the urge to do more than steal a quick glance at him when he continued. "What's a boy doin' with a man's weapon?"

Two of his friends sniggered in the background. I heard the sound of him stumbling forward a few paces and sighed as he closed in on where I sat. "Bet one could fetcha few coins for a blade like that. You buyin' us a round tonight, lad?" he asked.

"The sword isn't for sale," I said. Once again, the cloth in hand resumed the stroke that had been interrupted. "Go back to your drinking and leave me be."

"Listen to him, right? Thinks he's a noble's son and hasn't been taught any better." I finally glanced up at him when he paused and bent a few feet away from me. "You're just a bloody street urchin. You stink like a horse's arse, you do."

"Better than reeking of drunkard." A smirk curled the corner of my mouth, more of a dare than I was willing to admit to myself at the time. Still, a strange cause and effect played out in my mind, a series of events I hadn't been able to visualize since my father had been taken from me. It was as though a muse had woken from its slumber, summoned to come out and play again after so long in a box. My father had taught me the game while instructing me on how to wield a sword.

Anticipate their next move, he had told me. Form your reaction before they have a chance to act.

He reached for the sword's hilt, thinking he would catch me off-guard, and yelped when I captured his wrist in my hand. What started as surprise transformed into anger, but I dodged when I knew he would throw a punch and kicked him in the shin before clamoring away. He held his leg and swore under his breath. I lifted my weapon in warning, believing his next move would be to charge at me. This served to be enough of a deterrent. My attacker withdrew to where his friends stood.

They, on the other hand, scowled at me, indicating the altercation had not yet come to an end. One pulled a dagger, his eyes shouting malice while he advanced. I clutched the sword with both hands, a slight wave of nervousness running through me as I realized I was out of practice. Father had always told me I was nimble. I could only hope my wits remained sharp even if my blade skills had atrophied.

He swiped at the air to intimidate me and I lurched backward, catching myself before the clumsy maneuver could knock my footing off-balance. The others chuckled, one calling out, "He's scared of you, Nate!" and my first challenger adding, "Split 'em open an' see how he likes his belly bein' spilled on the street." I swallowed hard, attempting not to see that as a real possibility, and dodged another swipe out of instinct. Nate smirked, revealing a mouth full of rotten teeth, the ones that weren't missing. He thrust the blade again, forcing me to dodge the blow and I nearly tripped when my feet moved from dirt to cobblestone. It kicked up a cloud, which caused Nate to launch into a coughing fit.

A slow, wicked grin crossed my lips as I had the opportunity I needed.

Freeing one hand, I reached down and picked up a handful of earth, casting it upward blindly and watching as the greater portion of it hit Nate's face. He stumbled back, falling onto his ass and leaving himself exposed in the process. I dug my boot into his wrist, causing him to drop the dagger while he cried out in pain. I could almost see the wicked glint in my eyes when I scratched the surface of his neck with the tip of my sword. "Looks like I have another blade," I said. "Think I might have supper tonight after all."

"Smile while you can, boy," he said, punctuating the genesis of a threat with a groan. Whatever he might have said in addition fell by the wayside as the other men collected him, escorting him away with what little pride he might have had left. I picked up my prize and watched them leave in silence. The moment I felt confident enough to do so, I turned my back and sought shelter for the night.

The next day, I sold the dagger to one of the local smiths, the confrontation from the night before little more than a memory save but for the jingle of coins in my pocket. Whatever I should have feared was lost on me, swept to the side so I might muse upon how to spend my winnings. I walked into one of the inns and relished the first good meal I'd had since arriving in the city. By night, I strode into the tavern near where I'd had my altercation and purchased a pint of ale, hoping for a few hours more of warmth before I would have to bunk down.

As I sat at the counter, I surveyed the other patrons, allowing my gaze to jump from one to the other while taking note of each face. It had been two years since I had sat at one of these counters, and the recollection of the last time brought with it the chill of solitude as an unwelcomed companion. My eyes shifted to the barkeep – as though I needed to remind myself the tall, wiry man was not Old John – and settled on his wife as the spindly woman appeared to collect a pint for one of the tables. Still, I could not shake it, even when I decided against spending more money on food or drink.

I strode out the front doors and allowed my gaze to shift heavenward, my mind still lost in heavier things. Men rode past and other people strolled along the main thoroughfare, their presence failing to evoke more than my passing interest. I took a deep breath, in some effort to steady myself and place the past back where it belonged. It had me distracted enough that I failed to hear them approach.

"You're either brazen or stupid to come back here, lad," a familiar voice said, lobbing the opening gambit. As I peered down from my appraisal of the night sky, I spied the men who had been part of the group from the previous evening, of which Nate and his more outspoken comrade stood as their leaders. It was the latter who nodded toward the sword at my side. "We'll be collecting that and Nate's dagger. Hand 'em over and we'll let you leave with some of your teeth."

"I'd like to keep them all, if it's the same to you," I quipped while knocking myself from the throes of melancholy. The moment the words had been birthed, I realized the posture I had committed myself to and straightened my stance as though in recognition. Movement in my periphery told me some of the bystanders had paused to watch, which served to both bolster and rattle me. My hand settled on the hilt of my sword. "I won your dagger and sold it. Count your losses and find somebody else to threaten."

"What an imp." The man barked a laugh and cocked a thumb at me while regarding his friends. Something told me they had all shown up mostly sober, a thought I tried hard not to linger on. "He's working on getting gutted."

"More like you are." I raised an eyebrow. "Leave me alone."

"Don't think you're in much the position to make demands." Pulling back his cloak, he reached for his blade and drew it with a shrug. "I wish I could say I wasn't going to enjoy splitting you, but then I'd be lying." Pacing forward once, he held the weapon aloft. In that brief span of time, however, he had told me all I needed to know.

I didn't know if it was the alcohol or the benefit of having eaten, but some of the rust sloughed off. It was as though time had paused just long enough for me to weigh the man and epiphany struck out of the blue. I opened my mouth, saying, "Wait," just as he motioned forward. Mercifully, it was enough to get him to hesitate. I glanced quickly at the others, and then back at him. "Why don't we make a wager out of it?"

The man blinked stupidly. "A wager?" he asked.

I fought the urge to ask if he knew the definition of the word. "Yes, a wager." Pulling my sword from its sheath, I kept it lowered and pointed at the others with my free hand. "All of them step back. You and I can have a proper fight. Whoever wins keeps the blades."

He laughed. "You sold Nate's dagger. I get to rip that from your belly?"

"Make 'im work it off for you," called out a female voice from just inside the entrance to the tavern. My opponent and I peered over in unison at the barkeep's wife, who had chosen that moment to come outside. The presence of more people at the doorway with her and a few additional witnesses present around us suggested it no mere coincidence. Somehow, we had managed to capture a healthy amount of attention for the brevity of the exchange.

I glanced back at my opponent as he lowered his sword. "Work it off?" he asked, his sights still on her.

"Yes, make 'im indentured to you." My attention stole back to the woman, and followed the exchange as it bounced from one person to the other. She leaned against the door frame and folded her arms across her chest. "Ain't no good to you bleeding out. You take his wager an' if you win, you keep both the boy and his sword."

"What'm I going to do with an urchin?"

"I don't know. Clean your weapons? Tend your horses? Throw 'im a crust of bread for polishin' your boots, for all I care. Just sayin' he's better to you livin'.'" She pointed at me. "Other way goes, though. He wins, he keeps your blade an' you leave 'im the hell alone."

The man spat to the side and glared, but the woman held her ground, as though not the slightest bit intimidated by him. A smile tugged at the corners of my mouth. It was as though she had seen the same thing I did and made the same mental wager. He held his sword like an unpracticed amateur, his stance far too open and leaving too much to chance.

My gaze returned to the man as he looked at me. I shrugged. "Better than getting gutted," I said.

"I'll have you cleaning out piss pans," he muttered before raising the sword again. I mimicked his movements, giving him the impression of me being just as unknowledgeable as he was. Yes, it had been two years since I had sparred with my father, but both the blade and the knowledge I possessed were what remained of Richard Hardi. The sobriety I gained in the tavern turned into determination, kept hidden deep under my skin lest the other man become aware of it.

He lurched forward and I deliberately shifted away from the advance in a sluggish manner. When he thrust the blade, I twisted again, allowing him to catch my shirt and make a tear in it and acting surprised when he did. He licked his lips and grinned at me. "Sure you don't wanna give in now, lad?" he asked.

I shook my head, but said nothing else. Our blades clashed, but I let him nick the other side of my shirt after two awkward exchanges. I pivoted to the side, exclaiming when he came within a hair's breadth of cutting my cheek, and clumsily dodging his next advance. He laughed and when I looked at him with the most petrified expression I could muster, it only caused his laughter to escalate. My opponent opened his mouth, given over to another moment of grandstanding while still maintaining that open stance.

With the first word he uttered, the unholiest of grins swept across my face.

Tightening my grip, I surged at him before he could compensate. The sound of metal hitting metal interrupted him, a sudden onslaught almost knocking the sword from his hands from the first set of blows. His eyes widened and his posture turned defensive, the intensity of my strokes causing him to stumble backward and clutch harder onto his weapon. He motioned to swing his blade, but twisted too far to the side in the process.

Instinct took over where opportunity was presented.

I slashed his wrist and forced him to release the hilt with that hand. He cried out in offense and took his focus off his sword long enough for me to knock it from his grip with my father's blade. Fumbling, he finally letting it go, and I crouched before he had the chance to compensate. Both weapons ended up in my hands as I shot back to a stand.

"I believe this means I've won," I said.

He glared at me, wrapping his fingers around the wound on his opposite wrist and gritting his teeth. "You bastard," he said. Spinning around, he glanced at his cohorts, nodding at me. "Well, come on. Rough up the stupid little whelp."

The other men, Nate included, eyed me warily. "No, I don't think you'll be doin' anything of the sort," the barkeeper's wife called out, interrupting. She pushed off the door frame and wandered her way closer to where I stood. We exchanged a glance before she looked at the other men. "I think the boy is goin' to buy each of you fine men a drink and you'll be on your way after that." As she pointed at my opponent, her eyes narrowed. "An' if I see you 'round here again, I promise my husband an' the menfolk in 'ere'll give you worse than a cut on the wrist."

To say he looked crestfallen would have been understating the matter. He watched as not just us, but several of the people who had witnessed the confrontation filtered into the tavern, his eyes narrowed and teeth gritted. I spared him only one last look and nothing else, afraid to tempt my good fortune. The barkeep's wife placed a hand on my shoulder to coax me on, causing me to glance over at her. "I'm buying the drinks?" I asked.

A sly, amused smile traced a path across her lips. "You won yourself a sword," she said. "I think you can afford it."

I nodded, but as we strode back into her husband's establishment, I sensed a prodding to her words and found myself reflecting upon that. The drinks were purchased and I spared some extra coin for a room for the night, afraid that my challenger might return to exact his revenge.

When he didn't, I considered it a mercy. When I failed to see him at all again, I marked it off as the one true miracle ever granted to me by God and promptly used it to go about the Devil's work.

The next day, I sold that blade and returned to the tavern. A few of the men who had been there the previous evening paused to comment on the scuffle to me, one exclaiming that I was a 'tricky lad' and wagering to his friend that I could probably have him disarmed as well. The friend declined, but within the echo of their laughter, an idea germinated, bringing about a solution to my impoverished condition. An evening later, I wagered my sword against another man armed with a similar blade, and had him disarmed within moments.

Another crowd assembled to witness this. And a larger one the next night, who tossed money at me for the show provided. As I scooped up the coins, I thanked them with a bow and caught sight of the barkeep's wife in my periphery, looking on with a pleased smirk. The tavern filled with customers and somewhere in the silence, I realized I had made a tacit arrangement with her and her husband. I could not have been more pleased.

While those victories should've ensured my needs met for at least a month, the exhibitionist inside had gotten the better of me. Each night, I emerged at dusk and performed again, collecting my winnings and stretching the bounds of my imagination for how to spend them. Thoughts of my travels with Father danced across my mind once more, but this time as a buffet of forbidden fruits from which I could now partake. Women of ill repute enticed me into my first sexual endeavors. Merchants tempted me with better clothes and the barkeeper's wife with lavish meals, finding me all too willing to indulge myself. Once the fear of Nate and his ilk returning waned, if I had nothing left with which to purchase a room, I slept under the stars, content in my freedom for a time.

As the months turned colder, however, my disposition turned more desperate again. The crowds had begun to dwindle and with it, the amount of extravagance I could entertain without the fear of starving to death. When warmer weather brought another batch of travelers through the city, I took to the streets at once, determined to fill my purse before the chill returned to claim my source of income again. The first two nights bore modest earnings and by the third evening, I had determined to pull out whatever tricks I could to loosen their purse strings further. Strolling to my usual spot, I drew my sword and declared myself open for challengers should anyone be bold enough to take the gauntlet thrown.

That was when I heard gruff voice call out from the center of the crowd, "Think I might take you up on that offer, lad, if no one else is going to be brave enough to."

The people parted ways around him. I stood, regarding the tall man who emerged while feeling a nervous flutter in my stomach at the sight. His face bore two scars, one that cut across his forehead and another down his left cheek. He removed a set of gloves and I raised an eyebrow at the two fingers missing from his left hand, seeing before me an entire tome of stories waiting to be told about adventures I could have only dreamt about. A sword sheathed by his side, the leather bore enough wear to suggest that pulling the blade was a common practice.

My stomach threatened to sink into my boots.

He tilted his head, a full mane of brown hair spilling onto his shoulder and emerald eyes regarding me curiously. Given the amount of damage to him, his age was indistinguishable, but I assumed him no younger than his early thirties. "You're a scrawny urchin," he said once he had studied me to his satisfaction. He tossed the gloves to the side and removed his cloak, depositing it where his gloves had landed. "Doesn't seem like a boy like you should be causing the stir you've been."

My brow smoothed as a grin curled the corner of my mouth. I summoned as much bravado as a young man of my years could muster. "The name is Christian, sir," I said. "And that looks like a lovely sword. I should like to own it."

The stranger huffed, a smirk breaking out on his face. "Was about to accuse you of being educated for an urchin, but you just showed how much you still have left to learn." He drew his sword, the smile evaporating, but the amusement still present in his eyes. "Your move first, Christian."

I nodded, sliding my blade from its sheath as well. The crowd took several steps backward and watched with bated breath for our match to begin. I advanced forward with cautious steps, crouched low while taking hold of the hilt with both hands. A flicker of something indiscernible crossed my challenger's face before he assumed the same posture.

We both sidestepped each other. I thought of the times I exchanged blows with my father, knowing before the first clash of our blades that I was facing someone much more experienced than my normal fare of half-baked drunks. My challenger failed to close the distance between us, baiting me to make the final steps myself. I did so, but pivoted to the side with my final step, rightly anticipating he'd try to sneak a swing in with my guard down.

It missed. I lifted my sword in a retaliatory strike. The stranger shifted and managed to intercept the blow, a wide grin on his face when the first clang shattered the silence. "Not bad," he said, pushing off and taking a step away from me.

I furrowed my brow at the way he said that but shrugged the words off in favor of trying to visualize my next move. He made his before I could decide, however, and forced my reflexes to the test, with me turning one way and moving another to avoid two well-placed strikes. I caught one blow with my sword and started an exchange between the two of us, which lasted for a brief moment. Unfortunately, it also made me smugly consider I might actually be able to defeat him.

He seemed to sense it, because he changed his stance and came at me more aggressively. I failed to parry one shot and overcompensated with the next, leaving myself vulnerable to a counterattack. The sword flew from my hands before I could issue an objection and I gasped when I felt the tip of his blade touch the nape of my neck.

I shut my eyes, but still heard the smile in the way he spoke. "I believe I'll be keeping my sword for a little while longer, lad."

The audience erupted in applause. Opening my eyes, I fought to suppress a scowl as the crowd tossed their offerings to us, with the usual collection of other urchins attempting to pilfer a coin or two. I turned to face him, waiting for him to go around collecting the money that should have paid for my supper. Instead, he sheathed his sword and reached for his cloak, securing it around his shoulders before slipping the gloves over his hands again.

I frowned. "I suppose you'll be taking that," I said, pointing to where my sword lay.

He cast a quick glance at it and shrugged. "I don't have much use for it. I trust you know we'll be splitting the profit, however."

"Splitting?" Raising an eyebrow, I watched him scare off the scavengers and gather the remaining coins from the ground. "You aren't keeping it all to yourself?"

"Well, I could, but considering we both gave them a show, it'd hardly be fair." The subtle smirk made its resurgence when we made eye contact again. "Or, I tell you what, lad. Why don't I give it all to you and let you buy me a meal? Seems you scratch out enough of a living doing this, but you might consider switching jobs before you encounter a man willing to cut your throat."

My disposition soured. "Not much else I can do to make a living."

"Of course you can." He plucked the last pieces of money from the ground and walked over to me, waiting for me to extend my hands before giving the coins to me. I secured them in my purse and he watched, waiting for me to finish the task and collect my sword to continue. We started a walk for the inn, neither of us apt to talk until we made our way to the main hall, packed full of people with only a small table vacant for us to sit.

I eyed the other man warily while he made himself comfortable. The stranger waved over the barkeeper's wife, ignoring an inquisitive glance spared at me while placing an order for two ales and two plates of food. A few moments of uncomfortable silence followed after she left, until he finally cleared his throat and tilted his head at me. "So, out with it, lad," he said. "Who's out there looking for you?"

My brow furrowed. "I beg your pardon?" I asked.

He laughed. "Begging's not going to get you much pardon as far as I'm concerned. I find out some noble has money on your return, I'll tie you up and take you there myself."

It took a moment, but I finally realized what he had been asking. "Oh." I shook my head. "No, sir, I don't belong to anybody."

"Where do you belong then?"

"Wherever I want." I shrugged. "My parents are dead and I'm grown enough to do what I please."

"Yes, you are, but the rest of the world doesn't always agree." He paused to adjust his cloak, revealing an emblem in its crease. The sight of it startled me, forcing me to catch my breath until I reminded myself my father's killers neither wore black, nor bore the image of a rose. My new companion seemed none-the-wiser, glancing around the room first, then looking back at me and folding his hands on top of the table. "Who taught you how to handle a sword, then, Christian?"

Slowly, I relaxed again. "My father did. This was his sword."

"What did your Pa do for a living?"

"He was a traveling merchant, sir." I nodded toward the rose on his cloak. "What do *you* do for a living?"

He glanced down at it and laughed. "Might let you earn the right to know, but for now, let's just say I'm a mercenary and leave it at that. You can call me Roland."

"Roland what?"

"Roland nothing else. Too many names complicate things."

I couldn't bring myself to belabor the point. Giving the opinion an impassive nod, I allowed a lapse to settle in our conversation, grateful when our mugs of ale showed up. Roland took his in hand and thanked the innkeeper's wife while I sipped mine cautiously. My eyes didn't leave the strange man the entire time, not even to offer the woman with whom I had an unspoken business arrangement an explanation. Two plates containing meat and potatoes appeared before us shortly thereafter and while Roland took his first bite, I continued clutching the cup in both hands.

"So, Christian," Roland finally said, his gaze straying down to the plate while he broke off a piece of bread. When he spoke again, it was with his mouth half-full. "I'm to understand and believe you're nothing more than a fancy-talking, sword trained orphan street urchin, out here swindling folks for money. Is that correct?"

"I don't swindle anyone," I countered. "People either challenge me or they watch me. If they're entertained, they give me money. Sometimes, I sell the weapons I get and sometimes I let their owners have them back, but they always understand if they challenge me, it's my right to keep them."

"Honest business if ever I've heard of any." He nodded at the plate.

"Go on ahead and eat, lad," he said, brushing off his hands and sitting back in his chair. Roland swallowed the bite of bread down and allowed our eyes to meet again. "I'm going to say a few things and you're going to listen while I do."

Something about the way he worded the demand bore a level of threat to it. Another part reminded me of the tenor the conversations took when Father would settle into talking business with the buyers of his goods. The latter had me curious enough to pick up my fork and poke at a piece of meat. Roland smirked with approval. "Good lad," he said. "Now, I'm going to start off by saying I don't coddle people and I don't protect them. You pointed it out yourself. You're old enough to mind your own business. I have enough bastards suckling enough whores' breasts and I don't need another one, am I clear?"

Nodding, I fought the urge to offer a retort. Roland seemed to sense it and gave me a cautionary look before continuing. "Now, you say there's nobody looking for you and I'm apt to believe you, but if I find out otherwise, I will do exactly what I told you I'd do. Don't think your life is ever anything more to me than a few coins in my pocket."

I washed my food down with some of the ale. "I'm telling you, I don't have anyone who would offer you two bits for me," I said.

"I'd sell you out for one."

Deciding against calling his bluff, I shrugged again and continued eating. Roland took a deep breath, and the air seemed to change, switching from that first tenor to the second hinted at moments ago. He leaned forward in his chair, his presence looming closer to me with the volume of his voice decreasing enough to make him barely heard over the cacophony around us. "What are you planning on doing when the cold hits good and long enough to keep your crowds away?" he asked.

Somehow, I managed to suppress a wince at his question. "I'll make due, I guess," I said.

"You'll meet your death, more like it. Not as quick as some other people would, but at some point, you'll get desperate and either get caught stealing or wind up choking on a better man's blade. You could do better than that."

My gaze had drifted down to the plate of food, to avoid showing my hand too soon. With his words, however, I glanced back at him and raised an eyebrow, the action enough to spread a wolfish grin across his lips. "I can teach you how to use that sword of yours for money. Real money, not these coins people throw at you for show," he said. When I failed to attend to the plate of food again, he arched a brow back at me, mirroring my expression. "You ever kill a man, lad?"

"No, I can't say that I have."

"The thought bother you?"

This time, I couldn't conceal the reaction his question inspired. My eyes shifted to the far wall, then down to the table, a deep breath filling my lungs before being exhaled. Whatever Roland read of it, I neither knew, nor cared, but in the moments which followed, I saw the demons I used to entertain while working Jeffrey's farm; the ones who lured me away when I couldn't ward them off any longer. At the very least, I held them at a distance in using the blade, even for show. Each time I held a sickle or polished my father's sword while under my brother's roof, however, I wanted nothing more than to cut into the man who had taken Richard Hardi away from me.

Slowly, my gaze lifted, a look in my eyes even I could feel without seeing it for myself. Roland sobered and I shook my head. "No, sir," I said. "The thought of killing people doesn't bother me at all."

Roland tilted his chin in recognition of the inner darkness which had crawled out of my soul. Considering me in silence for a moment, we stared at each other as though waging a contest with neither of us apt to blink. After a few beats, the stranger nodded once. "Then I can make use of you," he said. The heaviness dissipated between us, leaving only a lingering undercurrent. Roland bit into his bread again. "If you think that's a better prospect than starving over the winter."

I hesitated for a moment before picking any further at my food. Regarding the mercenary seated across from me, I replayed the image I held of my father's killer and wondered if he might have been a mercenary as well, either in practice or in disguise. Yes, I wanted to punish the people who had stolen my father. I wanted to understand once and for all why he had become a target of such senseless brutality. And maybe – just maybe, I thought – sinking into their world might bring me to wherever such a group of men existed.

"Sure," I said, finally lifting a piece of bread to my mouth and tearing off a chunk with my teeth. I chewed as impassively as I could and swallowed as though nothing else had invaded my thoughts besides Roland's offer. "It's as good of a prospect as any."

"I'll secure us rooms, then, and we'll head out in the morning." Roland pushed out his chair and came to a stand. "Stay here and finish with your supper. Won't be anything else to eat until after we leave town."

"Yes, sir," I said, continuing the ruse of eating, unaffected, until Roland became engaged with business with the tavern's owner. Within an hour's time, I had a bed to lie on and a ceiling to stare at as I attempted to settle into to sleep. The scant amount of light which shone into the room kept me company as I made a promise to myself.

I would work on getting good at killing, I said, whispering the pledge out loud. And as the months wore on, I did, not flinching the first time I slit a man's throat for money. Regret remained as distant of a thought to me as backing down from my vendetta, one death after another desensitizing me to the thirst for blood being wrought in my soul. In my mind, they formed one less obstacle standing between me and my ultimate goal.

For when I found the man who had driven a sword through Father, I wanted to repay him the favor.

CHAPTER FOUR

"He doesn't mean to treat you badly, *amico mio*. Sometimes family doesn't know any other way."

My eyes shut briefly as I felt Paolo kiss the nape of my neck, one of his hands sweeping up my back in a soothing caress. Half undressed – clad in only boots and breeches while stretched out on my stomach – I could feel the fabric of my best friend's shirt skim across flesh, causing prickles to form where it touched. "Jeffrey is who he has always been," I murmured. "I neither expect our tenor to change, nor care if it does."

"So many lies spoken all at once," Paolo said, clicking his tongue. I could envision him shaking his head while his hands pressed more firmly into the muscle of my shoulders. "If you want to believe that, though, I won't try to convince you otherwise."

A moan threatened to crest the threshold of my lips. "Yes, please. Permit me my delusions and I won't challenge yours."

"You're the only one in this room with delusions."

His weight settled more against me, causing me to lower from my elbows and lie flat against the bed. The sensation of his fingers threatened to be my undoing, coaxing outward more than mere satisfaction, though I remained uncertain of how much I wished carnal desire to grace us with its presence. The next breath I exhaled betrayed me with the amount of tension it bore. It hitched as his hands coasted from my backside up to my shoulders once more "You're doing it to me again."

Paolo laughed. "What is it you think I'm doing?" His tone bore a playful amount of mockery to it.

"Tempting me, you scoundrel. Ruining all chance I might have of brooding." The internal battle continued its skirmish, leaving me to wonder in which direction I should land. I knew I had no desire to discuss my brother any further, but feared saying nothing would force me to succumb far sooner than I felt inclined. "When did you discover the sort of man you are?" I asked, in an effort to continue our conversation.

"You mean the kind that beds other men?" he asked. When I failed to answer, he took it as my assent. "My cousin and I used to sneak away together. When my older brothers and sisters weren't looking and his parents were busy. We'd run off into the woods and he'd ask to go swimming. That was his signal. '*Andiamo, Paolo.*'" Parting his legs, he straddled my waist, forcing me to shut my eyes again. "One of the times when we swam, he watched me drip dry and I could see where his eyes went. What made me nervous was that I never minded him looking."

A small grin curled the corners of my mouth. The kneading of his hands into my tense muscles finally coaxed pleasured noises past my lips despite myself. "That isn't fair," I said.

"What isn't fair? That I know how to unwind you?"

"That you do it so bloody well." Another groan rumbled from my throat when the massage intensified. I felt him start to dig into my backside and smirked. "You keep trying to convert me."

He laughed. "I'm not trying to do anything. *You* were the one who first kissed *me*."

"Yes, well... Just so you know, I do still like women. I don't think your hands are going to do anything to cure me of that."

When he lifted up from me, I was tempted to rise to my elbows again. A powerful grip grabbed hold of my shoulder, though, throwing me onto my back before I could fight against it. Paolo was on top of me within seconds, pinning me onto the bed, a devious grin on his face.

"You can like whatever you want. I know what your *cazzo* is telling me."

His lips met mine before I could issue a response, tongue exploring my mouth as I found myself responding to the aggressive way he kissed me. My hands lifted to touch his body, arms circling his torso as he lowered to press our chests together. I rolled him onto his back and fought to keep him there. "Don't act smug about it," I murmured against his lips as I mirrored the mischievous smile. "Or I might have my way and deny you."

"*Fai come vuoi,*" he responded before our kisses turned heavier, our touch more searching. His shirt and the few articles of clothing we still wore became forfeit, and landed on the ground in a heap just before our bodies merged. The remainder of my concerns went away for a time, lost inside the throes of pleasure well after we cried out with completion and curled up together. Paolo's arms felt warm, clutching me against his chest as his fingers carded through my hair.

"You'll figure out who these people are, *amico mio,*" he whispered as he held me.

"I hope so." My eyes shut, body and mind both given over to exhaustion. "I seem to be the only one who cares." The last thing I remembered was the sound of his heartbeat while the rhythmic rise and fall of his chest lulled me to sleep. When we woke the next morning, I put my time with Jeffrey behind me. I needed to face Roland and grovel appropriately for my disappearance.

I found him seated at a table in the corner, as I often did when the inn on the far side of town became our meeting place. Not much had changed about him from the first day I met him, save but for the gray peeking in his hair and the few wrinkles which had twisted his facial expression into a perpetual scowl. He shook his head when I approached, peeling an apple he turned expertly in his three-fingered hand. "Christian, Christian, Christian," he said without looking up at me. "I don't know what's bound to get you into more trouble, your spontaneous holidays or the way you and your thief fail to cover up what you do inside that bedroom."

Smirking, I slid onto one of the empty chairs next to him. "Are you afraid the clergy's going to demand my head?" I asked.

He huffed, finally placing the knife down and looking up at me with a raised eyebrow. "I think I might give it to them. Especially if there's a reward."

I propped my feet up onto another chair and shrugged as I crossed one foot over the other. "I don't expect I'm getting paid for the ambush the other night, so we can forego the lecture on my sexual appetites. Although, I must say, getting the guardsmen drunk *was* a rather brilliant plan."

"You're sensitive lately." Roland took a bite out of his apple. Reaching into his cloak, he pulled out a small, leather purse and tossed it onto my lap. "Is my best assassin being overworked, or is this some personal bollocks that has you acting like a spoiled nobleman's whelp?"

Shooting him a look of annoyance, I untied the pouch and shifted my attention to the coins I poured into my hand. I took a moment to compose myself, under the guise of counting, and dropped the coins back inside for safekeeping. "It's personal bollocks," I said, pocketing the money. "The sort you normally don't like me talking about."

"Oh, that kind." He sank his teeth into the piece of fruit again. "You can't go running off every time this becomes an issue. Business is getting busy and there're some jobs I don't trust to the others."

"I'm going to take that as a compliment." Raising an eyebrow, I motioned with my hand. "Come out with it. I take it that means you've got another one for me."

His gaze shifted from the apple to me, his expression unreadable. He seemed to be weighing something in his mind for a moment before shrugging and swallowing down another bite. "As far as your usual fare's concerned, this one's relatively painless. But maybe that's what you need to get focused on your work again." Without pausing in eating, Roland reached into one of his belt's pouches and pulled out a small scrap of rolled up parchment, placing it on the table. "I love when the nobles hand me these, thinking I know what the hell they say. Fortunately, he was kind enough to spell it out with his tongue."

"You should learn to watch the way you word things around me." I smirked while reaching for the message, unrolling it once I had it in hand. "Should I offer again to teach you how to read?"

"You can offer all you'd like. I'll respond the same way I always do.

If I learned how to read, what use would I have for you?" He grinned wolfishly as I sighed and glanced at the parchment. It bore a form of shorthand on it, something I couldn't fully interpret.

Roland saw my furrowed brow and cut me off before I could ask. "It's a house belonging to a knight in Exeter," he said. "He was a spy for one side and then defected, so now his former employers are up in arms about what he might have taken with him besides knowledge. They didn't expressly ask for his head –" He paused to sink his teeth into the apple. When he spoke again, it was with his mouth partially full. "– But let's just say if he was to wander in while you're knocking over a lantern, there might be extra pay involved."

With a nod, I reread the message. *Lawrence; Exe. NE of Cathedral. 10 Fire; 15 Other.* The latter designation nearly had my jaw hanging agape. I ignored the remainder of the message in lieu of my surprise. "They want to pay that much for this?"

"They want it done, I suppose. I asked to see it, for what it's worth."

"Lord Bertrand's enemies didn't consider his guards worth more than one each."

"Those were guards. This is a knight."

"That he is." My eyes returned to the ink scrawling for an additional moment. "Is this his description?"

"Must be. Tall? Light brown hair? Barely sired from his father's loins, acting like he owns a piece of the world?" When I saw him look up at me in my periphery, I nodded. "That's it, then. They said his house should be easy enough to find, but you can usually make the tongues wag at the taverns if worse comes to worse."

"Once again, with the wording of your comments."

"I'll not change the way I say things just for your benefit."

When his gaze failed to lift from me, I glanced up at him once more, raising an eyebrow at the expression on his face. There was a measure of severity present, the kind normally reserved for delinquent youths. One finger extended to point directly at me. "Be mindful, lad. Exeter isn't the place for one of your quests," he said. "You're a dog on a hunt and it scares me when you have the look of blood in your eyes. I don't know what's crawling around in your head right now. I don't want to know. I just don't want you bringing in a mess for me to clean up."

"I won't ask you to clean any of my messes, Roland. Besides, I have more fun tending to them myself." Kicking my feet down from the chair, I rose to a stand, rolling the parchment up once more and using it to salute him. "I'll be on my way and report back in three days' time. Will that be soon enough?"

Roland frowned. "I'm sending people if it's any longer." I turned to leave, tossing the contraband in the air and catching it as a leisurely stride directed me toward the exit. "Burn that!" he added, calling after me.

"At once, your grace." I spun on my heels to bow in his direction, winking before continuing to make my way out. The parchment found its way into the hearth and a whistle passed through my lips by the time I reached the stables. It didn't surprise me when I spied Paolo running a brush through his ebony gelding's mane. His brow furrowed at the expression on my face, a missed stroke causing the animal to shake its head.

I smirked at the way Paolo scowled at the horse, cocking a thumb in the direction of the inn once I had my friend's attention again. "He calls me spoiled, but indulges me like a favored son," I said. "How does he expect me to ever learn my lesson?"

Paolo huffed, lowering the brush. He put away the grooming implement after sparing a quick glance at our makeshift home. "Nothing will ever teach you anything that thick head of yours doesn't want to learn, Sir Christian of the Black," he said, reaching for the horse's reins and starting the task of securing them into place. "I learned that within minutes of meeting you."

I laughed, walking over to Tempest and preparing her for a ride as well. While Paolo's beast – which he had named Diavolo – endured the securing of his bit with patient stillness, Tempest forced me to pause our discussion to attend her properly. I narrowed my eyes at her once the task had been completed. She responded with a huff. "Funny you should mention Sirs," I said, finally continuing. "I'm to find a knight in Exeter."

"Are you working alone?" Paolo hefted his saddle onto the horse's back.

"Yes, sadly, I am." As I followed suit, I flashed a grin at him. "Ride with me for a time, though?"

"I don't think I should, if you're looking for lessons to learn, *amico mio*." The corner of his mouth curled in a sly grin as he mounted his horse, the action in defiance of his words. I mirrored his expression and he rolled his eyes at me as he gave Diavolo a nudge. Together, we bounded for the edge of town, the last vestiges of our village passing in a blur, our pace not slowing until we reached the countryside.

From there, sporadic conversation made up the journey to the largest city in the immediate area. It wasn't the first time fate had brought me back since I had begged for food as a street urchin, but the occurrences had been few and far between. I failed to make mention of it to Paolo. It lingered in the forefront just the same, threatening to bring wisps of memory in its wake as we slowed to a stop and steadied our horses. Paolo glanced heavenward, before peering back at me. "I should turn back, so I can return before it gets dark," he said. A small grin tugged at the corners of his mouth. "Don't get into trouble. I won't be there to tell you when it's time to leave."

My lips curled in a grin. There was concern in his eyes, yes, but mischief present in his tone of voice. "I might be a lost cause," I said, my smile broadening. "Mourn my passing when I die from curiosity."

His dark locks of hair moved with the motion of him shaking his head. A string of Italian preceded him gripping the reins of his horse tight and nudging him at the sides. Diavolo turned and sped to a gallop at his rider's behest, leaving me there to admire the sight of Paolo riding back toward town. It took until I turned my horse to face my destination again for my disposition to sober. The rest of the ride was spent lost in thought until the city gates appeared before me

There it stood before me, beckoning me the same way it had all those years ago. At once, I felt nostalgia seep into my bones, now that I had the chance to indulge it alone. "What say you we take care of business quickly so we can have a bit of fun?" I asked, leaning forward to stroke the horse's mane and chuckling when Tempest responded with a neigh. With the first nudge of my heels, she led us forward in a cantor, the sun dipping in the horizon with dusk threatening to take over soon. The air bore a chill, but not enough of one to make the remainder of the journey uncomfortable.

It was forgotten the moment I immersed myself within the walls of Exeter.

CHAPTER FIVE

The unwelcome scent of farm animals, human waste, and tanners had made its presence known long before I entered, and became barely tolerable as I guided my horse through the crowd. I had already flipped the emblem of my cloak out of sight, my hood drawn over my head, so I could study the people lingering in front of the shops. The day at an end, they hurried to barter their last transactions before retreating indoors for supper. A gnawing sensation in my stomach told me I'd need a meal myself before I could focus on the task at hand, prompting me to dismount in front of the first inn I encountered. I stabled Tempest after conducting a brief transaction to provide her with her own dinner, and slipped inside where I also purchased a room for the next two nights.

A plate of mutton and a roaring fireplace brought the warmth back to my bones, and a short nap restored my energy just enough that venturing into the night became less of a chore than it might have been otherwise. By then, most of the market traffic and loitering occupants had made their way indoors, leaving the streets an eerie quiet even in areas where more raucous affairs were taking place. The bells of the cathedral chimed, but I hardly needed their clamor to lead me where I was headed.

I needed only the light of the stars, and the ominous glow of a crescent moon hanging in the sky above.

On foot, I paced my steps as though a man about business, not wanting to be bothered. I recognized a tavern as I passed it based on the sounds drifting through the air, and smirked when I saw men entering what I knew to be a house of ill-repute. These offerings faded as the streets widened and vestiges of opulence opened up before me. It took me only an hour to find the first likely place where Sir Lawrence might reside, based on the information given. There were several routes back to the inn, which I tested in the event of needing to make a hasty departure. The slums and alleys provided both the fastest methods of escape and the most conspicuous due to the amount of people with no where else to be, further emphasizing just how attentive I would need to be to the task at hand. Survey complete, I steeled myself for the patience of inactivity and settled in to watch the homes by the cathedral, taking refuge in the shadows.

The longer I waited, however, the more a strange premonition washed over me, summoning memories I normally prevented myself from entertaining. For the first time in a long while, a recollection of my father's passing wafted through my mind like the unwelcomed ghost it was, setting me on edge. "It's all in your head, Christian," I said, scolding myself as I climbed an adjacent tree, and sat perched on one of its branches. My dagger remained sheathed, my thoughts shifting back to my purpose in being there as a cold breeze drifted past me, inspiring a shiver. Inhaling with slow, measured breaths, I gripped onto the branch, just in time for the front door to the home directly across from me to swing open.

I stilled myself instantly when a figure emerged from within. A tall, fair-complected man of average build with a nobleman's sword strapped to his side, his hair was light enough to give the impression he might almost be ginger, calling to mind the description written on Roland's parchment. A woman accompanied him – an unexpected addition, and yet, one that looked less than pleased to be by his side. Her hair flowed across her shoulders in dark waves of brown, a burnt sienna to his dirty, strawberry blonde.

He nudged her along toward the street, with her silence the only protest she seemed apt to offer. Furrowing my brow, I mused upon what would force either of them out at such a late hour, watching as they rounded a bend and disappeared from sight. Shaking off the last of the apprehension which had buffeted me, I jumped soundlessly from the tree and crouched low. Years of this type of work made and the fact that I had not observed any guards or servants made it simple to slip into the house undetected. Once inside I found myself in a large room that looked to be the great hall.

Lanterns remained lit around the house as did the hearth, ensuring that setting the place ablaze would be an easy task. As such, it gave me the chance to peer around its confines. The manor itself was larger than even Lord Bertrand's, with lavish stairs winding upward to a second story and high, vaulted ceilings on the main floor. Pausing first to check again for servants, and confirming their absence, I found the room which clearly served as a personal study and marveled at the opulence on display. "Perhaps I am being underpaid," I murmured while stepping lightly toward the mantle. The ambient glow from the adjacent room guided me while lighting one of the oil lamps. Putting away my tinderbox, I surveyed the area in greater detail.

Books were arranged along one side of the wall. A table bore a quill and ink, with several pieces of parchment laid out in a haphazard fashion. I stole a glimpse at these first and moved on to the shelves when I failed to see anything of consequence. Pulling one of the volumes down, I held it up and examined the pages before sliding it back into place, curiosity getting the better of me.

The next book bore interesting binding, but its contents were irrelevant to me as well. As I took the one beside it down, I caught sight of something from the corner of my eye which took me aback. Half expecting I might have been hallucinating, I stared at the emblem on the cover, and plucked it from the shelf immediately, shoving the other book back into place. The fire in the center of a circle – the mark of the men who had killed Richard Hardi – adorned the volume. "You're in bed with the Devil as well," I said softly, tempted toward a moment's indulgence and all-too-willing to submit.

The tome looked read-through, the spine relaxed and flipping open to a section of pages toward the middle as it rested in my palm. I saw symbols sketched next to lines of handwritten Latin, most of which I could interpret with only a fledgling knowledge of the language. Sitting on the edge of the desk, I turned each page, desperate to figure out what I was looking at while already knowing I would be taking it with me. Unfortunately, it caused me to lost track of time in the process.

I was startled away from my reading when the door creaked open, forcing me to tuck the book behind my back beneath my cloak. Glancing around quickly for an impromptu strategy, I remained mired in indecision long enough to be spotted the moment the youthful man entered the room with his lady in tow. He paused his steps and I fingered the hilt of my sword when he looked to be weighing his next move. "Well, how do you like this, Jane?" he asked. "A rat in the library. Do we have ourselves a literate thief?"

Still wearing the same attire as when I first saw him on the street, he drew his sword and pointed at me. His female companion lifted an eyebrow, an expression I mirrored when my gaze shifted back to him. "Should reading be reserved for the aristocracy, Sir?" I asked. The corner of my mouth curled in a grin. "Perhaps I was bored and in need of more enlightenment."

"I believe you'll be leaving with far less than enlightenment." He advanced forward a pace, causing me to step back. "What is the meaning of that emblem on your cloak?"

"Much the same as what I might find on one of yours. I imagine you have a fetching red one hidden off somewhere."

Sir Lawrence paused in his steps, his eyes widening at me. The lady looked troubled as well, and motioned to advance forward, but he took notice quickly enough for him to shove her backward several paces. "This piece of filth is mine to handle," he said. "Get into my room and prepare yourself. I haven't finished with you yet."

I furrowed my brow at the act which played out before me, Jane staring defiantly at him and Lawrence extending a hand to slap her across her face. As she rubbed her cheek, my temper flared, the distraction enough time for me to draw my sword from its sheath, the sound prompting Lawrence's focus back to me. He narrowed his eyes. "You know of the Luminaries," he said, "And yet you would challenge me. You must truly be an idiot."

"The Luminaries." I repeated the name as a reflex, hearing it uttered for the first time and caught up in revelation as a result. The bastards who had robbed me of my father bore a title I could finally speak. Whether or not surprise showed in my expression, I cared very little, and brushed it aside just as quickly as it had surfaced. "I might be an idiot," I continued, "But at least I am not a cretin like you."

He looked more insulted than offended. "A peasant thief with the audacity to judge the character of a knight. I'll be certain to remove parts of you before I finish you off."

"A man who treats a woman of noble birth like little more than a whore in my presence should hardly call himself a knight." My eyes shifted quickly to Jane, thoughts becoming splintered across several paths as her brow smoothed, her shoulders lowering to a more relaxed posture, before my gaze flicked back to Lawrence. "I thought your ilk were supposed to be chivalrous."

"And I thought yours little more than swindlers." The hand on his chest rose, a finger wagging at me in the process. "She knows who her keepers are."

"Knows, perhaps, but I can tell you right now which of the two of us she's probably favoring." A smirk lilted across my lips.

Lawrence gritted his teeth. "Enough. I grow tired of you." He gripped hilt of his sword in both palms again, his posture settling into an offensive stance. It was enough of a warning that I had time to draw my own weapon before he took a practiced swing, forcing me to dodge and side step away. I had not determined which of us would attempt the first blow, but that I had unnerved him enough to force his hand worked in my favor. Anticipating the next attempt, I cut to the side and jumped atop the desk, avoiding his blade in the process.

He spun around and glowered at me. I shook my head. "You're going to have me prolonging the inevitable just so I can keep toying with you," I said.

"Insolent peasant," he muttered. Lawrence regrouped quickly, swinging much more frantically and forcing me to dodge a second time. I leaped from the desk, disrupting the few papers still on its surface. Kicking a chair at him, I created an obstacle between us he needed to circle in order to get to me. When our swords finally clashed, I had him on the defensive, pushing him off and catching another blow with my blade.

"Who the bloody hell taught you your sword skills, a barbarian?" I asked.

"Quiet, while I kill you." His heels touched the fallen chair, prompting him to kick it backward and perilously close to where Lady Jane stood. I stole the chance to swing for him, not surprised when he parried and retaliated. One hand behind my back, I let him press forward, gaging each step I took with caution while my sword caught each blow.

Risking a quick glance to the side, I judged how to change our path before springing to one side the next time he swung. The maneuver granted us more room, and me a chance to weigh disarming him. Sweat beaded on his forehead. I pivoted one way first, then another, not having to raise my weapon to avoid the two poorly timed shots. He charged and I spun, and with that the door of opportunity swung wide open for me.

I jammed my heel onto his foot. As he winced, I clubbed him in the jaw with the hilt of my sword and sent him stumbling to the side. The action forced him to let go of his weapon with one hand, and as the other struggled with the sudden weight of the sword, I reached for his wrist. Lawrence shouted obscenities, pawing at me with his now-unencumbered hand for me to let him go.

In the effort to rear back for the fatal blow, I left him enough room to swing a punch for me. While I managed to maintain my hold on his sword-laden arm, my focus had been disrupted to my peril. I drove my blade forward blindly, making the most foolish of errors in the process, and paying for it dearly when he took hold of my wrist and squeezed. I emitted a cry of offense. My weapon fell from my grip just as I clenched my jaw. "Dirty, cheating bastard," I said, twisting his arm in retribution.

He cried out as well. "Just bloody give up and die," Lawrence managed in return.

I scoffed. Lifting a foot, I drove it into his knee and distracted him long enough to pull free of his hold. Despite the throbbing left in its wake, I reached for a dagger and swiftly pulled it, plunging it into his shoulder and forcing him to drop his own blade. He produced a blood-curdling scream even when I removed it and pressed the tip against his throat. "Now, which of the two of us is going to die?" I spat through clenched teeth.

All at once, the look he gave me spoke to me just how much I had underestimated my opponent. Something sinister danced in his gaze, a sudden air emanating from him which had not been present during the duration of our fight. The way the tenor between us shifted rang horribly familiar, reminding me of the man who had pulled a blade from his chest before murdering my father. A shiver of dread ran up my spine. The muscles in my throat began to tighten. An ungodly amount of pain surged through my neck, until my grip upon my dagger relented, sending it clanging to the floor.

I stumbled backward and clutched at my throat with both hands. Gasping for one last breath, I managed it, but felt another squeeze stop me from taking the next. Sir Lawrence stood straighter, blood trickling from the wound I had inflicted, but determination written all over his face. I barked out a cough, but started to feel dizzy, both confused and panicked that he wasn't even touching me and yet managing to somehow strangle me. The recollection of Old John falling to the ground served as a chilling reminder; unless I fought back, I would surely perish the same way the innkeeper had.

No, something inside of me seemed to declare. He would not take me down so easily.

The invisible fingers coiled tighter, bent on crushing my ability to breathe. At the risk of regretting the decision, I clawed at my throat while attempting to concentrate on the invisible force being inflicted on me. I imagined his hands and fought to grab hold of them, using what little strength I possessed to loosen their grip. At first, I wondered if this might be an exercise in futility, but at the precise moment that the world started to go black, the choke started to waver and air rushed into my lungs again.

I broke into a series of coughs, my survival instincts honed on the singular motivation to stay alive. My hands continued yanking and tugging and I knew the instant the hold broke as I collapsed. Still hacking and now, adding a groan in the process, I struggled onto all fours, clearing my throat while the room spun and my vision switched from blurry to half-focus.

The moment my gaze fixed on Sir Lawrence again, his brow furrowed. "You shouldn't have been able to do that," he declared. His gaze flicked quickly to Jane before returning to me. "Are you a sorcerer?"

I laughed as much as possible, my voice hoarse and another coughing fit punctuating the action. My hand clutched onto the edge of another set of shelves for support while I cleared my throat. "Yes, absolutely, I'm just posing as a mercenary to alleviate boredom," I said. Plucking my sword from the ground, I shakily rose to a stand. "I haven't the foggiest idea what you're talking about."

"What are you, then?" When I motioned closer, Lawrence raised a hand. The genuine look of terror on his face left me confused, but at a clear advantage. "Don't step any closer, or else."

"Or else what? You might sneeze at me?" The rapidly shifting dynamic forced me on the razor's edge. I took another step toward him. "I have orders to kill you."

"What orders? From who?"

"A fairly wealthy individual, needless to say, and I enjoy being paid."

"No." He shook his head, backing away a few paces until he hit the wall of books behind him. "Tell Talbot I'm getting close. Tell him to give me more time." His face contorted and he dashed to the side scrambling for his sword and lifting it with his uninjured arm. "This doesn't have to get bloody."

"Considering you just tried to kill me, I think this has to get exceptionally bloody."

"I can pay you better."

I laughed. "If I had a gold coin for each time such an offer has been presented to me, I would be able to purchase a noble title."

Sir Lawrence threw a desperate swing for me and my anger got the better of me. With one violent arc, I knocked the sword from his hand and when I thrust the blade forward, it plunged through his stomach, cutting through to the other side. His eyes turned wide and he stared at me with a macabre expression on his face. "The flame of the eternal will not be extinguished," he said.

As I pulled my sword from his stomach, Lawrence fell to his knees and then, collapsed onto the floor.

The recitation of those words startled me as I watched his body still. Their echo in my mind, coupled with the mention this man named Talbot – made me wish for the first time I had spared his life a while longer. Staring at the blood which pooled beneath his corpse, I sighed and wiped his blood from my sword. "Stupid, impetuous man," I murmured, unable to look away.

The sound of rustling in the background knocked me from my stupor, however. Turning around, I remembered Jane once more as she regarded me from the doorway, an unreadable expression on her face. Her gaze flicked from my sword to my eyes while I furrowed my brow at her, wondering what she intended to do. Everything about her posture suggested she might flee. But surely she didn't think...

Jane called my bluff. Spinning around, she pulled up her skirts and dashed for the front entrance, leaving me stupefied until she threw open the door. At that precise moment, my brain engaged and instructed the rest of my body that I might not want a witness to escape into the night.

Sliding the sword back into its sheath, I pursued her.

She had left the door wide open, which aided in my pursuit, but if I considered myself swift, she managed to be swifter, even with the folds of her dress conspiring to slow her down. Jane made a frantic dash in the opposite direction of the escape path I had planned, past the cathedral and into a less-familiar section of town. Swearing under my breath, I poured all I could into the effort of catching up, wincing when I saw her turn out of sight. I rounded the same corner she had, then skidded to a stop once I emerged around the other side.

Lady Jane had completely vanished.

The absence of her presence confused me at first, too many options opening up before me with no time for me to make the wrong choice. Spinning around once, I took a deep breath and stepped cautiously in the direction of an intersecting street, noting the area bereft of any sort of candlelight or hearth light from any of the windows I passed. Only the moon and stars provided light to me, with not a sound to be heard belonging to a fleeing woman. I dashed for the next road, then looked both ways and retraced my steps. In an act of desperation, I scaled the wall of an adjacent tavern and peered around from the rooftop, expecting to see a fleeing woman in the distance.

Nothing. Not a damn thing.

"What the bloody hell is happening tonight?" I asked aloud, fingers running up to comb through disheveled locks of hair.

My hand trembled as I lowered it. Swallowing back a slight surge of nerves, I stole one final look around and managed my way down from the roof. For a while, I was able to distract myself with the thought that unless I found Jane, my head might join the others mounted on pikes, but as hours passed with no sight of her anywhere, more unsettling thoughts came upon me, leading me back to Lawrence's house. Reflexively, I patted my back, feeling the book I had stolen still present in its hiding place. I had almost died, I told myself. And I had been accused of sorcery.

My brow furrowed. I felt the urge to produce the tome again, but knew to linger much longer ran the risk of sunlight unmasking me before more sets of eyes than just one. Shaking myself free of a thousand clamoring thoughts, I felt the embers of fatigue surging to a full inferno and reminded myself that fire is what had summoned me here. My final act, before putting the residence of the late Sir Lawrence behind me, was to set it ablaze.

Stepping out onto the street, I ducked into hiding before allowing myself to admire my handiwork. The lone house stood enough of a distance away from anything to spare any further property the risk of igniting, but if I had to be honest with myself, I held no fear of its destructive force. Something inside the glow of orange red whispered to me with a voice I had never heard before, its muttering indistinct, but present just the same.

The world around me had indeed changed. How much so, I had no notion of just yet. I felt it in my bones, though, and carried it with me as I slunk my way back into the inn and collapsed onto bed. It crept under my skin even as sleep threatened to overtake me. Something had invaded its way into me, foreign and yet, familiar at the same time.

I felt it tingle even with the first dreams I entertained for the day.

CHAPTER SIX

While I had known many a woman to disappear in my time, I had never come upon one who could truly vanish. After rousing the next day, I risked discovery to wade through the market, hoping to find the sole witness to Sir Lawrence's demise. Her lack of presence there didn't surprise me entirely – it had been a whimsical prayer on my part that she would simply stand out from the crowd. The more I combed the town, however, the more I began to wonder if I had imagined the noble lady at his side.

If not for the presence of a burnt out residence, I might have suspected I made the entire thing up. Blending into the crowd who had gathered to behold the charred remnant of the house, I noticed that the fire had extinguished itself with the job of destruction half-finished. If he carried anything vital, it had been rendered into ash – and any sign of foul play would no longer be apparent on his corpse, which should have met with our client's expectations. If I had to be honest with myself, my thoughts were not centered on the thoroughness of my job, though. Neither were they completely with Jane.

A shiver settled in my bones, amplified by the chill in the wind, while I recalled that sensation which had overcome me the night before. Taking a deep breath, I stared at my fingers as I released it, flexing each digit as though that might carry some clue with it. That sense of something having changed still lingered, with more secrets waiting to be shared. It was as though I had become aware of something taunting at me, lingering just out of sight.

"Are you a sorcerer?"

"Nonsense," I murmured to myself, sighing and lowering my hand, looking up to gaze across the sea of faces once more. When I failed to spot Jane, I wandered off. My stomach had started to gnaw at me hours ago and my head swam with agitation, threatening to split in half if I deliberated on anything further. After eating, I waited for night to fall, tempted to pay for company if just to stop the wheels in my mind from turning. In the end, I determined not even carnal pleasures would do me any favors.

If I could just find her, and figure out what to do with her, then this would all surely pass. Or such is what I hoped, but one hour begat several more in its wake, each more frustrating than the last. Time passed at such a breakneck speed – evening giving way to night – that I began to think living in the shadow of a cathedral had granted the woman some favor with the Almighty. She was going to send me away empty-handed. I knew it and yet, wanted to spit when the next morning broke across the horizon. Daylight stole the last grains of the sand the hourglass had afforded me and I knew better than to risk arriving late.

The path leading out of Exeter bore extra stones, it seemed like, making the ride more bumpy than it had been days ago. Rest stolen along the way could hardly be accused for being refreshing, and my horse's final strides back into town felt labored, as though the beast bore the weight of my folly and strained beneath it. I frowned when I arrived at the inn that night, hoping against hope that the man who kept my employ would spare me the wrath I knew I had coming to me. I had gotten distracted again, and could hardly argue my harrowing experience as any legitimate excuse.

He sat in his normal chair, though, as if expecting me.

A fire crackled in the hearth and several men remained embroiled in light banter while a cast of familiar faces aligned themselves around the wooden counter on the far end of the main room. I sighed as our eyes met – it would figure Roland chose that moment to peer toward the door – and the expression on his face gave all indication something had put him in a foul mood. Walking forward, I passed by where Paolo sat, clapping him on the shoulder as he worked on polishing off the rest of his supper. "Say a prayer for the condemned, *amico mio*," I muttered to him as I walked away.

My best friend looked up, but I gave him no opportunity to respond. Making a deliberate show of my stroll up to Roland, I finished it off with an exaggerated bow only a scant few feet away from where he sat. "The deed has been accomplished as you have requested," I said.

Roland's shoulders lowered, but the look in his eyes still entertained skepticism like an old guest he had long forgotten how to dismiss. "Sit," he said, extending a leg to kick a chair out for me. "I want details."

"Very well." Glancing down at the seat, I raised an eyebrow at it and fought the urge to reach for the edge of the table. Anything which gave away the knotting in my stomach would show my hand too soon and I knew better than to allow Roland any insight into my thoughts. As it stood, hours of travel had done nothing to help me determine what I might say to him. "What is it you want to know?"

If he noticed my unease, he gave no indication of it. "When? And is he dead or without a home?"

"Both, which means I doubt he minds what I did to his property. Sir Lawrence met with his timely end the evening before last." A grumble interrupted me, my stomach picking that moment to protest the scent of food and my lack of provision. I sighed at it. "This place brings out the glutton in me."

A smile cracked the corner of his lips. "I'd guess you hadn't had a meal since this morning, but you're always being led around either by your gut or your cock. Let me find where Mildred got to." He pivoted in his seat, glancing around the sea of faces. I felt a lightness settle in the air that bordered on excessive, threatening to topple again at a moment's notice. It was then that I realized how much my perceptions had colored the world around me, from the expression on his face to the tenor of the room. Even the way Paolo tried to get my attention in my periphery while Roland searched for the barmistress. One thing remained consistent through it all. I was being assaulted by my own conscience.

"Wait, Roland." I spoke the words before I could stop myself and cursed them the moment they escaped my lips. Roland turned to face me again and I winced at the way he raised an eyebrow at me. "Before we summon food on my behest, we should discuss what happened further," I explained.

"I'll have you get into it more once you've been served supper, lad," he countered. "There isn't any sense you starving for the longer version of what you just told me."

"Except that isn't all that occurred the other night." The confession prompted Roland to settle fully in his seat, his undivided attention focused on me. It summoned a flurry of nerves anew. "There was a lady. She looked to be of noble birth, at any rate. Our employers failed to mention he had taken up with company and she was present when he and I had our confrontation."

"Confrontation?" Roland furrowed his brow before dismissed the question with a wave of his hand. "What did you do with her?"

"You see, therein lies the conundrum." Clearing my throat, I fidgeted in my seat, unable to hold back the compulsion any longer. "Lawrence came upon me in his library and she remained present as we fought. I bested him, of course, but as I attempted to sort out my next move, she ran off."

"She ran off?" The repetition of what I had confessed bore a hint of incredulity to it. "Hitched up her skirts and fled into the streets?"

"Yes. She was out the door before I had even left the library."

"A noble lady was faster than a long-legged slip of nothing like you? You expect me to believe this?"

"I suppose if won't help when I say she vanished after that."

"I'll ask how much you'd had to drink before you set out that night." Roland sighed, any humor he might have summoned falling away into the most disgusting form of concern I had ever seen dance across his emerald eyes before. "Christian, you best not be lying to me. If she was aristocracy, they'll want your head. What in God's name have you done?"

Opening my mouth to speak once more, Roland lifted his hand to stop me from proceeding. He shook his head at me and frowned. "You bear our cloak," he continued. "If they come looking for you, I'll have no choice but to turn you over and they won't accept anything less than your life. I mean it. I will not be able to hide you away without threatening us all."

With a nod, I glanced away and said, "If you must, then you must."

"No, I don't think you're getting what I'm trying to tell you. You've bent the rules near to breaking in the past, but you have a woman who can whisper in the right sorts of ears and she knows you wore a mercenary's cloak. If she talks, there isn't a story that can be spun that keeps you from being drawn and quartered. Christian..." He narrowed his eyes at me. "Don't you dare tell me this has anything to do with your little quest."

I glanced back in his direction and held his gaze, weighing in my head what I should say. In some other reality, I saw myself confessing toward seeing the book, and fighting my way out of the clutches of death. I could hear my voice ringing in my ears, bearing the nervousness I felt over how I had freed myself, and how that feeling had attached itself to me ever since. Roland regarded me in silence, seeing the words lingering on my tongue and nearly willing them to life with his stare.

Shifting my attention away from Roland, I answered him only in silence. He sighed and shook his head, rising to a stand. "Eat a meal," he said. "And gather your things. I want you out of my sight until I know they're not coming for you."

He motioned to walk away. I shot to my feet. "Where am I supposed to go?" I asked.

Roland paused, his back partly turned to me. I watched his shoulders lift and fall, the sound of him exhaling an unpleasant note of finality. "That's your problem, not mine. Just tell Paolo where you wander off to, so I can fetch you."

"Very well." It was all I could think to say and yet, as Roland stormed for the stairs, I chewed on a thousand different responses, even after he had started his ascent toward the rooms. The sound of footfalls distracted me only enough for me to register Paolo in the corner of my eye. "What in the heavens am I to do?" I asked, caring very little for how crestfallen I sounded.

"*Non lo so,*" he said with a shrug. Paolo lifted a hand to scratch at the back of his neck. "Do you think you're in any trouble?"

"I don't think so. There didn't seem to be any guards around the knight's house looking for me, but Jane might not have told the authorities yet."

The weight of Paolo's gaze fell on me, compelling me to look his way. When he raised an eyebrow at me, I scoffed, shaking my head. "It isn't like that," I said. "Her knight referred to her by name."

Paolo hummed noncommittally, sighing to chase away whatever had prompted the tacit accusation. "And she saw what you did?" he asked. "Did I hear you correct?"

"Witnessed the whole blessed thing. Is it too much to hope she was a figment of my imagination?"

A frown tugged at the corners of Paolo's mouth as he considered something quietly for a few moments. Finally, he glanced back at me, a hint of resolve in his expression. "I will ride with you to your brother's house. You can stay out of trouble there."

"Not Jeffrey." Groaning, I collapsed back into my seat, both palms pressing against my temples before sliding up into my hair. I felt the urge to grab handfuls and tug. "I think lingering here and awaiting my impending death might be a preferable fate."

"Don't joke about such things." Paolo's frown deepened.

I sighed at him. "I'm frightened," I said, lowering my voice. "About a few things, some of which I don't feel like discussing right now. My brother has no sympathy for any of that."

Paolo shook his head and lowered into the chair where Roland had been sitting. "I know, but it might be for the best in other ways. It's far away enough for me to have time to reach before they do. If someone does come looking, we can get you somewhere safer."

"Is any place safe when the aristocracy places a bounty on your head?"

"You're asking *me* this question, *amico mio?*" My eyes met his in time for me to catch the solemn smile which traced across his lips. "There are many places you could hide if you needed to. The nobles are too distracted right now to look. You're in danger if you stay, but not in so much in danger that you can't run. I think Roland just wants you scared."

"Well, I hardly needed his help." For the second time that night, a full confession threatened to pour past my lips, suppressed only when I decided I didn't have the energy to relate it. Instead, I took a deep breath and exhaled it slowly, in an effort to settle my nerves. "I saw that look, you know. You're right, I did ask you that question, but I'll ask another. You've had to run from home before, but this is my problem, not yours. Why should you bother saving me from it?"

My friend shook his head at me. "*Non capisce una mazza,*" he said, the tone of his voice soft and latent with exasperation. I furrowed my brow at the unfamiliar phrase as he sobered. "Eat something. Promise me you'll tolerate your brother at least for a few days, *si?*"

"I will try, but I can't guarantee anything."

"No, of course you wouldn't." Paolo nodded at the door. "Meet me at the stables."

I wanted to protest – asking if we might tarry long enough for me to get a decent night's sleep – but the words locked up in my throat. I watched the way he stood, left bare by the concern in his gaze when he cast one last look back at me before trudging away. For just a moment, the concept of noble women and sorcerers drifted out of my mind, replaced by the image of my friend walking out of the inn, and the door swinging shut behind him. Taking a deep breath, I exhaled it slowly and summoned Mildred over to request a plate of supper.

My thoughts remained a muddled form of discord throughout the meal. As I slipped a few belongings into a bag, I included the spell book I had pilfered and sighed while slinging the strap over my shoulder. I found Paolo in the stables, readying Diavolo, and caught his gaze as I approached beside him. A silent discussion commenced in the look we exchanged. Even as I leaned close and kissed his cheek with reverence, I didn't know what we had resolved in the tacit conversation, except that he felt closer to me in that moment than any time beforehand. He reached for my shoulder and patted it. "Come. Get your horse," he murmured. "Let's get you on your way."

I nodded and turned for where I had secured Tempest, preparing her in silence and mounting her once I had secured my bag. For once, she behaved the first time I pulled at the reins and turned her to face the open doors leading out of the stables. We trotted up to Paolo's side and he flashed a small smile at me before whistling at his horse. With a nudge, we took off, both steeds entering into a gallop at our behest.

Along the way, I fought the urge to doze, allowing my mind to roam wherever it pleased when Paolo and I weren't engaged in conversation. We paused after dawn so I could splash some water on my face and picked a couple of apples. After stopping in a small village tavern for a meal, and to rest the horses, we pressed on as fast as the steeds would carry us for the remainder of the journey. By the time we arrived at Jeffrey's farm, the sun had begun another dip in the horizon, leaving the sky a mixture of deep reds and purples, threatening toward dark.

I secured my horse in the barn and Paolo tied his gelding to one of the hitching posts near the house. It was as he had Diavolo secured that Jeffrey emerged from within, holding Ida in his arms. Taking a deep breath, I steeled myself and moved to close the gap between us. "Good evening, brother," I said. Jeffrey furrowed his brow and clutched his daughter closer, almost spurring me to sigh. Even she didn't know what to make of the sight of me so soon. "Rendering you mute is a rare treat. I should keep this in mind should I ever desire to do so again."

Jeffrey frowned. "I have a hard time believing this visit is auspicious, Christian," he said.

"Pleasant to see you, too." Paolo assumed a position beside me, if just to scowl sternly at me and I sighed. My eyes shifted back to Jeffrey as I managed my best impersonation of chagrined. "I need to stay with you for a few days. I know this is abrupt, but I had nowhere else to go."

Jeffrey furrowed his brow, studying me in silence until he finally set Ida down. The little girl lingered by her father's side. "Should I ask what's prompted this? Are you in some sort of trouble?"

"When am I not? At the same time, I'd rather not discuss it. Not until I've had a proper night's sleep."

"I suppose I can wait until morning." His gaze shifted between Paolo and me before settling on my friend. "I don't think we've been introduced. I'm Jeffrey Richardson, Christian's brother."

"No, we haven't," Paolo said, closing the distance and extending a hand. His accent sprang fully to life, as it always did whenever he spoke his own name. *Paolo Bellini di Verona.* Christian and I are friends."

"A friend? I didn't know Christian had those." Jeffrey shook the extended hand, his gaze shifting toward the emblem on the other man's cloak before he released his hold on Paolo. My brother paced backward a few steps, reaching for Ida and clasping his fingers around hers when she lifted her arm. "Will you be staying with us, too?"

My friend tensed. "I probably shouldn't."

"At least rest up for the ride back." Whatever apprehension my brother fostered about having another mercenary under his roof, he seemed apt to attempt ignoring it. Instead, he nodded toward the house. "I'm afraid we only have the one other bed, but maybe Christian won't mind sleeping on the floor, since he's the one in trouble."

He cast a quick glance at me and I fought to bite my tongue. If Jeffrey was apt to offer hospitality, I figured I should not be the one to cast aspersions. When I failed to issue a cheeky retort, Jeffrey turned his back to Paolo and me. "Come inside," he coaxed. "Have a bite to eat. We'll save discussion for the morning, Christian."

"For the morning," I repeated, so as not to be completely rendered mute. Paolo and I exchanged a look while Jeffrey disappeared inside the house with Ida. Nodding toward where they entered, I reached to pat my friend's shoulder and garnered a sigh from him, the exasperation latent in it bearing affection despite itself. He motioned forward and I followed in his wake, shutting the door behind us and removing my cloak without further prompting from my brother.

Paolo mimicked the gesture, and together, we sat and accepted bowls of water to clean our face and hands before being offered what remained of their supper. After Jeffrey's wife took away the soiled plates, Ida bounded to us and yanked me by the hand. "Papa says I need to show you to your room while he tucks Ivette into bed," she said, adding another tug for emphasis.

I laughed and exchanged a smile with Paolo. "By all means, little bird. Lead the way," I said.

My niece nodded, solemn in her duties and silent until I opened the door to where we'd be sleeping. The satchel I deposited by the main entryway had found its way inside. I reached to pluck it from where it rested while Paolo bent and kissed Ida's hand, causing her to giggle. She bounded off and Paolo shut the door after watching her depart. I couldn't help but to smile. "She and her sister both are treasures," I quipped, setting the bag onto the bed long enough to ensure its contents intact before lowering it back onto the floor.

"I had nieces," Paolo said. "Nephews, too, but that was a long time ago." He sat in the sole chair in the room and reached to remove his boots while studying his modest surroundings. Apart from a bed and the chair, there wasn't much else besides four walls, a window, and a crude table poised in the corner of the room. Together, it formed a luxury most men of Jeffrey's station didn't enjoy – a makeshift room for guests.

I stole a glance around as well before peering back at Paolo, a small smile dancing across my lips. "This is where I slept for two years before running off to kill people."

Paolo snorted. "Your brother keeps it for you?"

"He harbors blind hope I might someday retire from this unsavory life and become like him."

We exchanged a smirk and a raised eyebrow, the joke not even needing to be stated to be understood. Paolo rose to his feet and padded to the bed, depositing his weight on top until he was settled supine atop it. I closed the distance and looked down at him with my brow yet upturned.

He looked up at me and grinned. "Your brother said you get the floor," he explained, lifting a hand to gesture with it. "Hospitality, *si?*"

"You are a scoundrel, *Signor Bellini*," I said lowering onto the floor and spreading out there. Paolo reached for me and I took hold of his fingers, compelled to bring the back of his palm to my lips. Something about clutching onto him made me yearn to curl into his arms, fatigue nipping hungrily and compelling me to relent. Our fingers remained intertwined until I heard the faint sound of him snoring, knowing he had succumbed and apt to do the same.

The sight of my satchel forced my tired eyes open, however, the whispers sprinting even faster than the compulsion for sleep and overtaking me first. Reaching for the shoulder strap, I pulled the bag closer and tipped it onto its side so I could open it. The sight of the spell book's spine compelled me to pull it out, and as I flipped to the middle, an English phrase caught my attention, causing my blood to run cold.

'The flame of the eternal shall not be extinguished.'

Lawrence's dying words echoed as an unpleasant reminder both of our encounter and my current predicament. Shutting it on impulse, I shoved it under the scant amount of room available under the bed and settled back into place. Moonlight from the windows danced across the wall and the rhythmic sound of Paolo lulled me back into a relaxed state, until my lids descended at last.

My dreams that night would be unencumbered. I could not help but to wonder, though, if they would remain as such for long.

CHAPTER SEVEN

I stole a kiss from him when he woke, hesitant to do much else where my brother could find us. As Paolo tended to his horse, I watched in silence, my mind too crowded to settle on any one thought long enough to indulge it. My heart turned heavy when he finished feeding and watering Diavolo and adjusted the gelding's saddle again. I almost said the words, '*Please, don't go,*' but choked them back with what little will I could muster.

"Be safe," I said, instead, walking closer when Paolo settled himself on the saddle and gripped harder onto the reins. One hand settled onto his horse's neck, brushing back its mane, while I regarded my lover. "I'll see you in a few days."

"One way or another, *amico mio,*" he said. A wink punctuated the comment, a moment of levity given over to such a sobering thought, making it easier for us to share a smile. I paced backward and he nodded, his focus shifting to directly ahead of him. With a whistle and a nudge, he coaxed the beast forward, until they both disappeared down the road.

Taking a deep breath, I steadied myself before walking back into the house. The door was open, combining the distant sound of children playing in the fields with the scent of dinner cooking in the hearth as I entered. Directing my attention toward the food, I strode closer, watching my brother's wife stir stew in a cauldron. Jeffrey stood beside her, already sweaty from work.

He glanced at me as I approached. "Good day, Christian," he said. "Your friend is on his way, then?"

His voice bore a convivial tone I immediately despised. "Yes, unfortunately so, but our employer is a harsh taskmaster. He would have become angry with Paolo if he lingered," I said. A yawn crested past my lips as I finally made eye contact with him. "Alas, you're stuck with me instead."

"Not much changed in nine years, then." He flashed a small smile before patting Anne on the shoulder and walking away. I followed him to the table, where a fresh loaf of rye bread sat cooling. Jeffrey pulled out a plate and a knife. "I trust you rested well, considering you look much less exhausted today."

"I did. Barely slept for the last three days and spent two of them in travel." I slid onto one of the bench seats. "As it is, I'm fortunate Paolo accompanied me here. I might have collapsed along the side of the road otherwise."

"Somehow, I don't doubt that." He thanked Anne as she walked over with scraps of cheese and meat, folded up into a cloth. She deposited it onto the plate and turned back toward the cauldron. It took my brother continuing for me to train my attention back to him. "Your friend is very... exotic. He said he hails from Verona?"

I nodded, both hands lifting to smooth back the locks of my hair. "Yes, he does. I know very little about his homeland as he prefers not to speak of it. He ventured to England about seven years ago and already knew English by the time we met."

"You two seem fond of each other. Should I accuse you of caring for someone other than yourself?"

"Accuse me of whatever you want. I will neither confirm, nor deny it."

"I believe there are times when you say things just to be contrary with me." Placing two large slices of bread onto the plate, he passed it over to me, inviting himself to sit in the bench directly across. Jeffrey nodded at the meat on my plate. "You're fortunate our lord's had excess. You've had a proper treat with us during both of your visits."

"A silver lining to the cloud." Regardless of my disposition, I did not mean the words to be wounding. Picking up a piece of bread, I ripped off the crust and popped a chunk of it into my mouth. "Out with it," I managed while chewing. "You're staring at me like a hungry dog begging for scraps."

"You did say we would talk in the morning," Jeffrey countered. "I was simply going to give you a chance to eat first." He sighed, his disposition sobering. Glancing at his wife, he caught her eye and nodded at the comely woman, causing her to straighten her posture. She checked the food one last time, then turned for the front door and walked toward it.

Jeffrey waited for her to disappear from sight before turning fully to face me again. "How bad is it, Christian?" he asked, his voice subdued.

I shrugged, attempting to seem impassive even as a knot formed in my stomach. "The potential to be terrible," I said, swallowing the bite of bread down. "More than likely, though, it'll only earn me a harsh rebuke. If I was in mortal danger, I don't think I would've made it here in such relative peace."

"Noted." Although my gaze fell from his, I could still sense the troubled way he regarded me. "From where is this rebuke coming?"

"My employer." I bit off some of the cheese. "Roland has been warning me to pay better mind to my duties than my hobbies and this particular instance proved him right."

"I wonder if I should bother saying I appreciate that there are others minding after you."

"Please don't. I think all of you fail to note I'm not a child any longer." Slowly, I looked up at him, casting a weary gaze at my brother meant to ward him off nagging me much further. Once the message had been conveyed, I turned my attention back to the food. "Paolo minds after me as well, Jeffrey, if you were going to thank anybody for bearing that cross."

"I think I should." Jeffrey paused, taking in a deep breath. I glanced at him again as I heard him release it with no small amount of heaviness. "I am weighing whether or not I should ask what would make an employer of scoundrels angry at you, Christian. I know what your hobbies have entailed. Did you have another brush with a cultist?"

"I did, yes. I was to kill him. It was as I was examining his library that he walked in with a companion. He met his end, but she fled before I could reckon what to do with her. "

Jeffrey somehow managed to bite back whatever comment I saw aching to brim past his lips. Instead, he clasped both hands on the table, far too close to my food for my comfort. "Perhaps God is granting you the chance to reevaluate your life. There's more than enough land here to work. It's a rewarding life."

"A dull and stationary one, you mean."

"It's stability. Why do you fight against that so much?"

"Perhaps I'm not a stable man, Jeffrey." Picking up what remained of the meat and cheese, I crammed it into the final slice of bread while rising to a stand. My brother looked up at me as I peered back down. "You are a good father and a caring husband," I said. "I am reckless, selfish, and haunted."

"I think you don't give yourself a chance to be anything else," he countered.

"No. But I recall trying to be you for a short time. It didn't work out very well."

Biting into the piece of bread, I set my sights upon the door. Jeffrey frowned, but didn't fight against my departure. I could already hear his objections circling around my thoughts anyway. The notion that there was a composed, quiet man somewhere deep in my heart bore all the earmarks of folly, a delusion I couldn't hold true as I knew myself far too well. As I stepped outside, I passed his wife and spoke to her without glancing her way. "I believe we're done disagreeing for the moment," I said. "I'm off to finish my meal in peace."

She opened her mouth to respond, but I didn't let her. Instead, I wandered down toward the fields and sat at the edge of them. Once I had finished eating, I spied where my nieces had run off to, smiling at them as they caught my gaze and waved me over. Another child – a boy; presumably one of the other workers' sons finished with his chores for the day – regarded me curiously, but helped pull me into their games for as long as my tired limbs would permit. Their squeals of joy lightened my disposition, laughter still ringing in my ears when I strode down to the stream to finish tidying up.

It wasn't until after I returned for supper that I felt the whispers return. Anne collected the bowls as we finished eating and the cups once the last of the ale had been consumed. The warmth of food and drink settled on my stomach for a time, but when the chill returned to my bones, I excused myself. My brother nodded and Anne regarded me in her usual silence, the smallest of mercies offered in that neither argued with my departure. Within a few moments, I had locked myself within the sanctuary of my room.

Sinking into bed, I nestled in until I felt comfortable. Faint strains of conversation drifted in from the main room. The last, lingering embers of sunlight filtered through the windows, though not enough to disrupt the pervasive darkness. I sighed, rolling to a stand again and searching through my satchel for my tinderbox and the candle I had stolen from Lord Bertrand. As it burst into life, the glow emanating from the wick comforted me, coaxing me to pull out the spell book out from under the bed.

I lowered atop the straw mattress once more, setting the candle aside and opening up the tome to its first page. Latin filled the next first few pages, with strange symbols jotted next to the words I had never before seen. Sitting up, I pulled the candle closer, flipping from section to section while trying to sort out what any of it meant. More of the same followed until I stopped on a page with a different sort of writing than had been on any preceding it.

The Latin was still there, but under each word was a broken up rendition of that term, hyphens separating each syllable with the occasional variance in the spelling. It wasn't until I recited in my head that I realized what had been done. "Pronunciation," I murmured, turning another page and seeing more of the same. I squinted at one phrase in particular, which seemed to precede both blocks of text, and mouthed the words first before giving unction to them. "*Evo... catio...*" I frowned and attempted it again with more confidence. "*Evocatio spiritualis.*"

A shudder raced up my spine like quicksilver, forcing the book to drop from my hand and onto the floor. I scrambled to collect it, knocking over the candle and having to refocus my efforts toward righting it before it could catch the bed on fire. Hot wax dripped onto my fingers and I bit back a yelp while placing the candle beside where the tome had landed. Swearing underneath my breath, I wiped my fingers off on my pants, eyeing the sigil on the cover with a measure of fear. "Witchcraft," I said, keeping my voice down lest my brother hear me.

"Are you a sorcerer?"

Shaking my head, I forced the question out of my mind once more while studying the hand I had burned. It caught me by surprise as I watched it tremble, but what shocked me even more was the realization of how desperately I wanted to try that again. "No," I said, picking up the book and shoving it back under the bed. I blew out the candle and rushed from the room, deciding to take a walk lest I act suspicious in front of my brother. It took hours for me to feel settled enough to return, and even then, I snuck in quietly to avoid notice. Slipping inside my room, I slept without touching the tome for the remainder of the night.

The next morning, I rose and found myself unwittingly forced into assisting my brother in the fields. The day had all but passed before I could seclude myself once more, the call of the spell book easy to ignore behind the veil of fatigue. It wasn't until the day following that I woke to find my fingers itching, something rippling under my skin as though apt to burst through the seams. I took a quick walk to the creek in some effort to abate it.

And yet, as I scooped up handfuls of water, even the sensation of the droplets stung in an odd manner. My breaths turned shallow and I toppled onto the ground in a seated position, attempting to figure out what had come over me. Vignettes passed through my thoughts, a discordant symphony of revelation pushing at invisible barriers and attempting to burst forth. The look of shock on Lawrence's face. The wary way Jane had eyed me and the change to the air when I beheld the fire consuming Lawrence's house. I forced myself to a stand, determined to make it back inside so I might make good on burying the book at last. After three days, the itch had become too much to tolerate.

As I stepped across the threshold, however, I saw my brother poised by the hearth and paused when he looked up at me. "Christian," he said, instantly stopping me from advancing any forward. A pregnant pause weighed in the air between the issuance of my name and Jeffrey continuing. "Could we talk?"

"Don't you have to get out to the fields?" I asked, but as my eyes rose to meet his, I saw what he held in his left hand and winced. He raised an eyebrow at me and I issued a shaky breath once I had taken stock of the full scenario. "Ah. I see you took it upon yourself to rummage through my things," I said, my gaze shifting briefly to Anne and the girls before my returning to my brother.

Jeffrey held the tome up as though to display it. The frown which overtook his expression bore a significant amount of weight, something dancing in his eyes I had never seen present there before. As I regarded him in silence, my brother scowled and I realized this would be unlike any of our other disagreements by the way the air shifted around us.

"What is this thing doing in my house?" he asked. "And when were you intending to tell me about it?"

CHAPTER EIGHT

W hile I had long since mastered the art of annoying my brother, I hadn't ever managed to inspire the sort of glower being directed toward me. I froze in position, as did Jeffrey, save but to gesticulate once more with the spell book. "Christian, do you have *any* notion as to what this is?" he spat when I failed to break the tense silence which had settled between us.

A frown tugged at the corners of my lips as I weighed my response to him carefully. Something told me this had the potential to turn rash at any moment. "I have some idea now, yes," I said.

"Then you brought this satanic nonsense into my home *deliberately?*"

The vitriol in his tone made me raise an eyebrow. I hazarded another step closer to him, waiting to speak until I was absolutely certain he wouldn't overreact in response. "Jeffrey, I might be risking angering you further by asking this, but how do *you* know what it is?"

"It doesn't matter. What matters is that you have taken this vendetta of yours far enough. You brought it under my roof, where my wife and children sleep, and I won't tolerate it." He gestured toward the girls with his unencumbered hand while finally lowering the book to his side. "I am throwing it into the hearth and we are not speaking another word of it ever again."

He turned his back to me, facing the fire as he did so. "Wait!" I barked the word before I could stop myself, the caution I had been compelled toward replaced by an urge to rip the book away from him at all cost. Dashing forward, I reached for it, scowling when Jeffrey yanked it away from the tentative hold I had managed. "You are not throwing that in the fire. I'm not finished with it yet."

"Not finished with it?" Jeffrey laughed, the sound devoid of all humor. "Have you gone mad?"

"No, I haven't. I risked my neck for that and haven't yet determined how useful it might be."

"Christian, I couldn't care less. It goes in the fire."

"*No.*" Making another swipe for it, I forced him to turn and face me again. Jeffrey tucked the book behind his back, freeing both hands to take hold of my wrists. I clenched my jaw, bucking against the restraint while cursing the strength working the fields had granted him. "You have *never* understood me," I hissed, not certain why I felt it necessary to say, but knowing somehow it needed to be stated. "Not in the time I lived with you and not in any year since. If you have no desire to help me, then *fine*, but don't call me mad for wanting answers."

"Answers to what?" he countered. "The same riddles that drive you to *kill*? Has it ever occurred to you that you're no better than any of those animals who came after father?"

"You *bastard.*" I ripped my hands away from his grip and swung at him before I could stop myself. The blow landed solidly on his jaw, knocking him backward and forcing him to clutch onto the mantle before he lost his footing. Jeffrey surged back at me, and I stumbled into the table as my brother pushed at me. Anne scurried away from us. Tugging Ida and Ivette with her, she circled the girls in her arms while Jeffrey and I sized each other up. "I can't believe those words came out of your mouth," I shouted. "I am *nothing* like them."

"The lies you tell yourself to rest at night." The volume of Jeffrey's voice rose to match mine. He pointed toward the door while speaking. "You cause injury to people for coin and you like it, brother. I know you do. You punish the world because you feel you were punished and you extend this anger back to me. I have no more contempt for you than you have for me, Christian. I might not grasp why you hold on to this malice, but you fault me for wanting nothing to do with it. And now you let yourself get seduced by the very thing that killed our parents?"

I opened my mouth to bark back a response, but stopped. As his words echoed in my mind, confusion overshadowed rage and demanded audience before my tirade could continue. "You mean the thing that killed our father?" I asked, my voice shaking with emotion.

Jeffrey furrowed his brow at me as though I was speaking nonsense. He issued several steadying breaths, in a defensive stance lest I come at him again, but still otherwise. "Yes, that was what I meant," he said, his gaze flicking to his wife before shooting back toward me.

"No, it isn't." I frowned and lowered my hands to my sides. Jeffrey relaxed slightly, and he and I remained locked in a stalemate when he refused to respond to the assertion. Shaking my head, I stole the chance to step close and reach around for the book, retreating a few paces once I had it in hand. I was grateful when he didn't try to stop me. "Jeffrey, why the hell did you say our parents? How do you know what this is?" I lifted the book before gesturing toward my chest with it. *"Tell me."*

"I *can't.*" At the same time, I heard resignation seep into his words, a breath exhaled after their issuance which made his shoulders slump. In the moments which followed, he remained silent, his fingers combing through his hair while he clenched his eyes shut. I stole the chance to peer toward Anne, experiencing a rare moment of kinship with her as she peered back at me, at an apparent loss.

My brother exhaled loudly, drawing our attention back to him. "Anne, could you please take the children outside?" he asked, his hand falling to his side and eyes opening to regard her. The look they bore had taken on a significant amount of fatigue and I felt a pang of sympathy for him. "They shouldn't have even heard this much."

She nodded and peered down at the two girls clinging to either side of her waist. "Come along, sweetlings," she said. "We need to go outside while Papa talks." I frowned at the way the girls nodded, seeing the fear they harbored and remembering belatedly that I had struck their father in their presence. Somehow, there didn't seem to be the right words to issue to either of them. I might have expected Anne's expression to be chillier toward me when she regarded me again, but she looked confused, and departed without another word spoken.

I sighed once I knew we were alone, nodding at the mark forming on my brother's cheek. "I lost my temper," I said, tucking the book behind my back, into the waistband of my pants, before it could become a point of contention again. "I apologize."

"I'm more used to you wounding me with words, not with fists," he retorted. Jeffrey trudged toward the bench seats and lowered himself into one, pointing at the one opposite from him. "I don't know if it's wise to tell you anything. It'll probably only encourage you."

"You'll forgive me if I balk at your condescension. They were my parents, too." Slowly, I lowered into the seat and took a calming breath, folding both hands atop the table separating us while doing so. "I have every right to know their fate."

"What you have a right to know and should know are different things, in my opinion."

Silence settled between us again, a more settled quiet than what had been present beforehand. I watched Jeffrey gather his thoughts, looking away for a short time before peering back at me and nodding. "I never forgave him for what happened," he said. "A lad of eight years and I hated him for taking our mother away. I know how close you were to Father. I never wanted to say anything ill about him, so I bit my tongue. But if you want to know why I went off on my own as soon as I did, that is why."

My brow furrowed. "I don't understand what you mean by that, Jeffrey," I confessed. "I've always been told mother died of a fever."

"Mother had fallen ill, but we'll never know if it would've meant her death. It wasn't the first time Father's habits had become a problem between them. You were only a baby when she first found out and I was old enough to remember the way they fought over it. I don't remember what set off the disagreement, just her in tears telling him she didn't want him meddling with that sort of devil work."

"Devil work?"

He nodded toward my back, informing me with the gesture that he also knew where I had hidden the book. "*That* nonsense. In his youth, apparently, he'd learned how to cast spells and spoke of it as though he was good at it. Mother was furious. She made him swear an oath never to use it again."

I blinked. "Is this why he was being pursued by them?"

"I have no doubt that's why, but whatever he had been running from finally caught up to him." Jeffrey punctuated his words with a sigh, his gaze shifting toward the hearth. "I know I've been dismissive of you, Christian, but I need you to believe it was for a good cause. Your curse might have been to watch Father be killed, but mine was Mother's death. It's been our burden to bear."

My brother became transfixed on the sight of the flames dancing in the firebox, lost inside his mind with a pregnant silence hanging between us. I reached forward, touching his wrist in an effort to coax him back. "What happened to Mother?" I asked.

His frown deepened as he shifted his attention back to me. "Mother had fallen ill," he said. "That part's never been a lie, it's the remainder that's been a half truth. I still doubt that she would have recovered, but we had no way of knowing for certain, especially when the band of men came looking for Father." As he took a deep breath, I settled in for a tale while Jeffrey gathered his thoughts. His gaze turned distant again, his attention drifting as he opened his mouth to continue.

"We were holed up in one of those damned inns," he began. "You know how they are. Each one is about the same as the one that came before it, populated by low-lives and travelers with loose women lurking around every corner. You and I used to make a game of hiding beneath the tables until the barkeep chased us either outdoors or back to our room. We had been threatened with a sound thrashing and ran up the stairs with so much commotion, Father had to tell us to mind ourselves around Mother."

I couldn't fight a small smile tugging at the corners of my lips. Jeffrey failed to share in my mirth, though. A haunted look overcame his countenance. "He was midway through scolding us when there was a crash from down in the main hall. And there was something about the panic and confusion on his face that made me wonder if he knew what exactly that was. Mother tried to get up. He said, 'Tilly, no, you rest.' When he looked at me, though, my stomach knitted into a hundred knots. 'Take Christian and hide,' he said. 'Don't come out until I call for you and don't make a sound.'

"I told him, 'Yes, Father,' and fought for your hand, nearly dragging you into the hallway. While you bucked and threatened to scream, I told you not to say a word and promised you apple cake if you kept quiet." A bittersweet chuckle passed through his lips, birthed quickly and almost bringing a breakdown of my brother's composure with it. Tears danced in his eyes. "I found us another empty room and forced us to crouch in the dark. At one point, I pressed my hand over your mouth while I held my breath.

"You finally forced my hand from your mouth to ask where Mother and Father were. I could hear how scared you were. You wanted to know what was happening and you begged me to let you go back to them and I tried to ignore you – I really did – but there were loud voices and awful noises and finally, I couldn't stand it any longer. I placed a finger against your lips. 'Not another word,' I said. 'I'll see what's going on.' And I left you there in that room repeating over and over that there'd be apple cake for Christian if he behaved himself.

"As I approached, though, those awful noises only got worse. I peered through a crack in the door and it was just in time for me to watch those last, brutal moments play out. Father had a man pinned up against the wall and had been reaching for this fellow's sword when suddenly, Mother began to scream. At first, I didn't know why. Not until another man came into view, approaching her bedside while Father was distracted." He paused, collecting himself even as a tear slid down his cheek. He regarded me again while swiping it away. "I swore for years I'd imagined what happened next. It wasn't until you told me about the innkeeper that I realized it was just as real as it had seemed to be."

"What did you see?" I asked, inching forward in my seat as if on instinct. Trepidation quickened in my stomach, but still, I felt as though my entire existence hinged upon the answer to my question.

Jeffrey shook his head. "The man beside Mother lifted a hand, and a gust of wind blew through the room that seemed to snatch the air right out of her chest. Father yelled –" His brow furrowed, gaze shifting away from me again. "– And I remember just how hopeless he looked when Mother gasped and fell still. He brought down those men with just a few simple words, but when he clamored to Mother's side, it was too late."

A lump had begun to form in my throat. I struggled to swallow it back down. "She was gone?"

My brother shut his eyes. "Yes, she was." It took a moment for Jeffrey to lift his lids once more, but when he did, the look in his gaze bore a chilling sobriety. "We forgot about you for a while. Father found you crying in a corner of the inn much later, but I..." He struggled to maintain eye contact, but lost the battle when more tears spilled over onto his cheeks. "I lingered by Mother. I couldn't accept the fact that she was dead."

It was the first time he had ever let on what pain he had borne through the years, and the only time I could recall any sense of connection with him. He glanced at me appreciatively when I gave his wrist a small squeeze, and we both sat in silence, him taking a few steadying breaths and finally sobering enough to speak again. "You need to stop this, Christian," he finally said. "These men are dangerous, as is your obsession with them. Burn the damn book. Go back to your mercenaries if you feel that will bring you peace, but stop pursuing Father's killers. I'm begging you."

My hand slunk away, retreating onto my lap. I sat back, raising an eyebrow at the strange juxtaposition of sympathy and judgment in Jeffrey's words and not sure how I felt about either. The warning they contained clashed headlong with the whispers growing inside my mind, and while I understood his aversion better, it did nothing to deter my curiosity. In fact, just as he had warned, it did the opposite. "They were our parents, Jeffrey. How can you expect me just to let that stand?" I countered. "I don't even remember Mother and if they stole *both* of them from us, shouldn't they pay for that?"

"Judgment belongs to the Lord."

"Yes, and he's done a smashing job of administering it, hasn't he?" Despite the sarcastic nature of my words, I could not help how subdued my voice had become. I sighed. "We both agree they're dangerous men, and yet you'd have me burn the book rather than use it. Father knew witchcraft, you say? Well, maybe you and I can as well?"

Jeffrey recoiled, the look on his face laden with revulsion. "As though I'd ever. And that is a lot to presume without bartering your soul attempting it."

"Perhaps not, actually." Leaning forward, I lowered my voice as though about to trade secrets with my brother. "The man I was sent to kill made an attempt on my life first and I broke his spell, all without knowing what I was doing. Ever since, I swear to you, I've been afflicted by this premonition daring me to do more, and I've been tempted to succumb. Because if I could thwart one of them without even trying, imagine what I could do if I actually studied the book and learned their magic."

"You're proposing to damn yourself," Jeffrey spat, "And to what end?"

"Theirs," I said, rising to a stand. My voice rose in volume once more, my feet pacing away from the table a few steps before I turned to face my brother again. "I might not be able to return to my life as a mercenary anyway, after this last fiasco. Some good might as well come of it."

"I think you're confusing the term 'good' with something else."

"I'm saying that I might have inherited Father's talents, and I'm not bound by oath to avoid using them. Admit it. A part of you wants Mother's killers to meet their end."

"No, I won't, because that part doesn't exist in me the same way it does you." Jeffrey slowly rose to his feet as well, making up the distance between us and stopping just short of where I stood. "I don't have the desire to exchange one form of bloodshed with another. Father was reckless. He played with darkness and it cost him our mother. In the end, he didn't even use his talents to save himself and do you know what I think?"

"Enlighten me."

"I believe it's because he was ready for his final judgment."

I scoffed. "He was sick," I said, "And concerned about me."

"He knew the evil of his ways and had finally made penance for them!" Jeffrey said, countering. His voice rose in volume, a defiance in his eyes as we stared down each other. "If he hadn't started down such a path in the first place, *nobody* would have had to perish."

"Listen to yourself. You hide your contempt under the guise of piety. Little wonder you and I have had not had many kind words for each other through the years."

Jeffrey retorted through gritted teeth, his words laced with vitriol. "Because you are just like him, Christian, and you don't seem to give a damn about anybody but *yourself.*"

He encroached on me a step and I backed away. As he closed the distance between us once more, I felt shivers run through me, my blood turning cold as the hearth behind me seemed to turn warmer. Concern ran as an undercurrent to Jeffrey's expression regardless of the callousness of his words, but I had closed myself off to it. "Then absolve yourself of my sins, dear brother. You are no longer responsible for my soul."

"Christian..." The evocation of my name was not enough to stop me from pivoting on my heels and turning for the door. Jeffrey remained standing in place as though frozen there while I stormed out the house, not looking back once during my entire march to the barn. Shutting myself inside, I flinched against the smell of the animals, plucking a lantern from the shelves where they were kept and setting myself upon the task of lighting it. As the glow from its flame filled the area around me, I sat on the ground and fought the urge to surrender into tears.

The spine of the book dug into the small of my back. I reached for it in frustration, tugging it out and tossing it onto the ground with groan. As it landed, the crease in its spine forced it open, splaying out more of its Latin gibberish for the eye to behold. The flame flickered enough to cast more light on it and I frowned, holding this new image in my mind of Father reading words just like this.

Whether it was this thought or the dance of the flame which compelled me to pick it up, I didn't know. Either way, the volume found its way into my hand again and I studied the page, sighing and flipping back to the page where pronunciations had been scrawled beneath foreign words. There laid the term again – *Evocatio Spiritualis* – daring me in defiance to speak it aloud again.

I swallowed down a lump forming in my throat. Temptation built to a fever pitch within me, compelling me to my feet with the lantern in one hand and the book in the other. My gaze fixed upon at the barn door I had just shut moments ago. "*Evocatio Spiritualis,*" I said, causing a surge of tingles to race through me, some unknown energy source creeping in through my skin. The words gained more clarity as I repeated them. My voice grew louder, my hands shaking as I glanced down at the next forbidden term scrawled in the book. Something wanted to escape – begged for it until I could hold it back no longer and barked out another phrase.

"Ventus, veni foras."

Without warning, the barn door flew open.

I clamored away, tripping over debris and landing on my backside while the lantern fell out of my grip. The oxen startled, but settled themselves as I twisted onto my hands and knees, still clutching the book. I righted the lamp before its fire could escape, my heart pounding in my ears. My throat felt tight and my temples throbbed, and a sheer, overwhelming sense of madness overcame me. I had no idea what I had just done. Somehow, I had tapped into whatever force breathed life into the mystical. And I wanted to do it again.

Coming to my feet again, I walked toward one of the animal pens and lowered my lamp onto a post. As a cold gust of wind blew through the barn, I dashed toward the door and shut it, racing back after this was finished toward my reading light so I could attempt it again. Focusing on the page, I held out my free hand. "*Evocatio Spiritualis*," I began once more. *Evocatio*. Evoking. Narrowing my eyes, I focused on the door again, drawing from the energy building in my chest. This time, when I blew the door open, it swung so far it knocked into the barn's side. The oxen voiced protest, but quieted themselves without any need for reassurance.

A sound of utter delight bounded past my lips. I shut the door again and flipped the page, finding another spell written out in a similar manner. Flames grew and shrank at my command. Winds blew through the barn and nature played out a chorus that seemed to have been written for me alone. I raved like a lunatic, repeating spells just to see the elements dance to the tune I intoned.

For a brief moment, I felt like a god.

CHAPTER NINE

With the first rays of dawn, I emerged from the barn alit with energy still crackling underneath my skin. The hair on the back of my neck stood on end, and prickles waxed and waned with every purposeful step I took back toward my brother's house. Jeffrey was in the fields, tending to his crops, allowing me the chance to slip into my room and gather my things. Whether or not my departure would be premature was of no concern to me. Whatever fate awaited me back in town, I was finished hiding from it.

Anne slipped me some food for the travel when I insisted I would not be staying. Ida and Ivette belabored me with kisses, and between the three of them, they kept me detained long enough for my brother to catch up to me as I readied my horse for travel. I took a deep breath when I heard his footsteps encroaching on me, not turning away from the task of saddling the mare and fitting her with bit and bridle. "You didn't have to abandon work just to see me off," I said.

The horse shifted her stance uncertainly as Jeffrey approached. I ran a hand along her mane to soothe her while my brother paused nearby. "Where are you going?" he asked.

"Back into town. You'll forgive me if lingering has sat poorly with me."

"Isn't that a risk for you to be doing? Your friend hasn't yet called for you."

I sighed, making a final adjustment to Tempest's reins before mounting her saddle. She shook her head as I settled into place and I held back my response until both beast and rider were situated. Jeffrey watched all the while, a sickening form of concern in his eyes. "Whether or not it's a risk," I answered, "I'm heading back just the same. Let the authorities seek me out if they so desire. They won't find me willing to go quietly."

Using my heels, I nudged Tempest forward. Jeffrey walked forward, though, touching her snout and forcing her to stop. She whinnied in protest and I glowered as he walked up to my side. "Please don't do this," he said. A shimmer overtook his eyes, an unspoken prayer contained within. "This is power that comes with a price. You and I have seen its cost firsthand and your fate won't be any different than Father's in the end."

Despite the sincerity of the plea, I found myself apathetic toward it and unwilling to apologize for the chill which entered my words. "I'll be careful, Jeffrey. That's all the promise I'm willing to offer." Giving Tempest a harder nudge, I gripped onto the reins when the mare surged forward, my posture stoic and only relaxing once I had passed my tree. I spared it one last glance, tempted to unearth the treasure box, but managing to resist the urge. I wouldn't be depositing anything inside it this time. In fact, my thoughts stole to the scroll left to me by my father, wondering if at last I might understand it.

"Another time," I murmured to myself before coaxing Tempest into a gallop.

We rode hard until we encountered a small village and paused there for a rest. I stole a nap along the way, seeking shelter from the sun under a tree, before progressing forward through the night. The sun had crested over the horizon by the time I approached town, and as I watched people come and go from the place my fellow mercenaries called home, I seized the chance to steady myself. "Please be here, Paolo," I murmured, lifting the hood of my cloak over my head and entering the inn.

The patrons nearest to the doors cast a quick glance in my direction, but the few people who sat further in ignored me entirely. I rounded a corner and dashed up to the second floor, my footsteps light and measured carefully so as not to rouse an air of suspicion. Passing one of the whores who made the inn a regular haunt, I avoided eye contact and failed to pause until I reached the final room down the long corridor. Lifting a hand, I rapped my knuckles on the door and waited for a response.

Within seconds, it swung open, Paolo furrowing his brow until he registered who stood before him. "Christian, what are you doing here?" he asked. "You weren't supposed to return yet."

Our eyes met across the short expanse separating us. While the sparks of energy had waned over the course of my journey, seeing Paolo caused them to ignite anew, bringing with them an added wave of shivers. Power danced inside my veins again and before I could stop the compulsion, I reached for his shoulder, pushing him back inside and kicking the door shut behind us. "I got tired of my brother," I said, my body pressing against Paolo's as my lips brushed against his. My satchel slid from my arm, dropping onto the floor. "Displeased with seeing me?"

The hand which had pressed upon his shoulder slid up to his neck. While Paolo regarded me with confusion, he failed to move away. "No, but I wonder if you lost your mind on the travel back."

"A distinct possibility. Or found it in the most pleasant of manners."

"Stop that." Our lips pressed together, the union tentative. I felt his hands settle on my hips, seemingly despite himself. "I am supposed to be preparing to leave."

"Where are you headed?" My teeth nipped at his bottom lip.

"A job. I had planned on coming to see you after." Paolo pulled me flush against him. I felt his lips curl in a smirk. "Aren't you sore from being in the saddle?"

"Not sore enough if you ask me."

"Roland is going to be furious when he finds out you're here."

"Remind me of that when I'm half of the mind to care." The desire for him gained palpable urgency, the urge to take becoming all the more present the longer our bodies touched. A shaky breath passed through my lips, one of my hands sliding around to Paolo's back to hold him firmly in place. Want collided with need within my mind and suddenly, it felt as though I had not desired anything nearly as much as I had him. And in that moment, it felt as though I could claim whatever my soul pleased.

"What happened at your brother's house?" Paolo asked, his voice a whisper.

"Everything. I have so much to tell you." A longer, more luxurious kiss commenced between us, my eyes shutting while my grip tightened. His hips rocked against mine, both of us falling prey to temptation at the same moment. Only the need for breath forced our mouths apart, and even then, we failed to drift very far. "Not now, though," I added. "There are more pressing concerns on my mind."

"Such as?" Paolo's hand slid down to cup my backside.

Another shiver raced through me like quicksilver. "Hearing you cry out my name"

"*Fai come vuoi, amico mio.*" Paolo pushed away from the wall, using his hold on me to walk us toward the bed. I marched backward obediently, tumbling atop the straw mattress when my knees hit the side and spilling onto it with Paolo. He grinned while settling above me. "The Devil's gotten into you," he murmured within the space between kisses.

I licked his lips and struggled for breath, not wishing to end the rolling series of embraces. "Are you calling yourself the Devil?" I asked.

"Not in you yet."

"Please allow me to make a petition."

He whispered something in Italian I couldn't quite make out. I opened my eyes long enough to see him pull his shirt over his head and reached down to untie the closure of his trousers. He made quick work of my cloak, lifting up only enough to allow me to toss garments aside and kick off my boots. We were both tightly wound by the time I kicked off my own breeches, our bodies warm and humming.

I cried out when he entered me, not giving a whit who might have heard.

Paolo's lips crashed into mine, in some effort to muffle me. My fingers tangled with the locks of his hair, holding tight while my nails dug into his side. He groaned and pushed further in, causing me to see stars dancing on the backs of my eyelids. I clutched onto him as though the wind might carry me off; as though the elements I now heard whispering in my mind might unravel me. Somewhere in the midst of this all, I forgot my name.

And remembered it again, when he whispered it harshly into my ear.

Our eyes met in the midst of a haze. Coils of tension wound themselves in rapidly-forming knots and I struggled to hang onto the moment, seeing its end far too close at hand. Something danced on the tip of my tongue, a strong impulse to speak whimsical words present through the rush of ecstasy. We moved in time with the pounding of my heart and he gripped onto me as words born in the throes of euphoria spilled past my lips. I lost myself within climax before what I said could echo in my mind, aware only of my own completion and Paolo's within me.

I had almost forgotten about it when I heard his voice again, his breath hitting the side of my face. "*Amico mio?*" he asked, the term of endearment suddenly a question, as though he was not yet capable of issuing a longer inquiry.

Air passed through my lips in lusty gulps. Paolo lifted up enough to look at me again, his eyes searching mine, as though skeptical and hopeful at the same time. I looked back at him, raising an eyebrow and heard my own voice again, speaking as though lost in the midst of a haze. "I love you," I said, committing to its issuance once more time. My chest tightened, but my gaze held steady, unwilling and unable to retreat.

If saying it once caused Paolo to be skeptical, hearing it again only served to startle him further. He furrowed his brow and I waited for some form of acknowledgement from him. "I think the time has come for you to tell me what happened," he finally said.

Paolo studied me in silence. I felt our bodies part and moaned involuntarily, floating for a few moments in a pleasant form of soreness as he settled next to me. An elbow bent and resting on the bed, he held up his head in one hand, remaining quiet. I took a deep breath and fixed my gaze on the ceiling, reflecting on the irony of peering up to the heavens. "I stole something from Exeter," I confessed, glancing back at him. "I didn't have the chance to show you before we left."

"What did you take?" His voice was soft, but even, making it difficult for me to tell what he was thinking.

A frown tugged at the corners of my mouth. "A spell book." I nodded toward the satchel left abandoned in the entryway of the room. "I can show you if you fetch my things."

Paolo arched an eyebrow. I sighed and pointed at the doorway and he finally mirrored my frown, lifting to a stand and padding to the door. Without moving, I watched him pick up the leather bag by its shoulder strap, the other hand flipping open its flap and digging through for a book. He turned it so as to look at its cover. "This is their mark," he murmured.

"Yes, it is," I said. "That is precisely why I stole it."

"You didn't tell me you found this."

"I didn't know how to talk about it at the time."

Paolo remained standing in place for what seemed like an eternity, the look on his face making it difficult to appreciate the sight of bare skin being afforded me. A sigh passed through his lips and finally, he strode back to the bed, sitting close enough to the edge for comfort. It prompted me to lift into a seated position. "Do you know how to talk about it now?" he asked, handing me the book.

I nodded and placed the volume on the other side of me, in favor of turning to face Paolo. "The kind Sir Lawrence nearly killed me," I began. Paolo remained impassive, but I watched him hold onto his breath for an extra moment before exhaling it. A small, wan smile tugged at the corners of my mouth. "I know I've told you a hundred times that the men who killed my father snapped the neck of an innkeeper without so much as laying a hand on him. Well, I experienced how firsthand in Exeter."

While he held his position, I saw something indiscernible trace across his eyes. His fingers touched mine and I interlaced them, clutching onto Paolo in some effort to center my thoughts. "For as many times as I have carried on about witchcraft being the culprit, I never expected to be proven right quite like that. I had him disarmed and suddenly, couldn't breathe. The world turned dark and all I could think to do was fight it, even if I had no idea how."

My gaze returned to him and our eyes met. "I broke his spell," I said. "And spent the time with my brother discovering that not only was my father a sorcerer, I am as well."

Paolo furrowed his brow, regarding me as though determining if I had gone mad or not. I gave his hand a squeeze, pulling mine back from his grip and holding it out before us. Shifting my attention toward my fingers, I focused on them while blocking out everything else in the room – the four walls, the bed beneath us, even the sound of Paolo's rhythmic breathing. Whispering words I had since memorized from Lawrence's spell book, I watched a spark jump from my palm until the final syllables had been birthed.

As flames rose from my hand, Paolo startled to a stand again, taking several paces backward. I glanced from the fledgling fire to my lover, unable to contain the smirk which traced across my lips. "Remarkable, isn't it?" I asked.

Paolo stared at my hand, his eyes wide. "*Dios mio*," he murmured with a nod.

"My brother would probably argue how involved the Almighty is in all of this." Shutting my hand, I extinguished the flames with that action. A sigh chased away my mirth, forcing me back into a much more sober posture. "My father had brushed paths with these men before, apparently, though my brother seemed not to know how they first met. All I can gather is he stole something valuable to them."

"The jeweled case he sent you away with?" Paolo spoke the question on the breath of a whisper, his expression still laden with incredulity.

I nodded. "I spent the entirety of my journey here solving the riddle. My brother says my mother met her end at their hands, too. All of my life, my father moved us around the country and it took until he fell ill for them to catch up to him. What other conclusion is there?"

"That you should leave the parchment buried and run." He swallowed back the lump in his throat and focused on my eyes again. Slowly, Paolo shook his head. "You shouldn't have come here. We shouldn't be anywhere near here if they know this is where they can find you. We can ride to London and be in France in a few days' time, or anywhere else in the world after that. *Amico mio,* they tried to kill you once. Who is to say they won't try to kill you again?"

We regarded each other in silence for several moments. While I had been able to shield myself against my brother's worried gaze, the same look in Paolo's eyes caused nervous flutters to dance in my chest. My hand lowered, touching the binding of the spell book, fingertips caressing the leather and using it as a reminder of what I had just done. An endless scope of possibility had been opened up before me, but as I held my breath, thoughts waged war inside my mind. I couldn't dispute Paolo's logic. Lingering would put me in the clutches of danger. Yet there I stood on the brink of uncovering my father's killers at long last. The vitriolic words I had cast at Jeffrey's feet felt impotent as I considered delivering them to the man standing before me.

He walked closer as though reading my thoughts. "Did you mean it, Christian?" he asked, kneeling before me and cupping my face in both hands. Paolo rested his forehead against mine. "Do you love me?"

"Yes," I said, shutting my eyes. My hand lifted from the book, coming to rest on Paolo's wrist. Tempted though I was to muse on how much three words could change an entire posture, I remembered how many times the man had compelled me even without them and groaned at myself. "I've shown my hand and now, I will be damned by it."

He failed to respond at first, though the quiet didn't carry any tension to it. My eyes opened as I fought the urge to be vexed with Paolo. "You truly want us to leave?" I asked.

"Yes, I do," he said, his lids lifting for him to meet my gaze. "I know you don't see the amount of danger you're in, but I do. If you can make fire in your hands, then they can do worse things."

"And if I leave, they've won. Nobody will avenge my father, certainly not Jeffrey."

"Do you think your father has ever cared about that?"

"No, but I have." I muttered obscenities under my breath as Paolo pulled away, his hands shifting down to clutch onto mine. He frowned and I mirrored the expression, the debate no less settled in my mind, even when I nodded. "He would want me safe," I conceded. The angry boy within me kicked at the ground and raged, but I held steady to the feeling of Paolo's hands, gripping hold of them tight. "You want us to go to France?"

"Wherever is safe," he said. I felt the tickle of his stubble on my lips when he leaned in and kissed me. His warm breath hit my face when he spoke. "Whatever you want to do with that book is what you want to do. I don't care. Take it with us, *si?* Learn more about it and maybe – *maybe* – much later we can find these men again, when we can be better prepared. Right now, it is too sudden and too dangerous."

"Do *you* mean that?" I asked, raising an eyebrow at him.

He nodded, managing a small quirk of his lips. "If it will get you somewhere safe, then yes, *amico mio,* I will promise you that."

While summoning the agreement seemed beyond me in words, the glower I gave him told him all he needed to know. Paolo kissed me again, and as I shut my eyes to return the embrace, I found my thoughts elsewhere, a rare occurrence with my lips so involved. '*I'm not nearly as scared as you are,*' I thought to myself. '*Perhaps not as much as much as even I should be.*' Still, I didn't have the heart to discourage him. Especially when he pulled away to gather our discarded clothing.

Even lacking the ability to issue an objection, I still couldn't deny my general state of being as I watched him hustle around the room. "I've barely had two winks of sleep in days," I said.

"Their first thought will be to come here," Paulo said. "If we ride north, we can stop along the way for sleep."

He handed me my clothing, waiting until I took it before reaching for his garments. I sighed and started to dress, lying flat on the bed until my trousers were secure and sitting upright to pull my shirt over my head. He was already half dressed by the time I reached for my boots. I slid them on, shooting him a casual glance as he fussed with his own shirt. "Are we to steal our horses from Roland?" A sly grin curled the corners of my mouth.

Paolo scoffed. "He would owe it to us, but no. I will leave money behind if I must."

"Perhaps I'll add an extra few coins to ensure he doesn't point the Luminaries to us."

When Paolo glanced up at me, raising an eyebrow, I sighed. "Sir

Lawrence shared that bit of information with me," I explained. "They also have some leader named Talbot, but sadly, I killed Lawrence before I could learn much about him." Discussing the matter further threatened to leave a foul taste in my mouth. I finished putting on my boots in silence and slipped on an overshirt before reaching for my cloak. "Whatever the matter, my father's killers have a name."

As I secured the cloak into place, the pensive frown on my lover's face deepened. He reached for his coin purse, avoiding my gaze as he did. "I will explain everything to Roland," he said. "Stay hidden in here or meet me in the stables." Bustling along without waiting for my response, Paolo opened the door and spirited into the hallway, his own cloak in hand. I found myself grateful he didn't see my expression as he departed, or force me to reassert my commitment to our departure. As it was, it took a few moments before I could summon the wherewithal to start packing.

Reaching for the spell back and my satchel, I slipped the tome inside and dug around for a spare shirt and pair of pants. The room still looked like a mess, the bed disheveled and the rest of our personal effects left discarded, causing me to wonder if this is how it had been when he left Verona. "Bloody hell," I breathed, attempting not to envision a younger version of Paolo tossing his belongings into a bag and racing off toward an uncertain future. It only threatened to add another item to a pile of mounting second guesses. Casting a quick glance toward the still-opened door, I threw my bag's strap over my head and strode from the room.

Surely, there had to be another way.

Bounding down the stairs, I didn't care if my heavy footfalls announced my presence before the crowd of usual suspects. Half expecting that Paolo was already engaged in discussion with Roland, I prepared to march up to the table to intervene. When I reached the first floor, however, I saw Paolo positioned behind one of the support beams, as if hiding from something. Cautiously, I crossed the distance between us and whispered, "What is it?"

Before he could answer, however, a sound pierced through the crowd which caused me to startle. It was a woman's laugh, but something about it sent a chill of dread up my spine while forcing my attention toward its source. There she sat, across from Roland, wearing a maroon gown and a cream-colored chemise, a hat perched atop a sea of dark locks, casting a partial shadow across her face. The carefree way my employer entertained her alarmed me almost as much as her presence, while still paling in comparison. It was her, the woman who had seen me kill Sir Lawrence in Exeter. Jane.

I felt my blood run cold as I hid behind Paolo. He cast a glance back at me and I gripped onto his shoulder as though offering a word of caution. *Be quiet.* In my periphery, I saw him furrow his brow at whatever expression must have taken up residence on my face. "Is that her?" he asked, mirroring my whisper, and I responded only with a nod, my heart racing and my palms turning sweaty. For as much as fortune had suddenly left me destitute, it vanished altogether the moment she turned her head and lined me in her sights.

A slow grin curled the corner of her lips. She glanced back at Roland, and flicked a hand in my direction, causing me to curse my existence more and more with every second that passed. "There he is right now," she said, speaking the words loud enough for it to carry, even though they were intended for Roland. His gaze shifted toward me and a look of surprise flickered past his eyes, telling me all I needed to know about how damned I was.

Weighing what I should do, I found myself frozen between the impulse to run and that part of me wishing to stand my ground. Jane settled the dilemma with her next words. "It would seem I haven't wasted my journey after all," she said, her smile broadening. Her gaze found mine again, past the barrier of my shorter lover, penetrating through me as though to catch me in a spider's web. I paled and gripped onto Paolo harder, as if to brace myself against the impact.

"Please, ask him to come and join us, Master Roland. I would like to thank him myself."

CHAPTER TEN

I had a split second to determine what my next course of action should be. While Jane had never appeared to be a scared waif, the woman who sat opposite from Roland bore enough of a regal air to suggest she had been vindicated somehow. This could mean I was truly being thanked, or might indicate just as much of a trap lying in wait as I feared. And the expression on Roland's face gave me no indication whether I should run or play the ruse. "Buy us time, *amico mio*," Paolo whispered, breaking me out of my stupor. "I will go ready the horses."

Slowly, I nodded, as though he could see the action with his back to me. My grip on his shoulder relented, my arm falling to my side. "Very well, then," I said, punctuating my words with a deep breath inward, intended to steady my nerves. My first steps forward bore caution, which took until halfway across the floor to abate. Jane and Roland watched in silence, until I paused a short distance away and nodded toward the noble lady.

She nodded in return. Roland remained seated while Jane came to a stand, extending her hand and allowing me to place a kiss on the back of her palm. "Milady," I said. "I heard talk of thanks, but confess I'm not certain what I should be thanked for."

Jane smiled and slowly lowered into her chair, the gesture bearing a striking amount of comfort given her station. The contrast of that against the setting knocked me enough from the throes of shock to steal a glance around. While the main entrance still bore a host of familiar faces, with none who stopped Paolo on his way out, I spotted a few men poised around the room I didn't recognize. Fighting against a frown, I glanced back at her in time to see her chuckle. "I think your employer might beg to differ after the story I just told him," she said. Her gaze shifted up toward me. "Sit and join us, Christian. That is your name, right?"

Roland nodded when Jane peered at him for verification. I struggled to maintain an even expression, all the while pulling out the last empty chair at the table and situating myself in it. "Yes, Christian of the Black is how most refer to me here," I said. "If they bother with titles at all. There aren't many of those spread around to peasant mercenaries."

"But men will cling to whatever recognition they get." Her eyes sparkled with amusement. She glanced between the two of us, motioning in Roland's direction when her attention settled on me again. "Now, as I was explaining to Master Roland, I rode in from Exeter to offer you a sincere thank you from both me and house Cavendish. The other evening, you did me a great favor. Lawrence had taken me away from my family home in Exeter and seemed intent on violence. I feared for my life until you appeared."

My eyes flicked to Roland quickly for appraisal. He raised an eyebrow at me, the look in his eyes imploring me not to question how the lady might be inclined to interpret the events of that night. "I told Lady Cavendish that she had just missed you," he said. "That you'd been sent on another job for me after returning from Exeter."

"Yes, which I am happy to report went well," I said, countering his quirked brow with one of my own. Reaching for the strap running along my chest, I lifted my satchel over my head and placed it on the floor beside us. A smile finally managed its way onto the surface, with as much honesty as I could give it. The game had been laid out before me. As it was, I had no other choice but to play it. Folding my hands atop the table, I nodded and assumed a much more agreeable air. "The man did appear to be boorish, if I could be granted the ability to speak ill of a nobleman."

"My family agrees, so you aren't breaking your station," she said, regarding me in silence for the briefest of moments. Finally, she relaxed her posture. "You needn't be concerned, Master Christian. My words to them bore some truth, but not all of it. Enough that my family understood you were hired by one of Lawrence's enemies and granted him a fitting end. They were so impressed, in fact, that as part of my thanks, I am to propose an offer to you."

My smile faded, given over to curiosity. "What sort of offer?"

"You're to be my guard for a time. Until I'm sure Lawrence's family won't attempt something foolish. I *was* betrothed to him and my family fears they might try to force another arrangement." Jane leaned forward in her seat, her smile turning cunning. "We pay handsomely, I can assure you."

I pursed my lips, pretending the thought of coin held any sway. "How handsomely? And for how long?"

"I think you're evaluating this proposal the wrong way, lad," Roland interjected, directing our attention toward him. His eyes settled on me with particular heaviness, his expression twitching as if wanting desperately to pass something from his mind to mine. We held this gaze for several moments, while I struggled to decrypt what he meant to say. Would refusing ensure my head on a platter? Or would accepting mean I might not have to flee? Neither seemed clear, but he refused to relent. "Worth any amount of money a noble would be willing to part with."

"You do keep trying to instill a sense of propriety in me, Roland," I said. "Perhaps one of these days it'll finally stick." I glanced back toward Jane. "My questions still stand."

Her smile faded, but I failed to register offense in the way she examined me. "At least a fortnight. Perhaps two. Your employer can set the price and I will assure it paid."

"You also know you're attempting to barter for the services of an assassin, right?"

"What better person to see a threat before anyone else might?"

I nodded, drawing a deep breath inward. My thoughts shifted to Paolo, who undoubtedly had our horses prepared by now. Stealing another look toward the strange men gathered around the room, I met her gaze once more while weighing any chance I might have for escape, reminded of how little I desired such a thing. "Do I have the liberty to consider this offer?" I asked, no more certain what I should do next than I had been when I rode into town. "I just returned, after all, and I admit I could use a short rest before embarking on another journey."

The wily curl her lips undertook tugged at the knots still present in my stomach. "I'll expect your answer by nightfall."

"By nightfall, you will have it." I lifted to a stand, fetching my satchel and ignoring Roland, despite feeling the weight of his stare on me. Hitching the strap over my head again, I then bowed to Jane, walking first to the stairs and bounding up them while watching for anyone set on following me. My gait back to Paolo's room remained confident, and as I shut the door, I failed to see anyone lingering in the hallway. My eyes shifted to the sole window in the room. Without hesitation, I strode to it, unlocking the shutters and seating myself on the edge of the sill. I twisted such that my legs dangled over the edge.

A race of nerves fought against the reminder of that fourteen year old boy who fell out of the window, fleeing for his life. I clenched my eyes shut and took a deep breath, thinking instead of the trees I'd climbed and jumped from over the years. This would be no higher than a few of them. Gripping onto the sill, I pushed off, clinging by my fingertips until the last minute before letting go to drop down onto the ground below. My knees buckled when I landed, but my posture held steady.

I peered toward the stables once I rose to my feet and walked casually toward them.

Nobody foreign passed me on the road, and the few who were present looked the other way when they saw the emblem on my cloak. I slipped away into safety, catching sight of Paolo in Tempest's stall and walking toward them, waiting to speak until I was nearly on top of them. Paolo spared me a quick look and I frowned in response. "Three men," I said, taking over in saddling my mare. "And she wants me to guard her. I smell a lie."

"If she already has men protecting her, I would agree," Paolo responded. He walked over to where he kept Diavolo's reins and walked them over to the gelding. "They know not to underestimate you. How did you leave?"

"From the window of our room. I claimed the need to sleep first." Once I had the saddle righted, I reached to pet Tempest's mane. She had yet to buck or protest, as though she had the ability to recognize urgency and push aside her normal petulance. I sighed. "You don't have to do this, Paolo. This is the bed I made."

"You say what you did in the room and then expect me to let you go alone. You are stupid, *amico mio*."

"I was not binding you to my fate." When Paolo failed to respond, my frown deepened. Something told me this was an argument I was poised to lose. My back remained to my lover, though, my eyes on the horse while I pondered her. "We are going to have to sprint. Tempest has barely had any chance to rest."

"Christian –"

"I know. I simply don't like the thought of laming her."

"Stai zitto e girate."

The way he muttered the words caused me to tense. I held onto Tempest's saddle, wondering if I shouldn't just pull myself onto the back of my horse and take off running. The compulsion wavered, though, when I knew that meant I'd be leaving Paolo to whatever it was he saw. Peering over my shoulder, I saw a silhouette in the doorway and pivoted to face whoever had joined us in the stables.

I recognized the tall figure from the great hall in the inn; one of the three men who had been keeping watch over Lady Jane Cavendish. He raised an eyebrow at me and I held my gaze steady, seeing the sword by his side and unafraid of it. As I lifted a foot into a stirrup, he pushed back the folds of his cloak. The interloper took a step to the side, revealing Jane behind him. She folded her arms across her chest, smiling at me as though Paolo didn't even exist. "You would risk laming the horse," she said, stepping further into the stables. "If you made it out of the town in the first place."

Slowly, I lowered my foot back onto the ground again. My eyes remained set on her, flicking only occasionally to the man by her side. "I see the need you have for guards," I said. "This one was not near silent enough."

He bristled and she laughed. "Caught *you* by surprise," she countered. Jane took two measured paces closer to us before stopping altogether. A sigh passed through her lips. "I was hoping you would accept the offer and allow us to talk on the road, but it looks like I need to have this discussion with you now." Her gaze shifted to Paolo before returning to me. "Come take a walk with me, Christian of the Black. I think you need to hear a vital part of my offer before you refuse it."

I looked toward Paolo in time to see him clench his jaw. My hand slid to Tempest's reins and I led her over to him, my other palm coming to rest on his shoulder and directing his attention toward me. "Take Tempest," I said, passing the lead over. "I will walk with the fair lady and hear out what she has to say."

More words were birthed and died just as quickly, none making it out his mouth. He glanced from me to her and grunted, which made up the entire assent Paolo was going to offer the concession. Taking hold of Tempest, he led her and Diavolo away as I paced closer to where Jane stood. "I hope trusting you doesn't end poorly for me," I added.

Her cryptic smile held steady. "Trusting anyone bears that risk, dear rogue," she said, "But I promise the nature of what I have to say isn't a threat. It's an opportunity."

"Fortune smiles upon me at last." I trudged forward when my sardonic response failed to make her anything but nonplussed. The man at the door held it open for us, waiting until we had both exited the stables before shutting it again. I squinted into the sunlight and nodded in the direction of the main road, an idle, morbid thought crossing my mind as we paced away. Whose blood would stain these streets before dusk, hers or mine?

"You're tense," she observed as we walked. Her guard assumed a position behind us, and if not for the fact that I had not been asked to disarm, the closeness of his shadow might have set me all the more on edge. She reached over and touched my face, directing my sights toward her. "If I wanted you dead, I would have come with more than a few men."

I raised an eyebrow, nudging away from her hand and offering her a cautionary look. "Dead, or to be made an example of," I said. "I know what happened in that room and it wasn't defending your honor."

"Oh, just because I know how to spin a tale to my parents doesn't mean I've started believing them." Jane's hand lowered to her side. If my inching away from her touch had made her angry, she gave no indication of it. She simply glanced away and led us further into town. "Just the same, I'm not lying. He *did* intend to harm me that night."

"I know. Believe it or not, I was concerned for your welfare."

Looking back at me, she quirked an eyebrow. "The moment before you had deigned to kill me?"

I shrugged. "You were a witness. And I had not yet decided that."

"It would've been a merciful death. Far better than Lawrence would've offered me and for much better reason. I'm hardly put off by reality, rogue."

My chest filled with air, in some effort to quell my nerves. "I rarely kill anyone I'm not paid to, milady. You would've been a victim of circumstance, nothing more."

"As such, I pray your forgiveness for running. But I wasn't ready to die yet." Her lips quirked before returning to her previous expression. Jane glanced around at the town surrounding us, the gesture pensive and yet, idle. "Why did you want Lawrence's book?"

I hesitated before providing an answer. "Is it unusual to be curious about such foreign words?" I asked.

Jane laughed. "That you know any words at all is a wonder. Most of your kind aren't literate." After gravitating closer, she lowered her voice. "Was that truly the first time you had wielded magic?" she asked.

My words matched the volume of hers. "You say that as though I cast a spell on him. As I recall, he was the one trying to do that to *me*."

"Yes, he was, which is what piqued my interest. He should've been successful." As I glanced at her, she raised an eyebrow at me. "It takes magic to break magic, and I've the suspicion you are only now learning this about yourself. You have a natural gift, and I would like to help you cultivate it."

Try as I did to suppress the urge to chuckle, one slipped through the cracks just the same. I paused my steps, turning to face her as I shook my head. "From where does this offer come? Your family? Wouldn't the church adore knowing they support witchcraft?"

Her smile slowly vanished. "Not from my family, no."

"Then from this group of people Lawrence mentioned. The Luminaries."

"Yes, you seemed to have heard of them. I was going to ask you about that." Jane regarded me from head to foot, as though sizing me up. "You know something more than you're letting on if you've seen their red cloaks before. You mentioned that to Lawrence. I haven't forgotten it."

"I've seen quite a few things in my line of work. Their sigil in the homes of noblemen, for one."

"Powerful people do flock to them especially in these uncertain times. All the same, if they were spoken of by the men you've killed, you did your victims a favor in ending their lives. Talbot wouldn't have been nearly so kind."

"Now, his is a name I hadn't come upon before Lawrence spoke it."

"It would've been the last thing he said if you hadn't driven a sword through him." Jane stole a glance around us again and directed her attention back to me. I held still during her examination, swallowing back a lump forming in my throat while wondering what had put it there in the first place. She drifted a step closer. "Have you opened the book?" she asked.

I watched her eyes dance with mischief and steeled myself. People passed us on the street, but not one of them paused, as if they knew they were better not listening in on our affairs. For a moment, I wished for an excuse to break this line of discussion while seeing none presented to me. "I did, yes," I said. "Latin. I confess I don't know much of it, considering how few times I find myself reading holy books."

"Mmm. Not quite aptly named, rogue." Jane tilted her head. "You feel it in your blood, don't you? It's been running through your limbs and into your gut ever since you broke his spell, whispering a secret to you that you're desperate to figure out." She glanced at the satchel, nodding toward it. "If I wasn't a lady, I would gamble Lawrence's book is in that bag of yours."

"And I would not take your wager." I smirked. "Peddling the Devil's fruit are we?"

"As though I would have to entice you. You plucked the apple long before you walked into that inn." Her posture straightened, an air of defiance settling over her. "Tell me the thought of learning more doesn't hold even the slightest bit of temptation."

She regarded me in silence, the look on her face offering a challenge I could not counter. I huffed, the sound full of derision, and glanced away. "From what I've heard of your people, it's better not to get dragged into their affairs."

"The Luminaries are hardly my people. I've been an accessory to them, but nothing more." The way she sighed prompted my eyes back to her, almost despite myself. "Knowing them has benefitted my family a great deal. In a time when many men would love to have our heads on pikes, they have sworn us their protection."

"Then what use do you have for mine?"

"I want more than just a shadow." She spared a glance at our silent companion, who stood far away enough not to be privy to the hushed tones of our discussion. Jane's eyes returned to mine. "I was once in the position of trying to learn without a teacher. It might have gotten me entrenched with that scoundrel, Lawrence, but it opened up another world to me."

When I failed to respond, she lifted a hand. This time when she touched my cheek, I remained still, feeling her fingers slide into my hair and trace the shell of my ear. Jane smiled while my eyes shifted from one local face to another, not certain how to dissuade her without drawing more attention to us. "Lie to me, Christian," she murmured. "Tell me there is nothing I can give you that you desire."

I took a deep breath and met her gaze again. "Do you think me that base of a creature?"

Her grin broadened. "I think there are many things a man can desire."

"And I think you hardly know me." At the same time, I found myself weighing her statement with a touch of seriousness. Nothing she could grant me, I attempted to say, but then I recalled those moments of second guessing before I chased Paolo down into the main hall. Certainly, I had the desire to uncover the secret portions of my soul, and here it lay before me. What the sixteen year old me craved when he donned a cloak and first slit a man's throat for money. One day I would have a blade pointed at my father's killer.

Jane chuckled. Her fingertip slid down my cheek and to my throat before her arm lowered to her side. "No, you are right," she said. "I don't know you." The grin still painted on her lips defied the way she turned on her heels, pointing toward her guard. Her words were directed toward the other man. "I suppose I have nothing to offer Master Christian. Would you secure us lodgings, Leonard, so we can be on our way in the morning?"

Leonard bowed and turned to depart. I sighed, watching them stride forward a few paces before finally capturing the bait laid out before me. "Wait," I said, calling out the word while not shouting it. Both the guard and Lady Cavendish turned to face me again, regarding me as I walked within earshot of more hushed words. I held up a hand to stop Jane. "You say you know the contents of that book, and how to instruct another on how to use it?"

She arched an eyebrow at me, considering me for a brief moment before responding. "Each man's book is personal to them somehow, but all of them contain the same basic spells," she said. "I can teach you, but your ability to use it depends on you."

"That is hardly a promise."

"No, it isn't, but I will say I'm confident enough to offer you the chance."

"On what basis?"

"Matters we can discuss if you agree to come along?" A grin spread across her lips once more.

The groan I produced might have been inspired by her, but it was directed more inward than outward. Folding my arms across my chest, I studied her in silence before finally allowing my thoughts to birth themselves in the form of speech. "I will agree to your arrangement on one condition. I determine when I leave. If this means returning money to your family, then so be it."

"I demand a fortnight, rogue. After that, we'll see just how eager you are to part ways." She nodded once, the gesture slow with her eyes set upon me through the entire motion. "We leave for Plymouth in the morning, then. Gather your things and be waiting for us at the stables come sunrise. I will return to the inn with Leonard and finish my business with your employer."

Nodding, I offered her that as my parting response and nothing more. Jane lingered in assessment of me, weighing something before turning to consummate her departure. As I watched her lead her servant back toward the inn, I caught sight of the stables in my periphery and shifted my focus back toward it. Another grumble threatened its way past my lips. How the bloody hell was I going to explain this to Paolo, I wondered.

Gritting my teeth, I trudged back to the doorway I had just exited a few minutes ago. Paolo had his back to me, a brush in hand he used to groom Diavolo in soft and steady strokes. I saw Tempest back in her stall, still saddled, but secured into place. "I don't need to see it to know it's there," he said, tilting his head to place me in the corner of his eye. "That look you get when you want to tell me something I'm not going to like."

I winced. Stepping closer, I paused by one of the empty stalls and leaned my weight against a post. "Perhaps because I'm not bounding to you saying we must be on our way," I said. A heavy sigh passed through my lips. "If I meet her terms, she won't pursue me any further. I'm apt to take her offer."

Paolo huffed. "It sounds like she filled your head with a lot of *cazzata*. What was her offer?"

"That I'm to spend a fortnight with her. After that, I'm free to leave."

"Don't treat me like I'm stupid, Christian. What was her offer?"

Swallowing hard, I looked away. "She saw me break the spell and she wants to teach me more about the book I stole. I was... inclined... to see what she knew about it."

"I see." Paolo shook his head and tossed away the brush. As he turned, his gaze failed to meet mine, set instead on the ground while he started a quick pace away from his horse. "I knew you needed to be protected from yourself. I never realized how much."

He motioned as if to walk past, on his way to the door. I caught him by the arm, though, and stopped him, forcing us to face each other. "Paolo, don't do this."

"*Figlio di puttana.*" Paolo tugged his arm out of my grip and finally looked at me, anger dancing in his eyes. I opened my mouth to respond, but he held up a hand to stop me. "I could say the same to you, but it never works, because you don't think with your brain. You think with your..." He gestured at my crotch before his arm fell to his side. "You want to take her offer. For what? *Per il bene di tuo uccello stupido.*"

I recoiled against the verbal slap, staring at Paolo while he clenched his jaw. "Do you think that is what this is all about?" Somehow, I held back the amount of vitriol with which I desired to issue the question. "My cock?"

"I prefer thinking that to the truth."

"What..." I trailed off when I saw tears dancing in his eyes. Touching his shoulder, I tried not to be offended when he shrugged off my hand, but it did what I had intended it to do. He looked at me again and the expression on his face made my heart sink into my stomach. "What truth, *amico mio?*" I asked.

Paolo issued a long, drawn out sigh. Both hands lifted, the heels of which rubbing at his eyes before his fingers slid up to tangle with the locks of his hair. He didn't speak until lowering his arms once more. "That you think, even for a moment, that this is a good idea. So, she knows spell books and witchcraft? She isn't the only person in the world who does."

"It isn't about her knowledge, Paolo."

"No." He took a deep breath, holding onto it until he summoned whatever strength it took for him to put words to his thoughts. "She knows the men who killed your father."

"Yes, she does." I stole a glance around, as if there might be spies hiding in the rafters, and lowered my voice. "Paolo, this is as close as I've ever gotten to them. Yes, we could flee and attempt to find them, better prepared, or they could continue to chase us like they did my father until they capture us. If we leave, I might never find them again or they might discover us when we least expect it. But if I go with her, I could end this now."

"You could end it now or die trying."

"I told her a fortnight. If I haven't found my father's killer by then, I will leave." My eyes settled on Paolo, fixed with his in a severe manner. "*You* know what this means to me. I have craved this chance since I first started wearing this cloak. If they're so willing to teach me, then why shouldn't it become their fatal folly?"

My friend and lover clenched his eyes shut, his shoulders slumping by a fraction while he took a deep breath. When he lifted his lids again, he looked exasperated and resigned. "I would be a hypocrite to tell you not to want this," he said, punctuating the words with a frown. Paolo placed a hand on the beam against which I stood, leaning into his hold. "It won't make the demons leave, though, *amico mio*. That much I know from experience. In the end, even when we get our revenge, you are still an orphan, and I am still an exile from my homeland."

"If I am to be an orphan, then I want them to bleed for it," I responded. Reaching out for him, I rested my palm above his heart and drifted closer. While I knew the stablemaster could enter at any moment – or any of the host of people whose beasts were tied up in the other pens – I allowed everything around me to fade. Within my thoughts, I envisioned the first time I had kissed him, seeing the inebriated young man I had been surge toward his friend here in these very stables before he could lose his nerve. "Please forgive me," I whispered, not needing the aid of liquor any longer to brush my lips against his. "I will return to you when I'm finished."

"Leave if it gets too dangerous. Promise me this," he said, failing to retreat. "Tell me where to find you and I'll let you go."

"Plymouth. She told me this is where we are headed." My eyes drifted shut. "I promise I will leave if the situation becomes more than I can handle. Is that a good enough vow for me to make?"

"Do you give me any other choice?" Paolo sank against me, a hand tentatively resting on my arm as even the sparse amount of space between us disappeared. The rest of the world ceased to exist while we kissed, his scent and taste overwhelming me until we pulled away. Even then, we opened our eyes to regard each other almost at the same moment.

"*Te amo*," he said, his palm lifting to touch the side of my face. While the hold was tentative, and the feel of his skin against mine far too fleeting, I experienced a moment of serenity unlike any which had crossed my path beforehand. He didn't need to translate what he said to me. I understood it perfectly. A shaky breath preceded him collecting his composure. "If we aren't running off together, then I have duties to attend."

"No wrath more severe than Roland's when he fails to collect a wage." The ache returned to my heart despite the levity of the moment. "I find myself wanting to ask you to be careful," I said, punctuating the comment with a laugh.

Paolo raised an eyebrow at me, his lips curling with amusement. "As though I'm ever the one who needs to do that."

"Look at the company you take up with. I might be a poor influence on you."

"Take your concern for me and direct it toward yourself, *amico mio*. Maybe then I won't worry so much." The quip bore a playful amount of teasing to it, masking the heaviness still apparent in the way he held himself. Patting my shoulder, Paolo turned his attention back to Diavolo, nodding in the direction of my mare while adjusting his gelding's saddle. "You should put away her things and go upstairs to sleep. The ride to Plymouth will wear you both out."

My smile broadened as I walked up behind him. My thoughts entertained the notion of sliding my arms around his waist, a temptation I managed to resist. Instead, I kissed his hair and retreated a pace afterward, turning my focus toward Tempest and ridding her of her bit and bridle. Even when she had been locked within her stall and settled into place, I lingered until Paolo rode off.

A yawn crested past my lips as I watched him depart, my disposition turning both solemn and fatigued. I considered it a mercy when the journey back to the room spared me the sight of either Lady Cavendish or Roland, and collapsed into bed with no will left to fight the onslaught of sleep. My eyes failed to open until dawn crested the horizon and even then, I felt refreshed enough only to trudge down to the main hall for a meal. Aches afflicted me from head to toe that barely had the chance to dissipate by the time I wandered into the stables.

She caught up to me as I finished grooming Tempest. The cryptic smile danced across Jane's lips again while her attendants separated to prepare her party's horses. "Are you ready to leave," she asked.

"As much so as I am ever going to be," I conceded. Once I had Tempest readied, I mounted the steed, gripping her reins tight. "The lead is yours once you are ready, Lady Cavendish."

She nodded with approval. Within minutes, we had begun a slow ride toward the crossroads leading out of town. As we pointed our horses southward, all but Leonard headed in the direction of Exeter, nudging their horses into a full gallop. My eyes lingered on them, until I felt the weight of Jane's stare directing my focus back to her.

Her lips curled, expression laden with amusement. I did my best to remain impassive. Settling myself deeper into the groove of my saddle, I glanced straight ahead while she assumed a place by my side. Something about the gesture unnerved me, providing my first hint that this might be as poor of an idea as Paolo warned it might be. All the same, I refused to reconsider it. My eyes remained set on the horizon, nodding in the direction of Plymouth.

"After you, milady," I said. "Let's be on our way."

CHAPTER ELEVEN

Long silences filled our southward journey, our horses walking at a brisk, but manageable pace. My mind wandered several times throughout the duration of the day, revisiting the suspicions I harbored while attempting not to entertain them for too long. Sometime around midday, Jane rode up beside me, jolting me back into awareness. "Leonard tells me there is a town an hour's ride from here," she said. "We'll pause for food there."

"Very well," I said, punctuating my acknowledgement with a nod and apt to leave it at that. When I failed to say anything else, Lady Cavendish allowed her mare to drift back beside Leonard and left me to my thoughts once more. A town came into view just a few miles further down the road, as Jane had indicated, and the same lack of conversation dotted both our time spent acquiring food and our journey forth. We rode onward until dusk, pausing before the sun fully set in the west to take up rooms.

Another long rest left me feeling much more rejuvenated. After passing through the market in search of food the next morning, I drifted back toward the open-air stable and fed Tempest an apple I had purchased as a treat. Jane found me a short time later, with Leonard in tow bearing a satchel which looked slightly more encumbered than I recalled it being last evening. If she gave any care toward his well-being, she gave no outward indication.

"The conditions of these towns are wretched," she commented once she was within earshot. The sigh which followed sounded heavy enough to nearly break her in two. "What I wouldn't give for the hospitality of a local Lord."

My gaze met Leonard's as he glanced over at me. While the look in his eyes managed to remain impassive, something about the weight they held told me I was being warned against commentary. Shrugging, I brushed my hands off and reached for Tempest's saddle. "Milady should be careful how loudly she announces her displeasure," I quipped, heedless of Leonard's displeasure. "Every scoundrel in town might assist in lightening your purse."

"The market does an adequate enough job of that, thank you." Jane smiled warmly at Leonard as he led her over to her mare's stall and secured the horse's accoutrements into place. "Although we did make certain to purchase a few things for us to eat along the way. We should be able to make it to Plymouth before supper."

"Always a pleasant expectation."

She ignored my response in favor of accepting Leonard's help atop her steed. It shifted its hooves to accommodate her weight while I shifted my focus away, in favor of surveying what I could make of the town around us. "Regardless of how much lighter your purse is, announcing it draws the wrong sort of attention," I added. Mounting Tempest, I nudged her out from her stall, gripping tight onto the reins to direct her closer to the exit. "Now, I have to be mindful of whether or not we're followed. Unless we're doing away with the charade of me being your guard."

Jane tsked, directing my attention back to her. "It isn't a charade, rogue," she countered. "I paid good money for your services." As she rode up beside me, her eyes danced with mirth, regarding me as though I might be little more than a child. "And really, if you think me some helpless waif, you do so to your downfall. Remember, I'm the one who's teaching *you* spells. Not the other way around."

Leonard snorted and settled onto his horse next. Together, the two progressed forward, a smirk dancing on Lady Cavendish's lips that her servant mirrored while riding past. Watching them depart, I sighed and Tempest snorted. "Yes, I hope she takes a nasty fall as well," I said, digging my heels into the mare's sides. She charged forward to catch up and from there, I devoted myself to a vow of silence. Unless the conversation shifted toward my purpose in being there, I wanted no part in amusing the woman.

The pledge held steady the remainder of the journey. We reached the gates of Plymouth, Jane straightening her posture as our horses carried us through. Leonard nodded to a man standing near the guards and in turn, the man mounted his own steed and raced ahead of us. I tensed and followed behind more closely, both unfamiliar with the town and my expected decorum as part of her entourage. It caused me to focus more intently on the townsfolk while attempting to appear nonplussed.

A few of them halted their activities as we rode past. The emblem on my cloak garnered a few stares, as well as some whispers, but Jane seemed apathetic toward them all. "This way, rogue," she said, leading us deeper into the city, and closer to its coast. She didn't wait for my response before quickening our pace.

Waves ebbed in the distance, bearing the glisten of the late day sun. The water stretched from one end of the horizon to the next, leading to heaven only knew where. I had never set my sights on so southward a horizon, nor fancied what might lie on the other side. Even the concept of Paolo being from a place called Verona failed to impact until that moment, when I realized I stood so close to where England ended and the rest of the world began.

Jane rode up beside me, prompting me to glance in her direction. Her expression bore a level of bemusement as our eyes met. "Did my guard fall asleep?" she asked.

"Surveying the land. Nothing more," I said. Freeing a hand, I pointed toward the road ahead of us, a predatory smile spreading across my lips. "Lead us onward, milady."

"Not much further now." She nodded once at me, head held high while she gave her horse a nudge. As she surged ahead of me, I took up a position on her left, set back two paces, but nothing more than that. Leonard mirrored my stance on the right, and together the three of us rode along a gently curving path, ascending one of the hills overlooking the town. As we rounded a bend, I found myself in awe, attempting not to pause while wishing an additional moment to marvel at what stood before us.

If the sight of the ocean had been impressive, my first look at her family's manor bore a whole other level of intrigue to it.

Surrounded by walls on each side, a set of gates remained opened and allowed us passage up to the imposing house. We rode until we reached its front doors, pausing by the horse which had belonged to the man we had spotted in town while a small collection of servants clamored toward Jane. She and Leonard stopped at the base of the stairs. I alighted from my horse as they did theirs, Lady Cavendish accepting the help offered and nodding at a young, female servant while handing her reins to one of the men. "I trust my father still tarries in Exeter?" she asked.

"Yes, he does, milady," the woman answered, tall and wiry with a simple dress hanging from her frame. The others seemed to be dressed similarly, all clean and well-groomed and instantly earning my distrust. The female servant gave another woman – this one a more matronly-looking one – a wide berth as she continued. "The manor has been made warm for your arrival, though, just as asked."

"Splendid," Jane said, allowing the woman to take her cloak. My gaze shifted away from Lady Cavendish and settled on Leonard, feeling the weight of his stare settle on me. The older servant had paused beside him and together, the two of them spoke in hushed tones. At first, I didn't know what about.

And then, the matronly woman stole a glance over at me.

Raising an eyebrow, I watched the two of them exchange information, Leonard leaning close enough to whisper in the woman's ear with her nodding intermittently while he spoke. I strained to hear anything being discussed, yet the issuance of my name from elsewhere prevented me from offering the conspirators more than another few moments of my attention. As I turned my head, I saw Jane smiling at me, her gaze shifting over to the duo as well before returning to me.

"You are easily distracted for a guard," she chided. At the same time, she arched an eyebrow and turned to line Leonard in her sights.

"Frances, if you could please draw a bath. And Leonard? Stable the horses so our guest can settle in."

Leonard's focus shifted almost more violently than mine had, as though he had been startled. "Yes, milady," he said, pausing after responding as though he had spoken before understanding the request. The matronly woman turned on her heels and entered the manor while Leonard strode closer to me. The amount of distaste evident in his expression left me to wonder what the servant's duties did not typically include stabling duties.

I handed the reins to Leonard as he extended a hand, chuckling as Tempest reared back and issued a whinny of protest. He gritted his teeth and held tight to her lead while the mare attempted to drag him forward. "It might be better for me to secure my horse on my own," I said. "She barely tolerates me on a good day."

"Leonard can handle an unruly mare," Lady Cavendish piped. She shot her servant a mild look of annoyance and he cowered accordingly, consigning himself to the task while obvious in his dissatisfaction with it. Jane closed the distance between us, extending a hand to rest on my shoulder and prompt me forward. "Into the house. You'll be shown to your room and we can talk over supper."

I glanced at my horse over my shoulder before sighing and shaking my head. "If he harms my horse at all, I'll carve him in two."

"I imagine you care more for that horse than you do most people."

"You would be correct in your wager." The expression on my face served as enough warning for Jane to turn her attention away from me again, focused more intently on leading her entourage past the threshold. I removed my gloves and held them in my hands while taking the chance to examine the interior of the house. The sight of what opened up before me forced me aback once more, leading me to wonder how many times I would be reminded just how out of my element I was.

High vaulted ceilings and a lit hearth greeted us on the inside. Several of the lamps had been lit as well, with the smell of food wafting through the house as a pleasant temptation. A staircase leading to the second floor laid directly in front of us, with rooms shooting off both to the left and the right of the front hall.

A large rug lay over the wood floor and tapestries hung from the walls, the area boasting very little in the way of furniture. I turned to peer at the door when it swung shut behind us, seeing that all but a few of the servants had followed us inside and now bustled to the next step of their directives. Jane walked up to me as I tracked the activity around me. "Now, I doubt this is your first time in a nobleman's manor," she said.

"The first time I have ever been invited to stay," I murmured, at too much of a loss to correct my subdued tone of voice. Each time one of the household staff passed us by, they cast curious stares at me, one or two of them eyeing me with revulsion. "They seem not to know what to make of me."

"Rogue, you smell terrible. I'm certain they'll like you better once you've bathed."

"Once I've what?"

Jane failed to answer my question. Just as I issued it, the matronly woman – Frances – caught Lady Cavendish's attention, motioning her toward the stairs while saying, "Your bath is being drawn, milady. Come and let me help you prepare."

"Thank you, Frances," Jane responded. She shot me a very quick glance, with that mysterious curl on her lips again before I became an afterthought. I watched them ascend and fidgeted at the glower Frances directed toward me before devoting her full attention to Lady Cavendish.

"If you could please follow me," a man chimed as he appeared on my right side.

I turned to regard him and raised an eyebrow at the way his eyes met mine, his expression both skeptical and expectant. Sighing, I nodded, not apt to indulge this charade any further while knowing I had no other choice. He seemed apathetic one way or the other, which suited me and made our trek to one of the guest quarters painfully quiet. We parted company without any ceremony, and once I was alone, I finally allowed myself to relax.

Placing the satchel on the floor, I unclasped my cloak and sat upon the edge of the bed. The mattress bore an unnerving level of comfort and fire crackled in a hearth; more tapestries hung from the walls of the room and the idle notion passed through my mind that perhaps I should take the lot of them down. I turned my head and spied a window, feeling some small sense of assurance for the first time since entering. Such was to be short-lived, however. When I tested the shutters, I discovered them unable to be opened.

"Will break you if necessary," I murmured, hanging my cloak beside my bed and sitting to remove my boots. After tucking away my weaponry, I pulled Lawrence's spell book from my bag, deciding to pass the time by reading. Lady Cavendish had mentioned supper and it occurred to me for the first time that she also said we would speak together during it.

"Surely she wouldn't have taken that much of a leave of her senses," I said aloud. Jane would have to be mad to continue entertaining me as though I was actually her guest, but the more I mused upon it, the more I realized how fitting it seemed to be for her. I thought of a woman bold enough to conduct business with my ilk and travel this distance with little more than a bodyguard at her side. A peasant mercenary dining at her father's table probably bothered her as little as everything else did. Not even two days into a fortnight and she had already proven herself beyond all expectation.

"I believe I might already be in trouble, Paolo."

An indiscriminate amount of time passed before a knock sounded on the door, waking me from a short-lived rest. The young, female servant stood on the other side, walking in with a folded pile of clothing in her arms. "Lady Cavendish wants a bath drawn and for you to change for supper," she said, setting the garments atop the bed.

I hid the spell book, tucking it behind my back to free both hands. "I have other things to wear, thank you kindly," I said.

The girl snorted and spared me a quick, derisive glance. "She says she doesn't want you smelling and in rags. Best to pay mind to what the Lady wishes." Just as quickly as she had arrived, the servant spirited out of the room, leaving a confused man in her wake. I had only a few moments to hide the book in my satchel again before Frances walked in to escort me away. Despite a heavy amount of protest, I found myself being stripped and forced into a bath, the water scalding and uncomfortable.

I gritted my teeth and attempted to shoo the woman away. Frances ignored me, directing the younger girl to trim my hair once it had been washed and barking orders that I was to have a shave, too, whether or not I liked it. As one of the men approached me with razor, I scowled and threatened to strip him of it.

"Ignore 'im," the matronly woman said. "Or cut 'im if he won't cooperate."

"Yes, ma'am," he said. The way he peered at me bore a plea in it, as if to say, 'Could we please do this the easy way, sir?' and though I failed to speak, I relented to the fussing. Still, by the time I had been shorn and shaved, and put into a fresh pair garments, I had built up enough anger to split among the lot of them. I decided, however, to save it for the source of my vexation.

They led me into the dining room while I adjusted the tunic which now hung from my frame. It had been dyed a deep blue, with a golden trim, and I only felt more ridiculous when I saw the way Jane studied me when I entered. "My, you do clean up very well, Master Christian," she said, standing on the opposite side of a table and regarding me with a frustrating amount of amusement. She tucked her hands in her sleeves. "You could have almost been a noble."

"I could have hung myself from a balcony, too, from shame," I said, giving the belt around my waist one final adjustment out of annoyance. "Am I to look like a fool during the entire duration of a fortnight?"

"For as long as I own your services." She lifted a brow at me. "Don't be so quick to dismiss it. You might find yourself relishing the attention."

"Not bloody likely."

The young, female servant scowled at me before hustling to Lady Cavendish's side. If my manner of speech had offended Jane, she failed to make note of it. "Always so pessimistic," she said. "I've met mercenaries with much better dispositions being paid far less." Jane nodded at her maid as she pulled out a chair. Lowering into the seat, Jane allowed herself to be pushed in closer to the table and pointed at the chair across from her. "I sent Leonard away so we might speak in private. Please, sit."

The servant who had rid me of my facial hair stood by a chair and pulled it out. He eyed me nervously and I sighed while giving in once again, displeased at how little control it seemed I had over the situation. "I think you have me confused for a man readily impressed by how much coin a person has to offer," I said, pulling in my own chair before the servant could be bothered. He backed away, at least smart enough not to fight me on this one concession. "If you wanted a more complacent guest, you should have wooed someone else."

"But I wanted you, Master Christian. Not merely a sword for hire." Her hands folded on her lap as she held a pleasant smile on her face. "Or have we forgotten my offer?"

"No, I haven't forgotten. In fact, I was reading before being rudely thrown into a cooking pot."

Jane barked out a laugh. One hand lifted to cover her mouth and I waged a battle not to give in to a smirk at the amount of delight the sound contained. As it stood, I managed only to be marginally successful in my effort. "Yes, I always boil my guests." Her hand lowered again. "Or perhaps I was testing whether or not you could chill the waters yet yourself. Have you learned much from Lawrence's book?"

I raised an eyebrow, the passage of the male servant from the room enough for me to realize what we were discussing in their presence. A steady stream of men and women shuffled in and out of the dining room, setting plates of food on the table and leading me furrow my brow at Jane. Once again, her apathy had me unnerved. "You are a rather trusting woman, milady," I said, flicking a quick glance at the servant closest to her.

Jane glanced at them. "Oh. Pay them no mind," she said, her pleasant, cryptic smile emerging in response. "They know better than to divulge our household affairs."

The younger female met my gaze while placing a loaf of bread before us. I watched her turn and depart, lost in the thought of such a host of people being so trustworthy. "I imagine they do. Speaking of cooking people in the bathwater."

"Now, let's not be so gruesome over dinner." I considered it worth noting that she didn't dismiss the implication entirely. Jane tilted her head. "You were telling me about your reading."

"Yes, I suppose I was." With the last of the food placed before us, all but one of the servants departed from the room. The final one who lingered – the man who had helped with my grooming – disappeared when Jane nodded at him, and with that, we were left truly alone. "So much of it is in Latin," I continued. A common trait between your sorcerers and the church. You both seem to take exception with the common tongue."

"Bound by our traditions," she said. Her smile faded, surrendering to a bout of sobriety. "Have you been able to make out any of it, though?"

"A bit." My eyes flicked quickly to a healthy portion of meat that had been placed upon my plate. "It still sounds strange for me to confess I've uttered such nonsense."

"And what did the words do when you spoke them? Did you sense anything different afterward?"

She lifted her fork and stabbed at a potato with an unaffected air. Reaching for my cup, I brought it to my lips and imbibed a sip of wine before reaching for my utensils. Manners and customs still eluded me, but mimicry seemed like it could cover a multitude of sins. "Far more than that," I finally responded. "They created fire. Wind, too, in gusts strong enough to throw open a barn door."

"Basic enough of a task, though impressive you were able to manage results even on your own," she said, the air turning pensive while she weighed my words. She continued to nibble at her food while musing and I finally gave into the compulsion to lift a piece of mutton to my mouth and take a bite. Her brow furrowed while I chewed. "I'd wager more that fire is your natural element, which is curious. Are you a volatile man, Christian?"

I snorted. "I believe most people would say that's accurate, yes."

"You do bear that posture. Like a storm passing through the night." Her smile broadened. "It begs the question of what made you this way, however."

"What made me what way? Volatile?"

126

"Yes. Tempestuous men always have some penchant for violence. This is why fire seems to favor them."

Her words rendered my tongue mute for a moment. I continued picking at my food while deliberating on her observation. "I had a rather unsettled youth," I responded, weighing my words carefully. "I suppose if anything contributed to the type of person I am, that did."

"It certainly would," she said, the smile on her face dissolving to a mere half-smirk when my eyes met Lady Cavendish's again. Hers seemed to be examining me, peeling back the layers one at a time in search of something. What, I had no way of knowing. "Many men have unsettled youths, even men of privilege. I think you're playing coy with me."

"Whether I am or not is my choice in the matter."

"Such bold words for a peasant. Did you never learn your station, rogue?"

A slow, mischievous grin spread across my lips. "I am no peasant, my good lady, neither am I a noble. No law binds me. If this means that I've never learned that station, then I will confess without hesitation."

"Miscreant." The sparkle in her eyes defied the issuance of the word, bearing mirthful appreciation. She set aside her fork and took her turn drinking from her cup. "Surely there's something you can tell me about this unsettled youth of yours. It might help me to understand you better."

"And why is such an understanding important?" I asked.

Jane sampled her wine, holding her gaze steady over the rim of her glass. As she lowered it, her posture straightened. "Magic isn't simple, nor does it seep from the skin of one man the same way it does another," she explained. Resting her elbow on the table, she cradled her hand in her palm and narrowed her eyes playfully at me. "The words in a spell book have no actual power in and of themselves. I could hand the book to Leonard and he could repeat the contents of every page, but you could make them do more than he ever could. Trust me when I say he's tried."

"And why is it that I can and he cannot?"

"I'm not completely sure, rogue, you won't answer my questions." Her smile broadened, an eyebrow arching again. "You were born with it, whatever the matter. Anybody who can break a spell without being taught inherited the link which binds man to magic. Before you even knew that you had such a thing, you went through the crucible, and fire became your friend. For what it's worth, I prefer water. This is why spend more time in this manor than the one my family owns in Exeter."

"I suppose that makes sense." The barest hint of temptation traced across my thoughts for a moment, weighing her small confession and prodding me to at least reveal something to her. Breathing a sigh, I determined that the barest of details would not be damning in and of themselves. "I watched a man murder my father. He had fallen ill and a band of mercenaries caught up with him. Needless to say, the experience has lingered ever since."

"Were you close to him?"

"Yes, quite. And I never forgave either God or man for taking him from me."

"Little wonder you bow a knee to no man. You won't even to a higher power."

The nonplussed way she responded to such blasphemy said much for her caliber, where it had been my intent to scandalize her. A smirk chased away the sobriety which had fallen over me, seeing before me a challenge to counter. "God has never given me a reason to. And milady spits in His face with her witchcraft, if we were going to listen to what the priests have to say."

Jane snorted. "They speak whatever words will fill their coffers. I'm not stupid enough to confuse the actions of men with the directive of the Almighty. Remember, rogue, I was raised around power. It creates the largest hypocrites of them all."

"Finally, something we both can agree upon."

"Will wonders never cease?" The way her eyes settled on me bore many layers to them. As we regarded each other, she gave me a quick, curt nod and glanced away, but I continued staring, weighing what might be racing through her mind. Jane picked up her fork and pointed toward my plate with it. "Finish your supper," she quipped. "I'll leave you in peace now."

"Yes, milady," I said, watching the shift in her demeanor and hesitating first before obeying her command. She ignored me and together, we ate in silence, consuming food and drink until we were both sated. Jane excused herself for the evening, permitting me back to my room, where I finally rid myself of her ridiculous clothing and flopped onto the bed in just my undershirt and pants. For some reason, I held no taste for reading further. Instead, I spent the time musing on Paolo, and what he might say about me sojourning in such lavish lodgings before I surrendered to the call of sleep.

I rose with the first rays of the sun and dressed again after relieving myself. A small grin tugged at the corners of my mouth while the thought occurred of the cavalcade of servants being forced to clean up after me. Making my way downstairs, I watched two of them wrap bread and dried meat into cloth and slip it into a knapsack. Jane oversaw them, dressed in riding clothes, and accepted the bag when it was presented to her.

"Ah, good, you're awake," she said when she turned to see me. "I'll have Frances fetch you a cloak. Go and get Lawrence's spell book. We're going for a ride."

She slipped the bag over her head and raised an eyebrow at me. I mirrored the expression, somewhat befuddled at the command. "Where are we headed toward, milady?" I asked, making quick eye contact with the matronly woman as she shot me a displeased glare.

"Out of town," Jane said, grinning when our eyes met once more. The look on her face was just as cryptic as ever, her demeanor just as carefree as she nodded toward the stairs. "Away with you, then. Time won't pause to allow us to dawdle. We have a light ride ahead of us and you have lessons to begin."

CHAPTER TWELVE

"A pity Leonard was unable to join us," I said as we passed through the city gates, leaving Plymouth behind. Before us lay the coast, and though I preferred the company of my thoughts to entertaining her in conversation, a few things yet had me unsettled. I had been asked to accompany her unarmed, and though her bodyguard had been present in the stables when we retrieved our horses, he made no attempt to shadow us this time. This left me alone in the presence of a noble woman.

Even my lack of piety couldn't ignore the taboo of our situation.

"Small mercies," Lady Cavendish responded with a small grin. As always, she appeared completely unaffected, both bound to societal contract and liberated from it. "Though if we're being honest, neither of us are that disappointed."

The cryptic way she issued the comment prompted me into silence again. We exchanged a glance before both of us looked away, entering another period of quiet I felt apt to recognize this time. The road stretched out for several miles, running parallel to the coast. Fishermen nodded at us as we passed and once I settled into the ride, I lost myself toward appreciation of the scenery. In the distance, ships sailed into the harbor, the air carrying the scent of rain with clouds rolling in from the sea. It wasn't until we ascended another hill leading eastward that I felt the first drops of rain hit my face.

"We're almost there," Jane said, breaking the silence at last. She glanced at me as I peered heavenward. "Perhaps it's time we picked up speed."

"I couldn't agree more," I said. In unison, we dug heels into our horses' sides and gripped on tight to the reins. Tempest galloped in tandem with her equine compatriot, leading me to the idle thought of how often she gave Paolo's gelding less cooperation. By the time we wove around to the top of the hill, the noble lady and I had been drenched from head to foot, and our mares along with us.

Jane led me to a cottage and took shelter with me in a small stable which had been constructed against the side of the house. Tempest shook her mane. I laughed as I lowered myself from her back and tied her reins to a hitching post. "Bloody animal. We're not much better off than you," I said, patting her neck before letting go of her completely. I walked up to Jane and offered her a hand, helping her to alight from her own steed.

"They need to voice their discontent one way or the other," Jane observed while lowering the hood of her cloak and shaking out her hair. She took a deep breath and pointed at the small house before us. "My secret hideaway," she explained. "My father's father built it to watch the ships sail into port. He wanted to travel, but never had much chance."

"A pity, that."

Jane regarded me with a raised eyebrow when she noticed the words had been genuine. I mirrored the gesture and followed along with her until we entered the cottage and stepped into the main room. "Light the hearth, rogue," she said, pulling off her riding gloves and unfastening her cloak. "Maybe we can get dry before the journey home."

"If the rain favors us with letting up by then," I said. Walking closer to the cold hearth, I knelt beside it and frowned. It had plenty of kindling available, and spied an ample amount of firewood stacked beside it, but as I freed myself the burden of Jane's knapsack, I recalled my tinderbox had been left behind in my satchel, my instructions having been only to fetch Lawrence's spell book. "I assume this means you have some flint somewhere."

"Cheating, are we?"

Her question caused me to peer up at her and furrow my brow. She nodded toward the firebox. "I thought you a pyromancer," she explained. "Light the hearth."

"As the lady commands," I said, mirroring the amused smile I saw spread across her lips. Jane turned her back to me and I directed my focus toward the dark pit, pulling off my gloves and drawing a deep breath in preparation. My hands extended outward, and softly I spoke speaking the words Lawrence's book contained, aware that the spell had become an old, familiar friend already. As such, it came as no surprise when a flame rose from the midst of the kindling, consuming a small patch of brush, but failing to ignite the logs in the process.

I narrowed my eyes and fixed my gaze on the fledgling fire. Reaching out to it with every measure of my being, I pressed it more into existence and jumped when the hearth roared into life. A bark of surprise sprang from my mouth, produced as I fell backward and crawled a few paces away from the sudden inferno in front of me. Jane laughed and dashed for the firewood, plucking a log from the pile and tossing it onto the pyre. "Rogue, I said light the hearth, not the whole cottage," she said.

Nervously, I chuckled, settling only when the fire died down to a manageable size. Jane glanced at me, and I grinned coyly at the bemused expression on her face. "I believe I might have overdone it," I said.

"You're a fledgling in need of control. At least you *didn't* endanger us both."

"This much is true." My eyes stole back to the hearth, watching the flames I had summoned lick over the logs and settle into a steady burn. Lifting myself up, I settled into a crouched position on the balls of my feet. Something inside of me swelled with pride, as though beholding the closest thing I would ever have to a newborn child. Jane stood beside me while I ran my fingers through my drenched hair. "How do we have the ability to do something so remarkable?"

"Remarkable or destructive?" We regarded each other again, her expression still bearing a hint of humor. She nodded toward the knapsack. "Bring that over to the table. We'll light a few lamps and eat first before we get started."

"As you wish, milady."

Rising to a stand, I lifted the bag with me and carried it over to where Jane indicated. She nodded, giving me silent permission to sit while she drifted toward the far side of the room, where a trunk had been situated against the wall. Lady Cavendish bent to open it, digging through it for supplies before shutting the lid. "Your first lesson will be control," she said, waiting until she had my attention to offer a knowing grin. "It seems it's become a necessity."

For as much as I wanted to bristle at the quip, I found myself smirking at it instead. "You said I was a fledgling," I countered.

"And I'd like not to die before you become a novice." Jane strode back toward where I sat and handed a candle to me. As she took a seat across from me, she arranged several others into a collection of brass holders and placed them in different corners of the table. An empty holder sat idle in the center, and Jane pointed at the charred wick of the one I held. "Now, concentrate on the size of the flame," she said. "We'll light these first before we have you attempt one of the lamps."

"Very well," I said, nodding. Another deep breath passed through my lips, my eyes squinting at the wick while I began to murmur the spell. Jane leaned forward before I could finish it, however, stopping me when she pressed a finger against my mouth.

Glancing at her, I raised an eyebrow. She smiled. "You didn't need the spell to cause the fire in the hearth to grow. Remember, this is your natural element. Speak to it from your heart."

The direction confused me enough to cause me a moment's pause. Jane nodded at the wick and I shrugged while focusing on the candle again. Everything else in the room ceased to matter, my entire attention being taken up by the item in my hand while I thought about fire, willing it into life. I thought of each time I had effortlessly turned a spark into a flame, and this time, rather than speaking words from a book, I heard my own voice in my head. *'Come now. Show yourself. You've cooperated with me in the past, now behave for me again.'*

Slowly, a flame sprang into existence, stopping once it had engulfed the wick altogether.

"Much better," Jane said, extending a hand to take the candle. I passed it to her, watching as she settled it into the empty holder and sat back in her chair. She pointed around at the remainder of the collection, the curl of her lips possessing a dare. "Now, let's see you light the rest of these."

With a nod, I lifted both hands and held them aloft, focusing on the candle nearest to me. The tingles I had experienced other times surged through my veins once more, my eyes dancing from one wick to the other while the words I used to coax each flame diminished into nonexistence. Jane watched the symphony of fire that I directed, and chuckled at my expression when I made eye contact with her again. The firelight cast a glow across her face I was certain she saw reflected back on mine.

For the first time since we departed from my town, I relished being able to share the moment with her.

We both stood and wandered around the room together, walking from lamp to lamp with me repeating the process anew each time. Lady Cavendish would point at one and once I had it lit, moved onto the one following until we paused by the last one and lingered near it. Jane's gaze bore a dare in it, not a word spoken, but the gauntlet taken by me as I flicked a quick glance at the lamp and looked away again. In my periphery, I watched light burst forth from within its sconce and directed a broad smile at her reaction.

"Now you're showing off, rogue," Jane said. She shook her head. "Hardly becoming on you."

"I thought plenty of women found that trait desirable," I countered as we drifted back toward where we had been sitting.

"You men all think that and we simply don't argue otherwise." At the same time, the way she peered over her shoulder at me bore sultry undertones to it. Jane nodded at the knapsack left discarded near my chair. "Take out our food and Lawrence's book. If you want to learn something worth boasting about, then we'll get started."

"As the lady wishes." Nodding once at her, I continued to the table and hefted the bag on top, pulling out the cloth-wrapped meal and tome it contained before setting it back down. It took a matter of moments for us to consume our bread and far less time after that for us to open the book and page through it. I chewed idly on an apple while Jane flipped to the beginning, forcing us to commence our studies there.

Painstakingly, she poured over each spell and pointed out many of the repeated terms so I might become more familiar with them. The enchantments which allowed me to manipulate fire became items of particular interest and made up our time spent in that first session. One taught me how to form a larger ball of fire. Another showed me how to toss it from one hand to the other. The last one had me focus on engulfing my entire hand with flames, a trick which both unnerved and captivated me as it failed to burn either skin or clothing. The natural affinity I had forced her to pause in wonder several times during our exercises.

"Yes. One of your parents had natural talents," she said as I closed my hand and snuffed out the fire. "I'm completely sure of it now, which leads me to wonder about their family lines. There aren't many with such a strong pedigree."

"My family has no pedigree," I replied, my smile fading. Lady Cavendish attempted to catch my attention, but I fought against it, flexing my fingers and peering at my palm before rubbing my hands together. "It doesn't matter," I added. "Even if they did, I'd have no way of finding that out. They're both dead."

The weight of her gaze settled on me, forcing my attention back to her in time to catch the curl of her lips before it faded. "You're resisting. There's something about all of this you don't want to talk about and it's only making me curious, Christian. Do you still not trust me with your secrets?"

"Not after only one day, milady. If I might remind you I have good reason not to."

"So you insist. Though how much so only leads me to wonder why you stress so much emphasis on it." Jane hummed, holding my gaze hostage – as much forcing me to look at her as refusing to glance away. I felt a shiver crawl the length of my spine, not knowing from where it came, but certain of its existence nonetheless. It didn't abate until she nodded and shut the book in front of us. "We should start back before it turns dark."

It took every ounce of self-restraint I could summon not to exhale a sigh of relief as I stood. Gathering up the book, I helped her snuff out the lamps and extinguish the hearth while she tucked the candlesticks and holders away in the trunk where she had retrieved them. Lady Cavendish assumed her regal air anew, carrying it out with her and maintaining a pensive silence with me again while we rode back to her family manor. Upon returning, I took out Lawrence's book to study for the remainder of the evening. My final thoughts before retiring were the same as they had been the previous night, centered on Paolo and how he might be busying himself.

Eleven more nights, I told myself, and then succumbed to rest.

The next day, we rode back to her cottage, this time with books from her personal library as well. The temptation had been present on the ride east to inquire as to why we never practiced in the manor; a question I answered myself as I recalled nearly razing the cottage. Both of us sat in front of that very same hearth after settling in, facing each other and holding hands while Jane taught me how to control the amount of energy I called forth. "You did well manipulating fire," she said, her eyes still shut, "But this is your natural element, and not every spell is a simple thought. Some have to be built upon, like stairs ascending to another floor."

"Very well, then," I said, allowing my lids to drift closed and my posture to relax into the exercise. "How do I go about building these steps?"

"By learning to clear your mind first. Take a deep breath. Release it slowly and take another until you are ready to proceed."

"And then what?"

"I want you to try to hold onto the energy which runs through you whenever you summon fire. Don't do anything with it, simply clutch it in your chest and keep it there. Are you ready to try that?"

"Yes." My chest rose as I drew in air and fell when the breath passed through my lips again. I repeated the process just as Jane had instructed, clearing my mind of anything but the invitation for my favored element to come out to play while doing so. A shiver raced up my spine, my grip on one of Jane's hands tightening as a surge of power raced through me. I let it fill me, but held onto it rather than expelling it as I normally had.

Jane clasped onto me in return. I could hear the smile in her voice. "Yes, like that," she coached. "Now let's see how long you can contain it."

"As the lady wishes." My voice became a murmur, issued with only partial awareness while I fought to sustain the amount of force building within me. Tingles raced up one arm and across my shoulders, surging to my other hand while threatening to crack my concentration. I winced against it. "I'm not sure I can do this much longer," I cautioned as a tremor settled in my limbs.

"Now, I want you to release it," Jane said, "But do it slowly."

"Slowly," I repeated while exhaling a breath I didn't know I had been holding. At the same time, I also ignored the very word I had issued back, feeling a rush race through me before I could stop it. Jane removed her hands in time not to be harmed, but the ensuing force pushed her one side and me, the other, causing us both to sprawl out across the floor. The lamps lit around us surged before dying down and the heat of the fireplace turned treacherously warm before diminishing. I lifted up on my elbow to regard Lady Cavendish. "Are you alright, milady?" I asked, unable to suppress the laugh which followed.

Jane slid up onto her palms and righted herself with a sigh. "Please pay more mind to *slowly* before you nearly incinerate us again, rogue," she said, taking a deep breath to compose herself. For as terse as she issued the words, there seemed to be a hint of awe in her eyes as she clasped my hands again, a faint humor flickering through her expression which set my mind at ease. "Let's try that once more, only this time, release it sooner so you can pace yourself."

I settled myself back into position in front of her. "Sooner. Understood." Nodding in agreement, I shook out the previous attempt from my limbs and tried once more. This time bore more success, the dispersal of energy more gradual and tapering off toward the end. As I opened my eyes, the final waves seeped from me, leaving me with a drunk and somewhat dizzy feeling in its aftermath.

Jane smiled at whatever expression must have been painted on my face, looking pleased. "Good. You didn't nearly char us this time." A good-natured wink followed the statement. Lady Cavendish sobered and let go of my hands, folding hers onto her lap. "These are the building blocks of a spell. There are many ways to channel power, but because you have the favor of the elements, I am teaching it to you this way. You use the power you gather to conjure magic. The bigger the spell, the more energy which is required. Just remember that, Christian. A spell is little more than a series of steps."

Rising to a stand, Jane hurried around the room, gathering our things. I lifted up to my feet to follow suit, slipping books into the knapsack I had once again used to transport them. "A series of steps," I said with a nod. "You said elements. I did mention I've manipulated wind a bit."

"Yes, I intend to have us experiment with that next. Beyond that, there is water, earth, and quintessence, although the last one is a more elusive concept. I think of it as that part of us which we feed into the magic we cast. Our spirit, if you will, and the driving force of the world itself. You'll struggle the most with earth, being such a volatile man, but you need to learn how to harness it just the same."

"And when do we get to that?" Shutting the bag, I lifted its strap over my head and raised an eyebrow at Lady Cavendish.

She replied with another cryptic grin. "Tomorrow, my rogue. For tonight, I have other matters to attend to. I'll show you my family's library in the meantime so you can busy yourself with reading."

"I believe I will do just that." Offering her a bow, I succumbed to a more genuine and pleased expression, unable to contain the amount of excitement bounding through me in the moment. We regarded each other with smiles before I set about the task of extinguishing lamps and Jane strode outside to ready our horses. The rest of the evening was quiet, with her absent during supper and taking solitary counsel in the courtyard afterward. I spent a few hours in the library before settling into sleep.

The following day, a spring found its way into my step, even if I tried to keep my outward appearance more reserved. We engaged in idle conversation throughout our ride through Plymouth and settled into our studies without the normal exchange of cutting remarks and posturing beforehand. I managed to summon a few gusts of wind, pleased with the advancement until the sound of thunder preempted us. We hurried from the cottage as quickly as possible and rode back to the manor, returning as the rain covered us in torrents, forcing us to seek out drier clothing in our respective rooms.

A knock sounded on my door almost immediately after I had finished dressing. "Her Ladyship wishes you in the library," Frances, the matronly servant, directed from the other side of the threshold, punctuating the order with her customary glare.

I nodded my assent and followed her into the room, regarding it now by the light of day. While I had examined it the night before, I still found myself in awe of the sheer amount of shelves and volumes it housed; more than I had ever regarded in my life. As Frances shut the doors behind me, I fell into the temptation to scan each spine. "The luxury of opulence knows no bounds," I said. "Although, I'll say this much, these are the few possessions I believe to be money well spent."

My gaze shifted to Jane in time to catch her laugh. The hearth crackled and filled the space with warmth, casting an inviting glow across everything it touched. I drifted further in the room as she crossed the space between us, her hair still damp and making her seem much more human in that moment. "Men wage battles," she countered, "But my father says knowledge conquers lands."

A faint chuckle passed through my lips. I stopped and regarded the deep woods and colorful adornments making up the rest of the room. "Is your family the conquering sort?"

"Aren't most families of nobility? There's a throne to be won after all."

"Thrones are for those who lack imagination. I can think of better things to aspire toward."

Her smile broadened, chin tilting upward while she regarded me with a glint in her eyes. "Irreverent peasant, we'll see how much you scoff at power when you realize how much of it you're capable of wielding." Jane relaxed her posture, her expression turning less severe. "Now, for the last exercise I had planned on teaching you today. Fire and air are your friends, but how well can they get along together?"

I peered around the room before looking back at her. "Is this a safe place to be venturing such a challenge, milady?" I asked.

"Remember, you're channeling their energy, not their appearance," she said, extending her hands out to me. "Keep that in mind and both we and the servants can live to see another day."

"Noble birth or not, you *are* a gambling woman." Nodding, I drew a deep breath inward and released it slowly. Reaching out for her hands, I took hold of them and rolled my shoulders once. "So, I am to summon fire first, then hold onto it while calling for air? Very well, then." My eyes shut, my focus given over to controlling the way my chest took in air and expelled it past my lips. I found myself in the darkness of my mind again, evoking my natural element and holding onto it with as much concentration as I could manage first before directing my focus elsewhere.

Reaching out toward wind, I attempted to capture it next, but it danced around me and evaded my grasp. A grumble surged from my throat, and after trying for it once more, my eyes opened. Jane lifted her lids as well and arched an eyebrow at me. "Is there a problem?" she asked.

"Yes, they seem not to want to play well," I muttered. "Fire was simple enough, but I couldn't claim the wind."

"Try it the other way around, then."

"I suppose it's as good of an idea as any." With a nod, I shut my eyes and cleared my mind again. Directing my concentration toward wind first, I felt for it and invited it closer, feeling it flit around me before settling into me. As my focus shifted to the second element, however, it escaped and left me back where I had started. "Bloody hell," I said, releasing my hold on Jane and pacing away from her angrily.

I felt Lady Cavendish stare at me as I ran my fingers through the locks of my hair. "Christian, you are doing exceptionally well for such a new student," she murmured in a soft, reassuring tone. "Allow yourself to make a few mistakes."

For as strange as it sounded to hear my name spoken in such a winsome manner, it still managed to lure my attention back to her. Jane reached out for me again and a sigh passed through my lips as I responded with a nod. Taking her hands in mine once more, I shut my eyes and spent several moments calming my spirit. The world faded around me. I focused on the cadence of my breathing and the beating of my heart, not bothering with formalities; simply calling to both elements and reaching out to them at the same time.

They came maddeningly within reach. Faintly, I heard myself mutter the words of the spell I had first learned, in an effort to draw them nearer still. Fire clasped onto me, but as I made a final push for the air, it dissipated through my fingers, dispersed when I let go of Jane again and shook my head.

"It isn't *working*," I barked, not mindful of either the volume of my voice or its tone. "I think I might be too frustrated to make another attempt."

Jane touched my chin and tilted my face up so that I might regard her. "You're trying too hard," she said. "Fire came easy and air likes to play, but doesn't want to be claimed. You aren't the first sorcerer to have this problem and you won't be the last. We need to train your mind and that will take time."

I scowled. "How many days can it take when we only have a fortnight?"

"We have as many as you're willing to grant this." Jane frowned when I turned away from her, but allowed me to escape. The weight of her gaze settled on me, but I chose to ignore it this time. "Christian, men spend decades trying to master magic. Nobody, not even the most talented, dies knowing how to do it all."

"I don't have decades!"

The way I shouted startled me enough to cast a glance at Lady Cavendish from across my shoulder. Her eyes widened, and my stomach twisted into knots at the confused look which surfaced in her gaze. Shaking my head, I turned my back to her once more and peered downward, ignoring her scrutiny as best as I could manage. "I don't want to talk about it," I said, thinking about the promise I had made to Paolo; the danger I knew I skirted against simply in being there. "I can just hear the questions you've ready to ask and I want no part in them."

Jane remained in place as I walked closer to the hearth. Resting a hand on the wall beside it, I watched the fire dance, my mind in just as much tumult as each flame licking against the wood. My chest filled with air, breaths taken in and out as I attempted to quell my anger again.

"Why are you so resistant toward opening up?" Jane finally asked, breaking the silence.

"I told you, I am not of the mind to discuss it."

"Regardless of whether or not you want to, I believe you must. You hold a secret in your heart that's distracting you. Christian, I'm never going to be able to help you focus if you don't let it go somehow."

I scoffed, but failed to move when I heard her pacing closer. She paused behind me, touching my shoulder in a tentative manner and prompting me to tense. The gesture bore overly familiar tones, ones which called to mind the impropriety with which she approached her own station. I felt my frown deepen. "Lady Cavendish, I couldn't answer your question honestly if I wanted to." My voice lowered to a soft, hesitant whisper. "I think I might have already said too much."

"By whose standards? You wanted a teacher and I've set out to be that to you. It's challenging to instruct someone so at odds with himself, though."

"I know who you serve and it isn't your family."

Jane sighed. Her fingertips slid from my shoulder to my back as she took another step closer. "You're speaking of the Luminaries, aren't you?"

"Yes, I am." I neither pushed her away, nor responded to her touch.

"And once again, the way you evoke them bears striking undertones. What do you think I am to them?"

"Does it matter, milady? I'm not an idiot. Whatever reason you have to be teaching me, I know it's to their ends somehow."

A soft chuckle passed through her lips. For how overt her actions had suddenly become, I didn't expect it when she drifted closer still, her other arm sliding around my waist from behind. I remained frozen in position, not sure if I should turn or pray she retreated on her own. The latter seemed not probable the moment I felt the sensation of her breath on the back of my neck, causing the skin to prickle. "You're smart," she said, "So I won't insult you by pretending otherwise. Yes, they want to invite you into the fold. It's what they do when they discover a gifted sorcerer without an order."

"They would find me apt to decline the offer." I attempted to ignore the way her hand pressed into my chest. Her lips touched my neck and a shiver blossomed from the point of contact to the base of my spine, forcing me to clench my eyes shut. Thoughts of Paolo crossed my mind once more and as much as I tried to latch onto the outcry of my heart, I became keenly aware of how long it had been since I received a woman's attentions. '*That you were a more jealous soul*, amico mio, *this would be easier to resist.*' "Milady, you would lead me down the path of temptation," I said, my breath turning shaky. "And then I would be guilty of sullying your honor."

"You assume Lawrence was patient enough to wait for our wedding night to claim those rights." An entreating tone settled into her voice. "Or are you distracting yourself with thoughts of my honor to avoid discussing other matters of discomfort?"

"Those seem to be plentiful in the moment." The hand on my back began a slow, taunting trek down my side, muddling my judgment further.

"I imagine they are." A light chuckle lilted past her lips before she regained some sense of sobriety. "Every man has a price, my darling rogue, though yours might be too high. Sir Christian, what *did* they ever do to you?"

"I can't say." Her fingertips threatened to graze against my hip and even my encumbered imagination knew where they meant to venture next. "Stop," I whispered. "I'm not in the mood to be kind if you persist in doing that."

"Has it occurred to you that perhaps my interest is in you?" she asked. "Maybe I want to know what it feels like to have a man I desire give to me what Lawrence only took. And what if I told you I volunteered to be the one to teach you when they proposed inviting you in, Christian? Does that influence your decision any?" Jane shifted her mouth closer to my ear. I felt her tongue give it a flick. "What you do with their invitation is up to you. You defended my honor, regardless of your motivations."

"What if I mean to kill one of them?"

"If you need suggestions, I've a list of a few I wouldn't mind dropping dead."

I couldn't decide whether to laugh or moan. My head tilted to the side, the act of submission not a conscious one, but one motivated by the need coiling in my stomach. Words fell from my lips as a murmur. "The man who killed my father. I don't know who the bastard was, but he bore their cloak."

"Why did they kill your father?"

"I don't know. He had something of theirs and managed to spirit me away with it before they ran him through. Lady Cavendish, am I in danger of needing to silence you again?"

Using the hold she had on me, Jane pushed me into a turn. I acquiesced, opening my eyes when my back hit the wall and her body melded against mine again. She peered up at me with a raised eyebrow. "I thought we had gone beyond such a need," she said, one hand trailing up my chest while the other toyed with my belt. "Their business is their business, not mine. If you want your revenge, I won't stand in your way of it."

She lifted up enough to brush noses with me. I spoke against her lips. "You would be an accessory."

"You flatter yourself. I would deny I knew anything about it."

One of my hands settled on her back. I shoved her against me further, allowing our mouths to dance without giving in fully to the compulsion to kiss her. "A lady's interests are her own, are they?"

"I leave the decision of your fate up to you. Perhaps you might change your mind after a fortnight."

"Doubtful." I held onto her for leverage, my body moving against hers, almost of its own volition. She mimicked the rhythm with her own, creating friction precisely where I wanted it to be. It took everything in my power not to engage her mouth with mine just yet. "I am still trusting you aren't luring me into a trap," I muttered.

"And once again, I repeat my warning that everything bears a risk," she countered. Reaching for my hand, she slid it down toward her backside. We continued moving against each other, her lips parting to gasp. "Tell me who you really are, rogue, so I know it when I cry out your name."

"Christian Richardson. Mercenary with the Brotherhood of the Black Rose. Assassin."

"Scoundrel." She bit my bottom lip and tugged at it before releasing it. "Sorcerer." Her arms both lifted, circling my neck as she whimpered. Jane threw her head back, inviting me with the sight of her delicate skin while she peered heavenward. "Irreverent peasant."

"Flatterer." I licked a line up her throat to her chin. When she looked at me again, I saw the lustful urgency in her eyes and felt it impact with what precious little self-restraint I had left. My unencumbered hand settled on the back of her neck, lips crashing into lips with wantonness. She held onto me and what had started as frantic turned downright manic within moments.

I hardly noticed it when she pushed away from me. Her hands reached for mine, pulling me with her toward the center of the room. She made quick work of my belt and I pulled off my tunic, tossing it and my undershirt aside. "I want you bare, milady," I whispered as I drew close enough to kiss up her neck again. "I want to sample the breasts of a noble woman."

"Have you ever undressed a woman of my station before?" she asked, laughing.

"No, though I will say I prefer the attire of peasant women now."

"Lazy men who want their needs satisfied without putting in any effort." Jane cupped me through my trousers, gripping onto the rigid evidence of my arousal without caution. The way she squeezed sent sparks of pleasured pain racing through my groin, her voice a harsh whisper when she continued speaking. "Rend the clothes for all I care, rogue. Show me just how much you desire claim over my body."

"As you wish." I strained to produce the words, and though the command inspired a wicked grin, I fought the urge to tug at the seams just as she had suggested. My hands pulled greedily at clasps and ties and the moment I had freed her enough to step out of her skirts, I felt a sense of accomplishment at what I uncovered. The body beneath bore flattering curves, her form displayed in naked splendor when she lifted her chemise and tossed it atop the rest of our clothing. Reaching for my hand, she used her grip to urge me down onto the floor with her, lying back once she had settled and beckoning me on top.

I paused to remove my boots, pulling off my trousers as well before crawling forward toward her. Our eyes met as I hovered over her, her gaze straying first to the medallion hanging from my neck before clenching shut altogether. My fingers thrust inside of her, provoking a cry from her mouth and her back to arch in response to the entry. Her nails dug scoring marks into my skin as I persisted. "Whatever it is you're doing, Christian, I demand you continue," she called out, heedless of the volume of her voice.

"As milady wishes," I responded. A loud moan pierced the air around us, the rhythm of my ministrations unabated until she pulsed around my fingers and panted for breath. Jane quivered and pushed me from her, inspiring me to laugh and furrow my brow as I settled onto my backside. She didn't bother to speak and I failed to ask of her intentions, having the question answered when she climbed onto my lap.

Reaching between us, she guided me inside of her and slowly settled into place. I groaned and gripped onto her hips, barely aware of the sly grin tugging at the corners of her mouth while her body rocked like the waves of the sea. I buried my face into her shoulder and tightened my hold on her while she clutched back, our movements turning frenzied; the rhythm one of unadulterated need. As I felt her spill over the edge, I did the same, pleasured sounds escaping my mouth through each pulse of climax.

I heard the smile in her voice as I rested my face against her shoulder. "Pause if you must, dear Christian," Jane said, "But you'll be doing that to me again before the night is through."

A devious grin spread across my lips. "Am I to be enslaved to you?" I asked.

"Show me your gratitude and I'll show you mine." Her eyes met mine in a deliberate fashion as I looked up at her, another shiver afflicting me when her nails raked against flesh again. "Let it out," she whispered, pressing her forehead against mine. "Let out the fire and let me teach you how to be a force to be reckoned with."

"Is that what this is?" I said, one hand sliding around to her back while the other one traced the contours of her body. My smile faded as I shut my eyes. "Catharsis?"

"It is everything we want it to be." She kissed me softly, only pulling away for breath. "Or nothing at all. Don't get so wrapped up in your thoughts. Regardless of what you want in the end, you have to forget yourself for a moment if you want to wield your gifts."

"Heavens do I ever."

"Then let me show you the way."

I kissed her back, apt to listen for the time being. For a few hours, I stopped being the son of Richard, or the conflicted mercenary. I was a man of magic, tapping into something larger than himself. Larger than Jane. Larger even than the act of our bodies coupling and ripples of satisfaction running through us after we became swept up together once more. I swore I heard the pulse of the world in the silence which followed, beckoning me toward distraction.

CHAPTER THIRTEEN

The next morning, I woke curled around her, one arm loosely hanging around her waist with furs draped across our naked skin. Squinting against the sun filtering through the windows, I blinked to clear the blur from my vision, seeing the hearth still blazing before us and wondering when either of us had thought to cover up. My mind raced to recall everything which had transpired the previous evening, fighting through a heavy layer of haze in the process.

I knew the moment that it had, though, when the first pang of guilt buffeted me.

She smelled inviting and felt warm. The way she shifted against me, still lost in slumber, was enough to stir the heart of even the most stalwart man and two wills warred within me as my hand settled against her stomach. The baser part of me wanted to pepper her with kisses, rousing her and losing myself in the bliss which had swept me under the night before. My heart convicted me, however, reminding me what I had left behind for the lion's den. This is where it seemed to have led me.

A sigh passed through my lips as I buried my nose in her hair. Jane stirred further and I shut my eyes, feeling my body betray me further the more she wriggled against me. Her arm shifted, and as her hand slid on top of mine, our fingers interlinked. She attempted to push my palm toward one of her breasts, which served to finally knock me out of my stupor.

I clenched my eyes shut and claimed back my hand. "I should dress and bring us food," I said, wondering if the excuse sounded as desperate to her as it did echoing in my ears. Parting from her side, I came to a stand and peered around the room for where my clothing had fallen. Jane shifted around to her back, and from my periphery, I saw her lift onto her elbows, heedless of the way it exposed the top half of her body. Or perhaps deliberate in the action, I told myself, averting my gaze.

"Christian, this is what I have servants for," she said. "I'm not employing you to wait on me."

"Consider it an act of good will." I flashed a quick grin, not making eye contact before resuming the pursuit of my pants. Finding them and the rest of my clothing, I placed them on a bench and slid my arms through the sleeves of my shirt. "Besides, my stomach can hardly wait for them."

"Is it your stomach or your mind afflicting you?"

"I'm not sure that it matters."

"I'd say it does, considering it isn't your cock."

The crass way she issued the words forced my attention back to her. She glanced downward and raised an eyebrow and I sighed while fishing out my pants. "Yes, well, what it wants can be attended to another time."

"Did my rogue suddenly get cold feet?" Jane twisted around until she was on all fours. I paused the effort to dress, captivated despite myself by the feline way she crawled to me, her licking her lips while closing the distance between us. Each inch claimed bore a wriggle to her hips, her backside high in the air and her eyes set on me as though I might be her prey. When she reached where I stood, Jane peered up at me. "Now, will you stop playing games and tell me what has you so startled?"

I opened my mouth to issue a retort, but my words fell short. Jane settled on her knees, glancing up at me with a devious grin tugging at the corners of her mouth. I read her intention and felt my knees go weak at the mere thought of what she meant to do to me. "We shouldn't be doing this," I said, my breaths turning shaky. "You are a woman of noble birth and I am a commoner."

Jane inched closer still. As she leaned in further, she pursed her lips and blew a gust of air against that part of me becoming more uncomfortable by the moment. I groaned and her smile broadened at my reaction. "Are we revisiting the topic of my honor?" she asked, tsking after the issuance of the question. "Tell me the truth and I'll give you what I know you want right now."

She lifted a hand, taunting me with her touch. I swore under my breath, clenching my jaw while her fingers trailed up and down sensitive flesh. "I have somebody." My vision swam, eyes wanting to shut. Mind desiring to give into oblivion again. "My feelings for you would always be muddled, Lady Cavendish."

"My rogue, your feelings for anybody would be muddled. You serve your demons first." Jane settled into a taunting rhythm with her strokes. "Do you think I'm in pursuit of a lover?"

"I don't know what you're in pursuit of." My legs threatened to wobble.

"Exactly what I'm doing to you right now. Nothing more. I'm using you for carnal pleasures. You're using me for my teaching. When you leave to do whatever it is you feel you must do to the Luminaries – either join them or fight them – then this ends. You only need to entertain me for what remains of the next fortnight."

"Entertain you, you say."

"Your payment in return for my instruction."

"I thought I was to be your guard."

"No, I'm paying you money for *that* part." I drew a sharp breath inward as coils of tension started to knit in my groin, heat pooling while my hips gave a rock. She smirked at the way my eyes fluttered. "Plunging between my thighs would be so much better arguing, don't you agree?" she asked.

"At this rate, we won't get to any actual instruction," I retorted, smirking despite myself.

"Pleasure me first and then, we'll get started." Her hand lifted, settling on the other side of my hips and tugging me down onto the floor with her. As I lowered, she reclined back and dutifully, I assumed a place between her legs. Crawling over her, teasing her lips with mine, I hummed into the kiss when I felt her dig her heels into me. Thrusting into her, I moaned and withdrew just enough for us to start rocking together, my inhibitions surrendered to her from that point forth.

I wore only a pair of trousers for the remainder of the day, when she let me wear anything at all. Lady Cavendish pulled out books while her servants brought in food, clad in only a chemise and apathetic toward what the commoners saw of her. Together, we sat in the library, resuming our work first on one of the large rugs before shifting to a spot of wood flooring sometime later. Jane fetched a piece of chalk and shifted around, drawing a circle in the middle of the floor and running lines through its center.

I couldn't be bothered to hide my arousal at the sensual way she crawled from one spot to another. As she provided me a generous view of her backside, I studied the curves of her body with unabashed appreciation. "Shall I spoil the moment to ask what you're drawing?" I finally asked.

"A casting circle." Jane peered at me from over her shoulder. "Sit in the center of it. I'm almost finished."

"As the lady wishes." I licked my lips when her gaze lingered and rose to a stand. Stepping into the circle, I realized the pattern in the middle of it had formed the shape of a star. "What is the purpose of a casting circle, if I might ask?"

Jane chuckled, reaching the edge of the circle with the piece of chalk she held. Placing it aside, she dusted off her hands and stood as well. I settled into a seated position while she strode to me and grinned as she settled in my lap, facing me. "It's to help you focus. Each of the five corners stands for the five elements I told you about," she said, the fingers of one hand idly toying with my medallion before she lifted both palms. "You're only going to summon fire and air. I'll help you with the rest."

"Quite the proposition to be saying with you seated like that." My smile broadened.

She clucked her tongue. "Be thankful I didn't have you get completely naked first. That would be a true test of your concentration." Her lips spread in a grin to mirror mine as I reached for her, intertwining our fingers. "Now, start with fire. Invite it in and reassure it that the wind won't extinguish it. You'll still have to coax air, but I think you'll have a better time of it this way."

"Worth trying, I suppose." With a nod, I shut my eyes, clutching onto Jane's hands tight while allowing my mind to go blank again. For as little focus as I should have had in the moment, I found my mind sharper, more in tune with the energy I attempted to summon. Fire filtered through me with ease, its wisps circling around as I focused on my natural element. Dividing my attention, I then saw the wind within my mind's eye and stared it down.

When it finally flew into the palm of my hand, it was all I could do not to bark out a laugh.

"I believe I have it," I murmured. "Now what?"

Jane hummed. I failed to open my eyes, afraid it might disrupt my focus. Her grip on me tightened and I suddenly felt a much cooler rush channel through me, a third type of energy merging with the other two. "Say hello to water, Christian," Lady Cavendish murmured. "See how much you can invite her in without my help. I'm calling earth to us now."

"What then?" My fingertips tingled. I admired the new presence and drew it in, wanting to hold onto it and surprised when it played into my hand as well.

"We will invite quintessence together, using our joined energies. Remember, this is the first step. Sometimes, you need it all and sometimes, you don't. You're powerful enough to do this the correct way, though, and I don't want you to cheat."

"Very well." I nodded and fell silent, allowing Jane to concentrate. Within moments, a firmer, much steadier energy meshed with the fluidity of the water, the intensity of the fire, and the playfulness of the wind. I gasped, unable to stop the impulse, and felt an impressive amount of power channel through me, running through my body from head to toe and back again. It seemed as though nature stood before me, asking it how it might do my bidding.

I found myself desperately wishing I had a task to assign it.

Jane whispered words I didn't recognize under her breath. Our grasp on each other tightened, and I felt what we had summoned slip from me to her, released in a slow, even manner until the world fell silent. As I opened my eyes, I watched her finish her words, her eyes shut and head tilted back as though issuing thanks to some deity on high. She lowered her chin, her lids fluttering open, and as she regarded me, I shivered under the weight of her stare.

Her smile turned devious, her gaze full of unspoken intention. "Now, my rogue," she said. "You can be inside me again."

I collapsed into bed that evening after consuming enough supper to sate an entire village. Books fell to the floor, but I paid them no mind, in favor of surrendering to the sweet embrace of rest. I would study more in the morning, I told myself. Perhaps even ask about attempting one of the more complicated spells in Lawrence's tome. In that moment, however, a fatigue unlike any I had ever experienced settled over me. It took the insistence of the servants for me to rise hours later, and even then, I ate slowly and without much motivation. When Jane failed to join me, I considered it a mercy.

She walked into the estate from her courtyard a short while after that. I followed her back to the library once she had eaten, and both she and I settled into a study bereft of sexual tension. Jane had me draw a smaller circle and place my palms upon its center. Lighting candles on each of the corners, she spoke to me of using other materials – crystals and herbs – to boost the energy granted by the elements. "First, I would like you to simply get accustomed to summoning them," she said. "Increasing their power is worthless if you can't harness them in the first place."

"I see the logic in that," I said. With a nod, I followed each of the instructions given to me. My first flirtations with water and earth forged tentative connections, the latter especially tricky, but Jane coached me with calm patience through each exercise. That night, I went to sleep without having bedded my teacher, but my spirit bore a sense of satisfaction just the same.

The next morning, I found myself being woken by her, the sensual creature having returned seemingly overnight. As she climbed on top of me, I groaned, taking hold of her hips while she rocked atop me, in search of a pleasure I was all too apt to provide. We kissed and she curled in my arms afterward, departing only when the servants summoned us to our meal. Instead of joining me, again, she excused herself to a bath and disappeared for the better part of the day.

My slumber was not to be nearly so restful that evening, however. I tossed and turned, waking in fits before sinking back into sleep again. Visions and vignettes plagued me, until I heard voices whisper and opened my eyes to regard who might be speaking. As I did, however, I immediately met with the eyes of a man I had never seen before.

His hair light brown and wavy, he almost looked to be my age with eyes as blue as crystals. Something about his gaze made my head swim. The world shifted in and out of focus, bearing the discordance of a dream as I furrowed my brow at him. "Your bloodline is a strong one, son of Richard," he said, his voice airy and distorted. I blinked while he reached out, unable to move against his touch, like my arms and legs had become trapped in mud. His fingers lifted to graze the medallion around my neck. "I admit, I've wondered what rock you've been hiding under all this time."

My brow furrowed, speaking with what echoed in my ears as a slur. "I haven't been hiding," I said. "I've been here the whole time."

"Sometimes plain sight is the best place to find cover. Though I see in your belongings that you have a mercenary cloak." The strange man relinquished his hold on the amulet, settling beside me on the bed. "I owe you a debt of gratitude. Lawrence had become a burden, but one not easily dealt with. I'm thankful for the enemies he made, for more reasons than one. If I believed in such things, I would call it fate."

"Who are you?"

"My name is Talbot. The lieutenant behind me is named Marcus. Sadly, you might remember him. I would apologize for having you bound to your bed like this, but I assure you, it's for his safety as much as yours."

Talbot shifted to the side, allowing me full view of the second man. My eyes flicked obediently to the other shadow, standing further away and out of focus at first. As my vision cleared, however, I felt a wave of recollection that threatened to break through the fog. A memory sped to the forefront of my mind, one relived far too many times for me not to recognize the man.

He wore the crimson cloak of the Luminaries, and peered down at me with derision, both arms folded across his chest. I drew in a sharp breath as I saw another time and place. An inn far away from here. My father, facing the window where I sat perched while a figure encroached on him from behind. I shook, struggling against whatever spell had been cast to hold me down as I saw this man – this *Marcus* – draw his sword and impale Richard Hardi with it.

My father's killer. At long last, there he stood.

"You bastard," I spat through clenched teeth. "I will tear you apart limb from limb."

Marcus seemed apathetic toward the vitriol in my tone. He glanced at Talbot. "Well, that confirms it," he said. "This is the urchin."

"Grown into a man," Talbot added with a nod. He glanced from Marcus to me while I seethed. "Christian, was it? Focus on me again when I'm talking to you."

Talbot snapped his fingers. My eyes shifted to him, driven by a force outside of my control, my posture relaxing without asking my permission to do so. "There. That's better," he said. "I need you to attend to what I'm about to ask you, because your life could depend on it. And you strike me as the sort of man who likes holding onto something as dear as that. Your father had something very valuable to me and Marcus told me that they couldn't find it among his possessions. Considering you slipped away from us, I think you have some idea of what I'm talking about."

My eyes narrowed. He might have gained control over my body, but my mind remained defiant. "I don't know what you're talking about," I countered.

Talbot took a deep breath and released it in a slow, exaggerated manner. "Far too much like your father." His movements quick, I barely had the chance to blink before his hand shot forward, clutching onto my neck with a grip tight enough to impede my breathing. My eyes widened while his expression remained impassive. "You know what I'm talking about perfectly well. I can see it in your eyes. You've carried it in your hand and studied it, and I imagine each time you've looked at it, you've had no clue what it is you beheld. I want it back. And I've been more than willing to leave a wake of bodies to get it."

"I do recall the one in particular you left." I strained to speak through the grip of his fingers. The man bore a strength I could scarcely believe was human. "You'll forgive me if that makes me resistant to tell you more."

"You know, Christian..." Talbot punctuated his words with a sigh, his gaze flicking away for a moment before returning to me. A deceptively placid smile crossed his lips. "Right before me, I see a lot of potential. You're a talented warlock. It's in your blood and you might live long enough to discover what that means if you cooperate. It would be a shame to break every bone in your body until you cried out where you've stowed what your father stole from me. Confidentially, even I would like you better in one piece." He lifted his unencumbered hand, settling his fingers over his heart. "I think you would make a perfect addition to our order if you set your petty vendetta aside."

"I have no interest in joining a collective of murderous letches."

Talbot laughed. "I hope you appreciate the irony of what you're saying. How many people have *you* killed?"

"My father was a good man."

"Your father had blood on his hands the same as the rest of us. You are *very* much your father's son. I know the little boy inside you has purchased this delusion that Richard was a hero, but let me dispel that for you. He wore a red cloak once, the same as Marcus."

My heart leaped into my throat, my eyes narrowing. Talbot slackened his hold on me, but kept his fingers wrapped around my neck. A response eluded me despite the increased amount of air I drew in, inspiring the smile on Talbot's face to broaden. "Oh, did he fail to mention that to you. I'm sure he burned the cloak at some point, but that doesn't change the fact that he wore one. I know you've at least sorted out he was a warlock the same as you, but where do you think he received his instruction?"

"I don't believe you," I countered.

"You do. You just don't want to. After all, you have to admit, it explains why we sought him out." As our gazes met, I felt my mind swim again, lost inside a sea of crystal blue. It felt like Talbot's presence loomed closer. My reason had been clogged too much for me to discern how much truth there was to the perception until I saw him lick his lips and tilt his head to the side.

A shiver ran the length of my spine when his cheek brushed against mine, his voice suddenly in my ear. "Tell me where the scroll is and I will unlock every one of your father's secrets," he said. "You relish the power of casting spells? You enjoy Jane's company? Tell me what is it you want the most in this world, and I will grant it to you."

"I..." I swallowed hard, a crease forming in my brow as something touched my arm, lifting and then settling on my chest. My vision hindered by my frozen state, my mind filled in the image of a snake, slithering its way down to my stomach and teasing at my leg. Drawing a sharp breath inward, I exhaled it in staccato. "I can't," I finally managed.

"You most certainly can. If you're anything like your father, a part of you wants to." A feather touch crept across my thigh. As it brushed over me, I moaned. "Believe me when I say I can make you want it that much more, just like I did him."

Distantly, I fought to cling onto something while still unable to move. "No. I can't."

"And why is that?"

"Because you weren't meant to know."

Cool breath hit my neck. I felt his tongue flick across my skin and gasped. "I wasn't meant to know where my own belongings were being hidden," Talbot said. He chuckled. "How audacious of you."

I gritted my teeth, as much against the question as my own reactions to the strange man. "He wouldn't want you to know," I said, threatening to chant the words if just to steady my resolve. "He entrusted it with *me*."

"Master..." The third voice broke through. I couldn't determine whether its owner should be thanked or condemned, forgetting for a moment who the speaker was. Another shaky breath surged from my chest while Talbot returned to my field of vision, glancing over toward where the other man stood. Marcus straightened his posture, his arms falling to his sides. "His mind is strong," he said. "The lady warned us of that. You could tempt him all night and he'll still mock us with his resistance."

A deep sigh preceded Talbot's response. "Is it his resistance which concerns you," he asked, "Or is it something else? You've always been jealous of Henri. It disappoints me that even death hasn't cured you of that."

Marcus bristled. "I simply think we are wasting our time. We should take him in and torture him."

"We should do whatever I *say we should.*" The way he spat the last few words brought to mind the snake again. Talbot slackened its hold on me until his hand finally fell away. My eyes rolled back as I heard the sound of a chair sliding against the floor. A shadow passed over me and as I attempted to focus on Talbot again, I found myself staring at his back, with him standing in front of me. "A natural born magician with an easy weakness to exploit and you want me flaying him first?"

As difficult as it was to see the posture each man took, something in the back of my mind registered tension. A staring contest that Marcus backed down from first; him leaning against the wall again with a huff and folding his arms across his chest again. Talbot strode forward and while I didn't hear whatever he whispered to my father's killer, it was enough for Marcus to nod and glance downward. "Yes, I understand," Marcus said, falling silent after this.

"You will understand or I will take back what I gave to you. Lest you forget I own your soul." Talbot lingered in his posture before turning to face me again. My gaze shifted to him, the action just as involuntary as it had been when he snapped his fingers. Talbot strode forward and crouched before me. "That mind of yours is steel, I will grant Marcus that," he said, lifting a hand to toy with one of the longer locks of my hair. He hummed. "I have no doubt your father has something to do with that. But it can be broken, Christian, and I *will* break you, one way or the other. If I want anything to linger in the back of your mind, it is this."

Talbot leaned closer to me. Our faces hovered nearly close enough to kiss, his gaze diving deep into mine. As the smile returned to his face, I felt darkness encroach upon me, attempting to pull me under. "Sad to say, that's all you're going to remember," he said. "At least, for now."

CHAPTER FOURTEEN

The bed shifted beneath the weight of someone settling by my side. As I felt teeth nibble on my neck, I jolted awake, scrambling away from the interloper as an impulse and into a seated position. It took a moment for me to figure out who I was looking at and even then, I had no discernable reason why I was startled to see Lady Cavendish. She sat upright and furrowed her brow at me. "Is something wrong?" Jane asked, issuing the words with caution as though I had taken leave of my senses.

Somehow, I wondered if she might be right. "I don't know," I said. It was the most honest response I could offer, spat out before I could think. My heart pounded in my ears, my chest rising and falling with lusty gulps while my frantic gaze shifted from her to the walls to the window to everything else in the room. Swallowing hard, I furrowed my brow. "Is it late?" I asked.

"No, not terribly, though my servants said you were impossible to rouse. I determined to come in and do it myself." Jane's expression turned amused, her leaning forward to rest her weight on the palm of her right hand. "Did you sleep poorly last night?"

"I think I had a bad dream, more like." Both hands lifted, pushing back the locks of my hair and lingering on my crown afterward. Something fought to break through the haze of sleep. A flash of an image. A man. The man who had killed my father. I winced against it, feeling my headache worsen as I pushed against the wall stopping it from being a clearer picture. "I think I dreamed of my father's death."

Jane frowned, regarding me with genuine concern. It cast a cloud against the playfulness her posture had sought to inspire, inspiring something warmer and kinder from her. "My rogue, why would your memories be so cruel to you within the safety of rest?"

"That I knew. I can't even recall the dream very well. I only see his face."

"I wouldn't forget such a face readily either."

My hands fell to my sides again as Jane inched forward. She straddled my lap, placing both hands on either side of my face while looking into my eyes. I furrowed my brow at the way she studied me, waiting for something that seemed to be hanging between us. When Jane motioned forward, however, it left the matter unresolved by anything but a kiss.

I sank into the slow motion of our lips together, and gradually the throbbing in my temples subsided. Jane pushed up her skirts and as we embraced, she shifted on my lap, coaxing out my baser urges. At first, thought eluded me, the desires of my body taking a surer stance the more she slid against me and especially as Jane guided me deep inside of her. The warmth and slick evidence of her lusts carried me over the threshold, into a shared moment of erotic bliss.

Later, however, the notion continued to trouble me, telling me something dire loomed over me from some uncertain direction. I sat with one of the spell books in hand, taking up space on one of the benches while watching Jane stroll out to the courtyard and disappear. The contents of each page failed to hold my interest, and the noble woman's absence for the remainder of the day bore conspicuous overtones. I frowned at my own paranoia and retired to bed shortly after eating supper.

The next morning, she met me down at the table for breakfast. We spent the daylight hours with countless books open before us, Jane explaining to me the basic mechanics of casting spells. I nodded and attended to the lesson with due diligence, pleased with myself when I was able to levitate a piece of parchment before incinerating it in midair. The effort met with applause and praise, Jane licking her lips while appealing to the sexual chemistry we shared again. While I surrendered without much thought, the tone of her actions continued to trouble me. We took dinner together later and she retired with promises of more to follow the next day.

Sleep eluded me, however. As I lay on my back, staring toward the window, I couldn't help the itch at the back of my mind, leaving me under the impression that whatever loomed over me would only worsen the longer I ignored it. Gone were the placid notions of my lover. As I sat up, I took a deep breath, tempted to wander without knowing to where. I found myself standing and pacing, until finally I dressed and followed the compulsion to leave the room. There were precious few places in the estate I felt at ease wandering into. At the very least, I reckoned, I could lose myself in the library.

The hearth crackled, providing the only light in the room while I slipped inside and shut the door. Wandering my way to one of the oil lamps, I lit it just by staring at the wick and repeated the effort with the other lamps around the room. A warm glow filled the area, illuminating the spines of countless books and drawing my focus to the shelves they occupied. I wandered past each one until I paused by the windows and pushed back the curtain to regard the grounds below.

While the dark of night shrouded most of it from view, the moon shone just enough for me to make out portions of Jane's beloved courtyard. Furrowing my brow, I spotted a collection of benches in the midst of varying flora – including trees and thorn bushes I assumed birthed roses during the summer. A small pool had been fashioned right in the center and a shiver tingled up from the base of my spine. Water was to Jane what fire was to me and something about the abundance of her element bore sudden suspicion.

"What is it you do out there?" I murmured to the empty room, narrowing my eyes in thought. An idea sprang forth, indulging my paranoia and perhaps, to a disastrous end. As the image of my father's killer resurfaced, however, I took a deep breath inward. "Forgive me, milady, but there is an ill omen afflicting me." Before I could argue against the impulse, I turned from the window and strode for the nearest collection of books.

Jane had pointed out which ones contained spells during one of our first lessons. I bypassed them, however, reasoning that if anything about her actions truly was nefarious, she wouldn't be so apt to hand me the keys to her undoing. Pacing from one bookcase to the next, I stopped at a collection of parchments that had been rolled up and tied shut with string. The first few I unraveled looked like nonsense, and a loosely bound book underneath contained notes, but nothing of use.

It wasn't until I spotted another volume bearing the sigil of the Luminaries that I had any cause for hope. Snatching it from its hiding place, I brought it closer to the hearth and sat in front of the fire. Some of the spells contained in Lawrence's book had been copied, and others excluded completely. I feverishly paged through and stopped at the unfamiliar ones, attempting to divine their purpose before moving onto the next one. One seemed tailored to draw the truth from its intended victim; another, to silence their tongue altogether. A little further, however, I stopped as I came upon a phrase I recognized and brought the book closer to my face. My eyes scanned over each word until I reached the end and took a deep breath.

"*Abscondita revelare,*" I said. Reveal the hidden. The rest of what I could make out granted the spell at least enough relevance to fulfill its intended purpose. Making mental note of the page, I shut the book and spirited over to a trunk where Jane kept her magical supplies. Collecting a few candlesticks and holders, I crammed them and a piece of chalk into a linen bag and strode toward the window again.

Unlatching the shutters, I leaned out as far as I could manage and lowered the linen bag before dropping it. It fell into a bush, which created a rustle, but masked the clang and rattle it would have made had it hit cobblestone. Once this was finished, I settled up onto the window sill, recalling my similar departure back at the inn and attempting to replicate that. I gripped onto the edge with both hands before swinging my feet over the edge. Peering at the cobblestone walk winding the perimeter of the courtyard, I aimed for it and jumped, grateful when I landed at the edge and not in the bushes.

My knees buckled, but I landed in a crouched position without much further ruckus than the scuff of my boots from impact. I failed to stand right away. Instead, I peered from one side to the next, eyeing the door closest to where I landed and holding my breath while waiting for someone to emerge. When nobody did, I scanned the remainder of the area, making mental note of two other doors, each leading into a different wing of the estate. All remained silent, giving me the confidence to continue forth. "Should have kept a dagger on me at the very least," I whispered while pushing to a stand.

I plucked the bag from the bushes and walked it toward the pool. A small shiver ran from the base of my neck, down the length of my spine, and while my rational mind felt compelled to blame the chilly air, I knew better. The area bore some sort of enchantment, lending itself to even more suspicion. I lowered onto the balls of my feet again and unpacked the bag, laying out the items within to my side and producing the spell book last.

After drawing one of the circles Jane used, I arranged her candles on each point of the star and evoked fire to light the wicks of each one. Flames rose and danced in the reflection of the water. The chill in the air started to subside and I took a deep breath, holding onto it as I opened the book and paged to the spell I had marked off. Slowly, I exhaled and kept my eyes fixed on the page while the rest of my mind went blank.

"*Ignis, veni foras,*" I said, reading the first line as softly as possible. The fire perched atop each candle danced, as though listening and responding with favor. Drawing a deep breath inward, I held onto it until more words flowed past my lips, reaching to each of the elements regardless of how tentative of a grip I had on each. Waters rippled and the wind blew in gusts. The earth beneath me bent its ear in my direction and as soon as I could clutch each thread against my chest, I continued onward, binding them by the sheer force of my need to find the truth.

I spoke the line which had attracted my attention in the first place. "*Abscondita revelare.*" Clenching my jaw and fixing my sights on the pool of water, I put as much weight upon those words as I could. The rest of the world gradually faded, drawing me into a deep form of meditation disturbed only so I could cast a quick glance at the next line in the spell. "*Occultorum revelare. Si dissolvant circumstantia falsa.*"

Energy channeled through me and flowed back into the ground

while the ripples in the pond became more agitated. My breathing became controlled, the words pouring out now in automatic as I focused more on their intention than their issuance. I asked to see what lingered just out of sight, in the corner of my eye without allowing me to capture it. The black waters drew me in, until everything within and without ceased to exist.

And in that moment, my mind filled with images.

Talbot. I saw him leaning over me, whispering to me and admonishing the man he had called Marcus. The man who had been haunting me since I woke with this unshakable fear. I felt frozen and accosted, filled with a rage I had to let pass through me despite my compulsion to grab hold of it. No, there were other things. Something else I had to see. The waters whispered to me, telling me not to let go just yet despite the fear joining my anger, telling me the awful truth that I had come so close to my own demise.

'*They want what you have,*' an indistinguishable voice spoke. One which sparked a hint of memory, as though I should know its source. '*Keep looking, Christian. There's more.*'

I followed the voice's beckoning. My thoughts pressed forward, deeper into the pool, allowing it to speak to me without influencing it. My mouth might have been yet chanting the words for all I knew, the strands holding the spell together tentative through my fledgling prowess. Still, I finally saw it emerge, a vision of the courtyard. And front and center was Lady Jane herself.

She strode toward the pond, dressed only in her nighttime garments, the hour late with a few lamps lit around the immediate vicinity. I watched as she paused beside the waters and took a deep breath, hands lifting and eyes shutting while words came pouring past her lips. Whatever incantation she spoke, it was one she'd issued countless times and the ease by which she evoked the power of nature inspired a pang of jealousy. The waters stirred and within a few moments, two figures came to life, hovering like spirits above the pool.

Jane opened her eyes and lifted her head to regard them. I fought the urge to tense as I recognized them; the two figures who had visited me by my bedside. Talbot spoke first. "It's been two nights since you spoke to us last," he said. An arm extended to his side, hand pointing toward the man beside him. "I was beginning to wonder if I should send Marcus to fetch you."

"No, Master, I promise my absence has been for good cause," Jane said. The way she bowed in supplication struck me as peculiar. A lady of noble birth who could not be cowed by a knight and her posture suggested Talbot had the ability to break her. She straightened to regard him again. "The rogue has settled in nicely, and relaxed enough to speak."

"And what has he had to say to you?"

Her lips curled, eyes dancing with delight. "It is him, just as you suspected. He confessed it to me this very night. I cast him into a deep slumber so I might tell you the news."

Talbot tensed, his eyes growing wide for a moment before settling back into an impassive expression. Marcus furrowed his brow, but remained silent. "And you believe he is telling you the truth?" Talbot asked.

"I have all assurances that he is," she said. "His anger for us burns bright and his lips speak vows that he will be your undoing."

"Such audacity. I wish him luck." Talbot folded his hands in front of his waist, a grin tugging at the corners of his mouth. "Did he mention the scroll?"

"No, but I managed to insure further proof that he's who he claims to be." A smile danced across her lips. "He wears the medallion around his neck, no doubt a gift from his father."

Marcus shifted his weight and frowned. "Is this why it was missing from Henri's possessions?" he asked.

"It would stand to reason ," Jane said with a nod. "Henri was smart. He made the most of spiriting his son away. I think the rogue is ignorant of everything else."

"But he didn't mention the scroll," Talbot chimed. He sighed and glanced away. "Don't ask him about it. He needs to trust you and that might raise his suspicions. I think I might need to pay him a visit and see just what we're up against."

"He's pliable." Jane's smile broadened. "Seeks solace as most men do."

Talbot raised an eyebrow. "Are you playing with fire, child?"

"Making preparations for my future, more like." The cryptic comment hung in the air between them. Talbot honored it with a nod and Marcus remained impassive. A hint of anger – perhaps even hatred – flashed across his expression and before I could wonder at it, Jane spoke again. "He won't give in to you easily. He resists just as much as he surrenders. Perhaps I should be the one to ask."

"No," Talbot responded. His eyes found her again, the gaze severe. "I will bring Marcus. I want to see this man for myself. He might prove useful to us in other ways."

"Master –," Marcus began.

Talbot lifted a hand to rebuff him and Marcus responded by scowling and slinking back. "You said he has natural talents," Talbot continued, "I trust this is still proving to be the case."

Jane nodded. "It is, Master. He is a pyromancer, first and foremost, but his abilities are barely tapped. He could be an exceptional sorcerer." Her eyes shifted from Marcus to Talbot, her posture turning uncertain. "Marcus is right to doubt, though. You could torture the information from him or I could lure it past his lips. But if you think him useful to the cause as a soldier, I believe even I am skeptical."

"I forgive your doubt, but not his." A paternal grin spread across his lips. "Continue to secure your future, child. I, on the other hand, will mind our interests. The only mistake I have ever made with regard to his bloodline is to grant his father a choice. I won't make that error a second time."

"You will force him across the veil?" Jane asked, arching a brow at Talbot.

"I will keep him alive until he tells us where he's hidden that accursed scroll," he replied. "After that, though?" His grin turned cunning. "I will convince him of our ways. I think our dear Christian fancies himself a stronger man than he truly is. Everybody has a weak point."

"And you intend to find his?"

"I intend to press a finger on it until he cries out for mercy."

The images faded, swept aside like smoke. I watched as they dissipated, startled when the candles blew out and the night stilled around me. Blinking several times, I tried to focus on the dark of the courtyard again and heard my heart thundering in my head, felt my stomach twist into knots. My mind spun dizzy with a thousand thoughts, each colliding with the other to gain a place of primacy.

I fell back onto the cobblestones, my limbs protesting how long I had remained in the same posture. Each breath I took stung, my chest turning tight while I struggled with my next course of action. "Clean this up," I whispered to myself. "Get back inside before anyone realizes what you've done." A nod preceded me lifting up again, reaching to gather my materials and toss them back into the linen bag. Retreating to the far side of the courtyard, I slung the bag over my shoulder and studied the estate's exterior.

The seams in a few of the bricks granted me just enough leverage to scale the wall to the window sill and pull myself back inside. It took a matter of moments for me to have everything put away and even less time for me to slip back into the confines of my room. After shutting the door, I collapsed on the bed, the composure I had kept tightly wound slipping, my hands beginning to shake and chest filling with air in lusty gulps.

Every impulse told me to run. Gather my things and ride hard and fast for home. "They'll be after me the moment I depart," I said just as soon as the notion crossed my mind. This left the chance I could reach Paolo, perhaps even set us on our way to London and the hell out of England, but a pang of guilt rippled through me as I considered the one thing it would not permit me to do. "Jeffrey," I said. Our parents' killers were after the scroll and now that they knew about me, my brother would become an unwitting accomplice. "What have I done?"

His words of warning made my stomach turn. Every harsh word spoken about Richard Hardi came to mind almost at once just as the recollection of Talbot's words echoed in my head. He had once worn a red cloak. Had put us all at risk and now, I doubted everything I had once held as gospel. Rolling to my side, I drew my knees up to my chest and clutched onto them, wishing I could apologize for every conviction I had harbored in blind faith. I had walked into the lion's den on my father's behest. And as the name Henri joined the list of revelations, I realized I had never truly known the man at all.

I shut my eyes only to silence the world around. The cacophony failed to still, but fatigue made its presence known regardless of how little I wanted to rest. I was trapped in a quandary and my state of mind made reasoning a way out virtually impossible. Slowly, I began to relent. I saw Paolo within my thoughts. I envisioned Jeffrey, and Anne, and the girls, and felt the weight of each precious life settle on my shoulders. Succumbing to sleep, I did something I had not done the entirety of my adult life.

I prayed that whatever gods existed would help me find a solution.

CHAPTER FIFTEEN

I bore no doubt that Jane knew something was awry with me the next day. I couldn't look her in the eyes without seeing her deceit and wondering how many times she had regaled my enemies with tales of her conquests. Pursing the notion any further threatened to ruin my appetite. As such, we ate in tense quiet for the better part of the meal.

It took until she had finished eating for her to break the silence, clearing her throat as she polished off the last of her drink. Setting down the cup, she folded her hands atop the table and leaned forward. I stole a quick glance upward in time to watch her arch a brow at me. "Is something the matter, my rogue?" she asked. "You look troubled."

For the lack of a better place to look, I stared at the piece of bread I held in my hands, tearing at a piece and continuing my slow pursuit of consuming it. "Simply lost in thought," I murmured between bites. "Apologies, milady."

"And what has you lost in thought? Did you have another one of your night terrors?"

"Not another one, no." It took a considerable amount of effort to force a smile on my face. I met her gaze more fully, certain the attempt at reassurance had been anything but. "Though, I did have some trouble settling in to sleep."

Jane nodded. "A shame, truly." Her lips curled, the first time in days I had seen her cryptic smile. "Will you be attending to your lessons today, or do I need to distract you?"

"I'm not much of a mind for either, milady. I think you have me worn out."

"We have such precious little time left. You shouldn't be squandering it." I felt her eyes take on more of an air of scrutiny. Suddenly, I became aware of the fact that we were in the midst of a contest. She rested an elbow on the table and cradled her chin in her hand. "If I give you the chance to rest today, we will have to spend the better part of tomorrow immersed in study. You do understand this, yes?"

I nodded. "I understand and I accept it. Heavens, is the fortnight almost finished?"

"Just a few days left. Unless, of course, you decide to stay."

I almost asked if I would be allowed to leave. Tension settled between us, even as my smile broadened. "Then I will make certain I'm ready for our lessons tomorrow." Finishing off the remainder of my bread, I stood and bowed before her. "Might I take a walk around the grounds? I think being outside would help my disposition."

"By all means," Jane said, though I caught the slightest amount of tension in her posture. Her lips failed to say it – attempt to run and I will find you – but a flicker in her gaze communicated the threat well enough. She tilted her head and I straightened my stance, uncertain if a chill had settled in the air or if my imagination had fashioned it. "Be in your room tonight," she added. "We'll take supper there."

"As you wish," I responded, turning before my grin could falter altogether. I passed two of the servants on my way out the front door, feeling the weight of each questioning gaze feed my paranoia. The grounds opened up before me, the sun shining almost in mockery of my mood, though nothing could taunt me more than the sight of the wall surrounding the manor. My skin crawled, feet itching to run as fast as my legs could carry me. It took only moments for the debate of the prior evening to smother the temptation and extinguish it wholly.

The grounds themselves were bereft of people, save but for a host of men assigned the task of minding the wall. They paid me idle notice, not pursuing me when I wandered around the other side of the large house and toward the stables. The stable boys glanced in my direction before returning to work. My shoulders slumped as I caught sight of Tempest in one of the stalls and even as I approached the far end of the property, I found myself musing on the riddle while coming no closer to its solution. A faint wind rustled the few leaves remaining in the trees and distantly, I heard the waves of the shore while realizing my world had become a prison.

A hissing noise chose that particular moment to knock me from my thoughts. I blinked and scanned around the immediate area, attempting to discern its source as my brow furrowed. When it sounded again, I peered up toward the branches of the nearest tree and walked closer to it. A figure hid within the remaining foliage, only visible as I closed in on it and squinted past the sun. "Who goes...?" I began, until I adjusted my position enough to enter the shade. Once I did, there was no mistaking the identity of the person perched above me.

My heart leaped in my throat, tears threatening to sting my eyes while I breathed a relieved laugh. Paolo met my gaze just as I opened my mouth to speak, lifting a finger to his lips and winking. Swallowing hard, I peered around, in search of Jane's servants in case any of them were close enough to spot or hear us. One stood near their quarters, but appeared to be distracted by a piece of wood he picked away at with his knife. "I'm not certain if there's any good place for us to speak," I whispered as my gaze returned to my lover.

Paolo nodded and pointed toward the corner of the property. I raised an eyebrow and he gestured more emphatically, an exasperated sigh passing through his lips. "*Non capisce una mazza,*" he said, his voice even fainter than mine had been. "Follow me."

I nodded, surrendering to the ghost of a smile. Paolo didn't wait for any further acknowledgment from me before slipping down the branch and landing within the shade. Instead, he walked along the line of trees lining this part of the property, prompting me to stroll beside him within the light. We failed to make eye contact through the entire trek, not pausing until we stood at an angle that took us outside the one interloper's line of sight. Paolo leaned against the trunk of a larger oak and I stopped beside it, my gaze falling to the ground. "How long have you been here?" I asked, keeping my voice low. Another thought invaded my mind just after I issued the question. "Does Roland know you're here?"

"I've been here for two days," he said, "And yes, he does. He asked if the bed had been lonely and I told him he keeps denying me while you will not." Hearing the amusement present in his voice made my heart lighten, even if just a little. I had missed his levity. His voice gained a measure of sobriety as he continued. "I haven't been able to get any closer to the manor, but I've hoped you would wander outside. Have you been kept busy, *amico mio*?"

I winced at his words, not certain if they bore an accusation to them or if it was my own guilt-laden conscience filling in the subtext. Exhaling a shaky breath, I lifted my head to peer toward the horizon. "I have been a fool. That I had a better defense than my own stubbornness, I would present it."

"I know you're stubborn. Why do you think I rode down here?"

"How did you know where I'd be?"

I chanced a glance at Paolo in time to see him smirk faintly. Relief washed over me when he failed to look vexed. "Men speak when they've had too much to drink," he said. "Somebody told me where to find the manor when I arrived."

"That they do, though you have your own magic in the way you lower their inhibitions." A faint smile crossed my lips, wobbling as it bloomed and threatening to make my sight glass over again. I wanted to reach out a hand to him and feared doing so. Clearing my throat, I nodded once more and pushed my fingers through the locks of my hair, finally damning the consequences enough to meet his gaze. "We are in trouble," I said. "All of us. Roland might even be counted among that lot."

Paolo raised an eyebrow. "Christian, you were in trouble the moment you left town."

"Yes." I breathed the word with exasperation, directed at myself. "Perhaps even before then. I wished to wrestle with the serpents and underestimated their cunning. Now, they are poised and ready to strike." Pausing, I drifted closer to the tree, placing a hand on its trunk. "I don't think I have much time left. I am wise to them and them, to me.

There have been two men circling while the lady has kept me distracted."

A frown overtook his expression that I mirrored instantly. "One of them is my father's killer," I added.

"*Merda*," he said, a deep sigh following the issuance of the word. Profound fatigue settled in his eyes, which shifted away from mine as he shook his head. "Please, let go of this once and for all, *amico mio*. I beg you. You will get yourself killed if you stay."

"I'm keenly aware of that fact." Turning slightly, I extended a hand, attempting not to move much beyond this. As I touched his fingers, they closed around mine, bearing the texture of the gloves he wore. Paolo glanced back at me while my frown deepened. "I'm outmatched and in a difficult spot, though. Yes, if I stay, this man – this Marcus – will strike against me with his master at his side. And I've experienced enough at their hand to know they will have their way with me. If I leave, however, my brother will be in trouble. They want the scroll my father gave me and now that they know who I am, they will pursue you all until they find Jeffrey."

"When they find Jeffrey, they will find the tree."

"Yes, they will. Whether it takes them a day, a fortnight, or a season, they will. And whatever it was my father died to protect will perish." Evoking Richard sent hot pokers stabbing through my heart. I shut my eyes against the pain, not wanting to consider my father's own duplicity at a moment when there were more pressing matters before us. My lids lifted again and I swallowed back a lump in my throat as I regarded Paolo again. "Jeffrey's family shouldn't suffer my folly."

"I agree." Paolo gave my hand another squeeze. "Should we send one of the brothers to protect them?"

"They will perish in the effort, even if they flee. Jeffrey has the same gifts I do – I'm sure of it – but no will to use them."

"Then we will need to bring them with us." The emphatic way he nodded threatened to break through the melancholy which had settled over me. He looked at me as if waiting for my affirmation and silence settled between us as I considered the possibility. I had already determined fetching the scroll would give the Luminaries ample chance to catch up with us. But perhaps there was another way, I told myself.

A faint memory danced across my thoughts, stealing my gaze away from my lover as my eyes undoubtedly turned distant. I recalled the night my father had been murdered, remembering him taking one last, lingering look at me before pulling the medallion he wore over his head and putting it over mine. "*Don't ever take this off,*" he had said. "*It'll keep you safe.*" It had been so long since I had remembered the directive that I failed to consider what was meant by it.

'I haven't been hiding. I've been here the whole time.'

'Sometimes plain sight is the best place to find cover.'

Without giving the matter any further thought, I let go of Paolo's hand and reached under my shirt for the medallion. Pulling it over my head, I glanced at it for a moment, noting the times both Jane and Talbot had touched it. The fact that something so simple could captivate them, even if just briefly. "I have an idea," I said. My eyes lifted to find Paolo's again. "I need you to trust me and ride ahead of me, though."

The frown returned to my lover's face. "I won't leave without you," he said.

"You have to. For my brother and his family. Please." I thrust the gold chain into Paolo's grip and took hold of his hands with both of mine. "Leave now and ride for Jeffrey's farm. Give this to him and tell him he is not to take it off, whatever he does. He needs to leave at once and get the devil out of the area, but anywhere else he goes, he should be safe. They won't be able to find him."

"How are you so sure?" Paolo raised an eyebrow at me.

"It's kept me safe thus far. I think that was by design. My father was able to avoid his cohorts for years, and I, since his death. It's the best I can hope for right now, and considering they now know where I am, I have no use for it."

Paolo sighed, but he nodded. As I let go of his hands, he slipped the chain and medallion into a pouch and shut it tight again, looking back at me once the task was finished. "What else?" he asked, the question filled with resignation.

I released a breath I failed to notice I was holding. "See my brother off and unearth the scroll. You know where I keep it. You have to remove the rock concealing its hiding place and find the spade I keep hidden near it. I am going to make my escape tonight and ride on until I reach a point where we can meet."

"Not town. It won't be safe there." He frowned in thought for a brief moment, glancing away first, then back at me. "Ride to Taunton. There is an inn on the western edge of town with a horse painted on its sign. Give them my name and I will ask for it when I arrive. If I get there first, I will wait for you."

"What is in Taunton?" I asked.

"The first place of rest before London. Then far away from England, *amico mio*," he countered. His gaze bore weight to it, settling on me as though issuing an ultimatum I would be unable to refuse. "If I leave to do this, you are promising me you'll be in Taunton. You are *promising me* that we will leave this all behind here. Looking for these men. Looking for their trouble. Play with the spells if you want, but please, promise me we will do it somewhere else. Somewhere safer."

The severity of his words settled into my heart, calling to mind the plea he'd made to me before my journey to Plymouth. My entire existence since I had been fourteen had been to see revenge through to its bitter end and now, the quest had come to fruition. I couldn't outrun myself any longer. Paolo and I would never be what my father and mother had been, but standing before me was the closest thing to a normal life I would ever entertain. Whoever Richard Hardi had been and whatever led him to become the man who raised me, in that moment, I felt as though I had stepped inside his shoes.

And I was thankful for another chance.

"Warn my brother and I promise you I will be in Taunton" I said, the words bearing conviction at last. "You and I will leave the Luminaries far behind us."

"*Gratzi*." The tension left his body as he spoke the word, fatigue giving way to gratitude and exasperation to relief. He reached for my hands again and drew me close to him, as much apt to damn the action as I had been only a short while ago. I shut my eyes and pressed my lips against his, a cauldron of emotions bubbling and boiling beneath my skin at the feel of his kiss. Relief did not deign fit to pay me as much of a visit. I was too keenly aware of how much trouble I had been through and how much waited on the other side. Smelling him and tasting him, however, gave me the first glimpse at hope I had experienced since waking. By the time he pulled away, I felt a spark of life reignite within me.

We regarded each other and I lifted one of his hands, bringing the back of his palm to my lips. The lump in my throat bobbed as I swallowed back the heady mixture of sentiment and anxiety pulsing through me. Exhaling a deep breath, I nodded at him. "Let me go and prepare," I said. "If we're to make it that far, I'll need to have a plan of escape."

"What will you do?" he asked.

"Attempt to beat a sorceress at her own game. And hope like hell I still have my blades when I return inside. I wouldn't be surprised if she was taking this chance to disarm me."

"You doubt me, *amico mio*." Paolo smirked, releasing his grip on me and pushing back the folds of his cloak. I watched him produce a sheathed dagger and pass it over to me, his expression never wavering. "I'll bring you a sword in Taunton."

"Thank you." A grin lilted across my lips as I lifted the ends of my shirt and tucked the dagger behind my back. Once it was hidden away, I dropped the tunic back over my waist and smoothed out its folds, punctuating all of this with a nod. Shifting my sights toward the horizon, I took a deep breath while considering my escape further. "I'll need to find a road that doesn't wind through town."

"You entered from the North, *si?*"

As I glanced back at Paolo, I peered at him with a quizzical expression and nodded. His smirk broadened. "There's another road if you go further west," he said. "At the crossroads, turn north. It will intersect with the main road outside the city gates." When I continued to regard him in stunned awe, he continued. "I knew we might have to escape, so I plotted our journey. What do you think I've been doing for the last two days?"

A delighted laugh sprang past my lips, as softly as I could manage it. "Ever the resourceful one. I best send you off before I risk getting us caught," I said, mirroring his smile. "As it is, I want to find a way of thanking you that would get us put in the stockades."

"Show it to me in Taunton. This way we are already fleeing when the authorities come after us." Lifting a hand, he brushed the backs of his fingers across my cheek. "*Te amo, amico mio.*"

I smiled, reaching to pat his hand. "I love you as well, Paolo." Apt to indulge the sight of him for an additional moment, I lingered in his touch until he finally pulled his hand away. The air carried a weight to it, something which afflicted my steps even when he scaled the wall and I turned away to return inside the manor. It seemed as though the gaze of every servant settled on me as I strode past, weighing me in a conspicuous manner even as I ignored them.

My expression remained impassive; neutral to the point of being blank. Even if my heart was heavy, my mind remained focused and on my way back to my room, I avoided any potential altercations which might force me to show my hand. It wasn't until I shut the door that I afforded myself the chance to relax.

Pausing to catch my breath, I reached for the dagger I had hidden and stowed it inside my leather satchel. A quick perusal of the rest of its contents proved what I had feared. I found no evidence of any blade I had carried with me to Plymouth and considered it unlikely I would discover them hidden anywhere in the room. My pensive frown deepened, eyes scanning what I did have at my disposal while my mind worked to develop a plan. Yes, I knew I could kill Jane, and now, the odds were stacked in my favor that I could slit her throat before she worked a spell against me. At the same time, my stomach sank at the notion. She might have been a conspirator, but I had not yet become a cold blooded killer.

"Cannot allow her to stop me, though," I murmured, lifting a hand to scratch at the back of my neck. As I spotted Lawrence's spell book, I walked over to it and brought it with me to the bed. Settling on the mattress again, I flipped it open and paged through the contents, careful to examine each spell contained therein. Most seemed liable to backfire, or not to be enough to detain a much more studied sorceress. "Be of some benefit to me, Lawrence. Surely you could do better than choking people."

Each page I flipped threatened to snuff out the fledgling hope Paolo had ignited. I gritted my teeth and skipped to the end of the book, wondering if working backward might offer some revelation scanning forward hadn't. As I stopped on one, I poured over the notes penned in the margin about it, able to soothe my racing heart. "This should do it," I said, fanning the flames if just to inspire confidence within me. I had no chalk to draw a circle, nor time to practice evoking the elements less apt to incline their ear. All I had was a passionate plea within me, begging for this to work.

I gathered what makeshift materials I could assemble in the room. Repeating the spell a hundred times over, I set myself toward memorizing it in the intervening hours. A chill raced through me as I waited, solidifying the last parts of the plan within my mind. As the sun began to set in the horizon, the smells of supper wafted up to my room as if to remind me that time had run out. I could only hope magic would be on my side that night.

Because if that failed, I didn't know what would become of me.

CHAPTER SIXTEEN

The blankets had been smoothed over my bed by the time the sound of footfalls made it to my room, candles lit to compliment the roaring hearth in providing equal parts light and warmth. I lay on my back, idly reading Lawrence's book when the door swung open, the young, female servant entering with a man following in her wake. The latter carried two platters, both of which he set down on a small table before bowing and making his way out.

I raised an eyebrow at the remaining servant when she turned and departed as well. Within moments Jane entered, pausing to shut the door behind her before directing her attention toward me. The first moment our eyes met bore a level of tension to it, her evaluating me and me doing likewise to her for several seconds longer than our usual glances. This told me our game had commenced.

Attempting a smile that felt belabored by fatigue, I set myself to the part I had rehearsed while waiting for her to arrive. "Good evening, milady," I said. "How has your day been?"

"Rather odd with you so absent from it," she offered. Her cryptic smile made its first appearance as she strode to the table and pulled out one of two chairs, slowly lowering into it before focusing on me once more. Jane folded her hands atop her lap. "Has the rest helped your disposition?"

"Yes, considerably. I already feel in better spirits." Placing the book aside, I rose to a seated position on the bed first before walking to the empty chair. Jane's eyes lingered on me, studying me as I settled in and shifting to my gaze when I peered back at her. "Apologies for my earlier behavior. It's been some time since I've been so tired and I've been told I get ornery when I'm fatigued."

"Hardly ornery. Distant, more like. I had to wonder what was clamoring on inside your head." Her smile broadened as she plucked an apple from the platter in front of her. Lifting it to her lips, she took a bite, then nodded toward the food as if to silently direct me to join her. I nodded, mirroring her grin, and paused to evaluate what had been prepared for supper.

A bowl of stew had been placed on each platter, flanked by the normal addition of bread, cheese, and apples. Something about the stew made me suspicious. I picked up a piece of cheese and started to eat it, making eye contact with Jane again as I swallowed down a bite. "I was thinking I might tarry for an additional few nights," I said, breaking the short silence that had settled between us. "Considering I've missed a day's worth of lessons. I think my evocation could use some additional practice as well."

"If you have any hope of confronting the Luminaries, it surely could." For a flicker of a moment, genuine delight accompanied the rest of her expression. She bit into the apple once more and waited until she swallowed before she continued speaking. "Will your friend worry about you? The one I saw you with in the stables back where I retrieved you?"

I shrugged. "Perhaps I might send word to him of my plans so he doesn't. It wouldn't be the first time we've been on separate tasks for a period of time."

"What does he do?" Jane raised an eyebrow.

My grin turned into a smirk. I paused to finish off the cheese and reached for another piece. "He's a thief. I'm an assassin. When we're working together, my job is usually to rid us of any guards or potential problems while he obtains whatever it is we came to snatch. It's lucrative. Roland gets to charge extra for our services when we're paired up."

"Slippery devils, both of you, then." She sat back in her chair, studying me in silence before lifting a foot and having it settle on my thigh. I tensed only from surprise, which spurred her to laugh. "You get this amusing look on your face when a proper woman advances upon you. Men are so predictable. Both receptive and offended when they're not the one making the first move."

"I think the greater concern is that my mind shifted from conversation toward other things." I popped the rest of what I held into my mouth and dusted off my hands. Both palms settled on her leg once unencumbered, running up to the hem of her skirts and advancing beneath the folds. "At the same time, you show your hand, milady. It's quite apparent that you missed me."

"Perhaps." One arm lifted, elbow coming to rest on the table top. She touched the corner of her mouth with her fingers and shifted her focus down to my hands. "Perhaps I've simply grown tired of pretenses. Us speaking of menial things like thievery and killing over a meal I can wait to consume. I'd much rather have other things first."

"Other things, indeed." Humming, I slid forward in my seat, deliberately shifting her foot to rest on my crotch. Her knee bent while my gaze darkened, my thoughts repeating the mantra that I needed to forget who and what she was for a time if this was going to work. I licked my lips as she pressed the bottom of her slipper against my length. "I thought I could focus on resting," I said. "Alas, I grow impatient with myself. A day or several, either way I've not had you in far too long."

"Your cock seems to agree with you, my rogue." Her foot lowered from my chair, ending her ministrations for the time being and affording me a chance to regroup. I attempted not to look too relieved. Instead, I advanced closer to the edge of my chair while she did likewise to hers and placed both hands on my thighs. "Though your mouth indicates I'm not keeping you waiting enough," she added. "Which am I to listen to?"

"To hell with my duplicitous words. Listen to my cock."

I surged forward before I could lose the nerve for it, pressing my lips hard against hers and taking her in a wild, decadent kiss. Her taste settled in my mouth, her tongue sliding inside to dance with mine while I lifted a hand to grip the back of her neck. Not bothering to withhold a moan, I parted the kiss only to issue it forth and tugged her closer while plunging in again. Jane lifted slightly from her chair, coming to rest on my lap with her palms settling on my shoulders this time instead.

My other hand swept across the fabric of her dress, over one of her breasts and around to her back. She bit at my bottom lip and I groaned, shoving her more flush against me, allowing my actions to turn needier. Lady Cavendish didn't seem to mind. In fact, the more adamant I got, the more she responded in kind, until I was left to wonder which of us was doing the seducing. Her mouth pulled away from mine so she could arch her back. I kissed down her neck to her throat and licked a trail back up to her ear. Pleasured noises lifted into the air, a response to the way my teeth teased at her skin.

"Hold on tight," I murmured, forming the only warning I felt apt to give her. Both of my arms wrapped around her while hers circled my neck. As I stood with her, Jane's legs settled around my hips, clenching my waist to offer leverage as I carried her. My first steps compensated for the added weight and the rest bore the apathy of an incensed lover. Throwing her down onto the bed with reckless abandon, I acted as though I had forgotten both her name and her station in life as I became swept up in her.

If Jane cared, or was any the wiser to me, she failed to make it apparent. She laughed as she hit the feather mattress, bouncing once before I could settle on top of her. I straddled her, pulling up the ends of my shirt and tossing the garment aside before leaning in close to her once more. Jane smirked and nipped at my lips, acting as though something hadn't just caused her to tense. "What happened to that medallion of yours?" she asked between languid kisses.

I engaged her lips with mine for an especially long period, pushing up her skirts and allowing my fingers to dance up her legs. She broke the embrace with a sharp intake of breath when my thumb teased between her thighs, sliding against the slick evidence of her arousal. "I took it off," I said, nipping my way over to the side of her neck again. Biting down hard, I smirked when she quivered, her body shaking in a manner which finally proved I had earned the upper hand. Jane's nails dug into my upper arms while I continued teasing with my fingers. "It's in my satchel for safe keeping. I didn't realize you fancied it."

"V-v-very much so." Jane clenched her eyes shut and whimpered. I slid my thumb against her one last time before inserting longer digits into her. A loud moan served as my reward, prompting my teeth to blaze a trail down to the crook of her shoulder. While my hand worked on pleasuring her, I stole the chance to refocus my concentration. She dug channels in me and I felt the wounds weep small amounts of blood, but still, I managed to settle into a cadence with my ministrations bereft of any influence from her.

When my lips moved this time, it was not to kiss at her skin.

She called out my name and I whispered the words I had memorized, making certain not to say them louder than the noises she produced. Jane bucked her hips and shifted to force me deeper inside her, but I continued my rhythmic strokes undeterred. As each word passed through my lips, I focused more and more on the spell and less and less on her, missing the moment when she surrendered to oblivion. Her body slid up and down the sheets while I failed to pause.

"What are you doing, Christian?" she asked. I heard the question distantly. She gripped on harder and I smirked while repeating the spell I channeled over and over again. Each element came to me as I evoked them, the plea of my heart earnest and focused on something other than my selfish whims for a change. I wanted to get out of there. I wanted to ride to Taunton and know my brother's family was safe. I wanted away from this circus and to put the nightmare of nine years to bed at last, regardless of whether that counted as a win or a loss.

All I needed to do was bind her to that bed.

Her hands fell away from me, thrown to each side while I reclaimed my hand. Jane let out a surprised cry and I forced my palm atop her mouth, lifting up enough to look her in the eyes. Whatever my gaze conveyed to her, it was enough to instill a look of fear in hers while her brow furrowed at me. I spoke the final words in Latin, lids drifting shut while the last of the energy I had gathered passed out from me and into the air around us. When I regarded her once more, I could not help but to smile at my handiwork.

Jane could not so much as shimmy, let alone force herself out from under me. I drew a shaky breath outward and released it slowly. "You are going to be trouble when I have to remove my hand," I said, tsking as I studied her. She scowled and I sobered while considering her. "Were you to deliver me to them tonight? Shake your head or nod."

The spell prevented her from issuing more than a small nod. At the same time, the answer sufficed. I frowned in response. "You knew I was wise to you," I continued. The confused expression on Jane's face caused me to pause and re-evaluate the presupposition. I raised an eyebrow. "Or you weren't sure yet, but your friends determined to act before I did become wise." When Jane looked more confident of this, I nodded and sighed. "My, look at us. Back to where we began, with me sorting out what to do with you."

She screamed something into my palm, her eyes wide as she did. I furrowed my brow, keeping my hand atop her mouth even when she persisted. Her head shook from side to side as much as possible and her eyes welled with tears, her emphatic speaking continuing despite the impotence of the action. A pang of temptation raced through me, wanting to know what she might be saying, but suspecting I would live to regret allowing her even a chance to cast magic against me. "No," I said. "I've listened to your poison tongue long enough."

Using my knee as leverage, I reached down with my unencumbered hand and tugged at the bed sheets. It took gritted teeth and determination for the fabric to rend, and an additional shift of my leg for me to free a panel of cloth entirely. As I pushed the linen beneath my other hand, I crammed it into her open mouth and muffled the few words she managed. "... Going to regret..." was all I could make out before I silenced the noble woman.

"My one regret is following you into this pit," I retorted. Once I had her sufficiently gagged, I lifted up from the bed, swinging my leg over Jane and placing my foot down on the floor. Keeping attentive watch over her for several lingering moments, I ensured she truly couldn't move and frowned against the compulsion to ensure it. A few more rips and a short time later, I had her limbs secured with something other than magic, setting my mind at ease enough for me to progress onward.

Jane cried and whimpered as loudly as she could manage while I shed the clothing she had forced upon me and took out what I had worn down to Plymouth. After slipping my legs into my pants, I thrust my arms through the sleeves of my shirt and sat on one of the empty chairs to put on my boots. The dagger Paolo had provided slid into the empty slot on my belt nicely, and once I had my cloak secured in place, I was ready to depart. Giving the dark folds of fabric an additional adjustment, I touched the embroidered rose and nodded once to myself.

"Time to leave," I murmured to myself, collecting the remainder of my things and thrusting them into my satchel. I stole the remaining bread and cheese as well, cramming it in with everything else, and affixed the strap over my head. As I approached the closed door, I unsheathed the dagger and stole a deep breath.

The last moment before the plunge, I reminded myself, and once more, I was the assassin.

Opening the door, I didn't miss one step in surging from the room and toward the first figure I spotted. It was the second of the two servants who had accompanied Lady Cavendish just a few minutes prior, poised by the stairs and shifting in my direction as he heard the incoming footfalls. I skidded to a stop behind him before he could fully turn, wrapping an arm around his neck while placing my blade against the peasant's throat. My unencumbered hand clapping over his mouth, just as it had with Jane. "Your mistress is alive, but your future has suddenly become in question," I whispered harshly into his ear. "I need a sword and an escort out. You are going to keep as quiet as possible while helping me with these requests, or I'll be glad to show you the color of your blood before you perish."

He nodded as much as he dared without slicing himself in the process. I strode forward with him, descending the steps one at a time in a careful, measured pace while watching for any potential complications. Nobody stood at the foot of the stairs, and not a soul awaited us as we wandered through the great hall. The servant led me past the entrance and toward one of the side rooms, gesturing at a shut door as we approached.

"Open it," I said, keeping the volume of my voice low. "And bring the sword to me."

I slowly allowed him to step out from my arms and kept a wary eye on him while he opened the door. Lingering at the entrance, he pivoted to scowl at me. "Go in and get one yourself," he said. For as bold as he was to spit the words at me, he at least had not been daft enough to say them at full volume.

"I'm not a fool. Armories only have entrance. You would shut me in the moment I entered."

He narrowed his eyes, but wisely offered no further rebuttal. Walking into the small, dark room, he emerged only seconds later holding a sheathed sword. "You call me the fool, but I think you're a worse one than me," he said. "The Luminaries will have your head."

"If only I didn't have something of theirs. I'm certain they would otherwise." Ripping the sword out from his grip, I secured it on my hip and kept the dagger pointed at the servant. Without taking my eyes off him, I nodded toward the front door. "Now, the escort out. You're perilously close to retaining your life if you continue to cooperate."

I watched the lump in his throat bob as he nodded. He turned his back partly to me, keeping me in his periphery while leading me back to the great hall. We came within inches of the doors when another set of feet paused at the bottom of the staircase, a gasp preempting any chance I had of silencing the newfound interloper.

Frances, the matronly woman, cried out in a shrill voice, "The rogue is escaping! Find the Lady of the house!"

As I spun around to catch her in my sights, my captive rushed at me, attempting to dislodge my footing. I stumbled backward, swiping the blade at him and missing him with my first attempt. While he failed to knock me over, he caught me by surprise enough to throw a punch that narrowly avoided connecting with my jaw. I gripped tight onto the dagger's hilt and thrust it forward, catching him in his shoulder and pulling it out before swiping the blade across his throat.

Blood poured from the wound. He reached with both hands to clutch at it and fell over when unable to support his own weight. I cast a quick glance at the woman, in time to see her retreat backward and up the stairs again. At the same time, the clamor of footfalls told me this was about to get perilous fast. Wiping the crimson staining the blade on my cloak, I shoved the dagger back into its sheath and ran for the doors.

Pushing them open, I spirited onward, feet moving at full speed while the sparse light of the setting sun shone the path toward the stables. Shouts rose from the manor behind me, producing enough urgency to demand I continue running, knowing that the moment Jane was freed, I faced the risk of being detained despite my best efforts to avoid it. Guards poured out of the servant house. Two men by the stables saw me approach and unsheathed their swords, the taller of the two racing forward to engage me. I drew my blade and sped to meet his advance.

Anticipating his first blow, I ducked out of the way and used my momentum to spin around. He presented his back to me long enough for me to swing at it, cutting into the fabric of his cloak and scratching him deep enough for him to cry out in pain. He stumbled forward and I thrust the blade through him, retracting it just as he fell forward. His sword dropped to his side and I picked it up while turning to face his compatriot.

The other man scurried away from the pens, distracted momentarily by the horses as all but Tempest reacted to the sound of violence and the smell of blood. I readied myself as he swung for me, lifting one blade to engage his sword while thrusting the other into his stomach. It remained inside him, abandoned when I shoved him to the side and cleared the path to Tempest's stall. The mare whinnied and reared, but appeared more unnerved by the other horses than the source of their agitation.

"Good girl," I said, wiping the blade clean before sheathing the sword. I reached for her saddle. "I apologize for the journey ahead of us, but it's necessary. Perhaps somebody in London town might give you a better home."

She snorted as I secured the saddle on her back, but cooperated. I had her bit secured in her mouth at the moment the next set of guards reached us. "Be good and wait for me," I said, patting the mare before leaping over her gate. As I landed on the other side, I produced the sword again and nodded at the first contender.

He wasted no time in coming for me.

I lifted my sword to deflect his first blow, pivoting out of the way from the next attempt and managing a swipe across his upper arm. He emitted a yelp of pain and turned to face me. Another series of blows yielded a moment of vulnerability, which I used to my benefit. Thrusting my blade through his chest, I pulled the sword out as I heard steps and a swooshing sound behind me.

I dove to the ground, aware of a slice which cut across the back of my neck. The onslaught afforded me no chance to recognize it with anything other than a wince. Rolling out of the way of the next plunge downward, I scrambled to my feet in time to parry this guard's next attempt, exchanging blows with him while gritting my teeth. His miscalculated his next swipe, and fortune smiled down on me when the unexpected failure put him at a loss. I knocked his weapon from his hands and slashed across his throat, freeing my concentration just in time for me to spot a final guard fleeing from the stables.

Dashing for him, I produced the dagger Paolo had given me and threw it at him. When it plunged between his shoulder blades, he fell to the ground and I nodded, satisfied enough with the effort to direct my focus back to my horse. "Let's get out of here, girl. What do you say?" I murmured, cleaning off the blade again and securing it into place before jumping the gate again.

Tempest protested as the volume of the other horses rose to cacophonous levels. I stole a moment to calm her, finally assessing the cut on my neck as well and breathing a sigh of relief once I realized it would bleed, but hardly kill me. "No time to bandage it," I said, although thoughts of finding the first apothecary past Plymouth danced in the back of my mind. All I needed was to make it out of here. And I could taste freedom at last.

I opened the gate and mounted the horse. Gripping onto her lead, I squeezed her sides, grateful when the mare cooperated and trotted out of her enclosure. We turned to face the exit and another nudge launched her forward; another tug of her reins turned her toward the road leading out of the manor. As we galloped for the path leading into town, I freed a hand to draw my sword and stared down the last resistance the fortress had to offer.

The guards protecting the wall watched me charge for the open gate. Both scattered out of the way, granting me clear passage to the other side. I ignored the arrows sailing past, shot from the direction of the tower and barely missing me. While it bore the promise of more in its stead, I refused to slow, even to change direction, for fear one of them might hit. We continued at this pace until we put Plymouth at our backs, and even then I urged her not to stop just yet. Not until I was certain we hadn't been followed.

We stopped, at last, by a tree on the outskirts of town. I produced an apple taken from my supper and fed the mare, petting her mane as she ate and walking beside her for a short while, to make sure the sprint hadn't lamed her. "We need to keep going, girl," I said, frowning against the words, speaking them as much to myself as to the horse. The sun had fully set by then, leaving nothing but moonlight for us to travel by. After breaking off a piece of bread and eating it, I mounted Tempest once more and nudged her on at a significantly slower pace.

Rolling hills and forest surrounded us on either side of the road headed north. Fatigue threatened to settle on me as we rode through a smaller satellite village and toward a larger town on the horizon. As we broke through another patch of forest, entering the far side of Tavistock, I felt the wind blow a chill through me and clutched my cloak shut against my body. The moorlands in the distance looked eerie at night, and just as I was tempted to chastise myself for the bout of nerves, Tempest reared and attempted to stop.

"Come on, girl," I said, squeezing my legs against her sides and prodding the reluctant mare onward. She sped back to a trot, but the chill turned frighteningly worse. Tempest halted and as I observed a strange hush to the collection of shops around us, I felt my heart race and nudged the horse again and again, trying to prod her along, but to no avail. Not a single soul inhabited the streets. And as a rush of air pierced through the night, the mare lifted up to her hind legs too quickly for me to compensate. I felt the world tip backward and only had the presence of mind to grip her mane in some effort not to spill out of the saddle.

It proved not to be enough, however. As Tempest listed to the side, I lost my hold and the ground rushed up on me, impacting with one solid smack which radiated through my entire body, blossoms of agony springing up from my shoulder before dispersing elsewhere. I groaned and rolled to my side, struggling to catch my breath and grateful when flexing my fingers didn't inspire fresh jolts of pain. The mare landed beside me, producing a pitiful whine, and as I glanced at her, I saw a bolt protruding from her front thigh, bearing a glimmer as it reflected the lights of a nearby inn.

"What the bloody hell..." I began, but just as I wheezed the words out, I heard footsteps approach and felt a boot press hard into my shoulder, shifting me onto my back. It shoved down further, until I cried out for its owner to stop, and only then did my vision focus enough for me to regard the source of my discomfort. The ends of a crimson cloak came into view first, and then the rest of the man's figure until my eyes met the gaze of my attacker.

My blood ran cold when I saw who it was.

The man who had haunted me since I was fourteen, whose memory fanned the flames of the quest which spanned the entirety of my adult life, peered down at me, a wolfish grin spreading across his lips. Something predatory lingered in the look he gave me, twisting my stomach into knots and freezing me into place for the time being. Marcus tilted his head as he regarded me, everything in the gesture suggesting he had weighed me and found me wanting.

"Well, if it isn't the whelp," he said, raising an eyebrow. "Not much better than the loins you sprang from when it comes to planning your escapes, but I'll give your father credit, he at least knew how to be evasive."

"How did you...?" I started, but found it difficult to finish the question.

"Find you? Please, the noble whore might be little more than an amateur, but you're even less skilled than her. I'd been setting out to pay your friends a visit. Now I'm glad I lingered." Marcus learned forward, sobering significantly as he looked into my eyes. My vision swam, my mind clouding faster than I could compensate, leaving me no recourse but to offer as much resistance as I could. He grinned as he sensed the struggle taking place within my head; the way my limbs turned to mud the same way they had at his master's behest. It was as his lips parted that I saw them, however.

Two sharp daggers hidden in a sea of otherwise dull teeth. I recalled the blade Richard had thrust through his chest, but seeing the points of his canines bore further testimony to the otherworldly. My thoughts cleared enough for me to compare the mental image of this man with the creature peering down at me. I gasped as an epiphany struck. He hadn't aged a day since I was a fourteen year old boy.

I knew I had underestimated the skill of my adversaries. Now, I found myself debating their humanity.

My foe locked his gaze with mine, his grin never wavering. "Now, tell me, whelp," he said, "What did you do with the medallion?"

CHAPTER SEVENTEEN

"I beg your pardon?" I asked, before I could stop the question from drifting past my lips. It bore honest confusion in its cadence, something I couldn't mask even if was in control of my full mental faculties. I furrowed my brow, eyes narrowing. "What of it?"

Marcus sighed, the sound bearing no small amount of exasperation to it. "This is the problem with you amateurs," he said. "You don't know the value of something when you steal it, and you pay no mind not to lose it." He clucked his tongue at me and shook his head, the action rueful. "I told Master to remove it from you the other night, but he didn't want to raise your suspicions. Now, look where that's gotten us."

I opened my mouth to speak, but he afforded me no chance. His foot applied more pressure to my shoulder, provoking me to bark out a cry of protest as the discomfort bordered on pain. The man – if he could even be referred to as such – laughed at the sound I produced. "Despite how much he claims not to believe in it, Master has himself convinced that destiny brought you to us," he added. "Personally, I think he just has a soft spot for hopeless idiots, given his penchant for your family line."

"Funny you should say that," I managed, even as the pressure intensified. He let up only enough to allow me to talk. Several fevered gulps for air passed through my chest before I could continue. "His predilection for hopeless idiots, that is. I suppose that would explain your presence in his camp."

"Only children attempt to unnerve grown men with such retorts." For as nonplussed as he made the comment sound, the lift of his boot and the swift kick of his foot against my face seemed to suggest I had rattled him just the same. Fresh pain blossomed from the point of impact, but as the action forced my head away, I felt my senses swim back into coherence once more. He lowered his foot and crouched enough to touch my face and point it back to his. "Have you never figured out how to be a man?"

My head swum anew, but not as pointedly as it had before he kicked me. I felt blood trickle from my nose and smiled despite the grief. "What use would that serve me?" I asked. "I wanted to grow up to be a thorn in your side."

"As though an insect like you could bear that power."

"Which is why you cowed when Talbot pointed out your jealousy toward my father, am I correct?"

His hand wrapped around my throat and gripped it tight. It hindered my ability to draw in air, but loosened his attempt to place a hold on me. The bindings on my limbs loosened and my senses pulsed in time with the beating of my heart. If I could continue to fan the flames of his wrath, I stood the chance of getting the upper hand. My chin tilted in defiance even as his hold on me tightened. "Kill me," I added. "Go on, and face your master's wrath. You wanted the scroll? Does the medallion have some worth to you? Only I know where you can find both."

"I should flay you for the answers," he retorted. The two sharp teeth in Marcus's mouth grew in size until they perched above his bottom lip, his gaze screaming wrath. My focus wavered as shock rippled through me, my expression undoubtedly the reason why Marcus chuckled. "You throw barbs which have no meaning to you about items whose sole worth to you is sentimental. Bah." He scoffed. "Just like Henri. One little flicker of humanity left in his heart and he used it to betray us."

"That makes your blood boil, doesn't it?" My voice came out strained, but with defiance still present in my tone, even in the face of something utterly terrifying. "Talbot fancied my father quite a lot, I'd wager. Has a soft spot for me because of it and won't allow you to harm a hair on my head. What is his directive? That I be captured and brought in unharmed? He relished that small taste of me he stole, didn't he?"

Marcus growled, but with that, the final vestiges of his hold on me broke. I lifted a hand, and without much thought, grabbed his wrist at the exact same time flames licked up my fingers and to his arm. The other man hollered with offense and stumbled backward, releasing me from his grip. As air filled my chest again, I emitted a series of coughs and stumbled to my feet, narrowing my eyes at Marcus as he seemed to recover at the same time.

We stared down each other, both weighing the other for our next move.

I reached for the hilt of my sword and drew it. While I hardly expected the action to be intimidating, the way Marcus smirked unnerved me. He pulled his own blade from its sheath and in the moments which followed, I assessed him better. Clad in the same sort of attire I wore, he had the added benefit of a breastplate over his chest that his cloak partially concealed. His movements were fluid, heedless of the armor he wore, which added another item to the list of otherworldly attributes. My gaze flicked to the flame-within-a-circle embroidered on the fabric before matching his once more.

Marcus nodded toward my weapon. "Did your father teach you how to wield that?" he asked.

Fighting the urge to tense, I mirrored his grin. "Perhaps what I first learned of it," I said. "I promise I have only improved since then."

"Same cocksure attitude as him, too. I hate it." The long, sharp teeth remained exposed as he paced to the side, forcing me to counter in the opposite direction. We started to trace the outside of a circle with our movements while unable to look away from the other. "Do you really think you'll be able to kill me?"

"I aim to attempt. Repeatedly, if I have to."

"You don't even know what I am. Did your father spare you the details of his youth, whelp?"

I bristled, attempting to keep the reaction to myself. "He certainly left out any mention of what unsavory friends he once had."

"Don't insult me by referring to him as a friend." Marcus chanced a step forward. I allowed him to claim it, while readying myself for whatever his first move would be. While my mind had cleared enough for me to fight, I couldn't anticipate what his opening volley. It set my nerves on end, becoming both a benefit and a curse. My horse lay wounded on the ground nearby, jerking and whinnying in pain. I could feel the cut on my neck sting each time I exerted myself. But my senses remained attuned to the man before me.

He came at me with no further warning, the flurry of blows an onslaught which put my reflexes to the test. For as much as I had observed the unencumbered nature of his movements, they shined all the more with each strike, forcing me to twist and step back to prevent further injury. Our blades impacted and pushing off only resulted in more intersecting blows. I pivoted away from one counterstrike. Surging at him, I attempted to put him on the defensive, but he responded by nearly knocking my blade out of my grip. As I struggled to regroup, Marcus laughed, sweeping a leg and using it to knock my footing out from underneath me.

I fell to the ground with an unceremonious thud.

Marcus thrust his blade at me. I rolled away in time to avoid being stabbed, but not soon enough to avoid him cutting into the fabric of my cloak. Kicking at one of his legs, I distracted him enough to scramble to my feet and lifted my sword in anticipation of another strike. My opponent stepped back unexpectedly, however, shaking his head while daring to turn his back on me. "And Talbot wants you turned," he said, his tone rueful.

"Turned? What does that...?" I began, but just as I issued the question, the ground beneath me rumbled and shifted my footing. I saw small trench dig itself through the dirt which separated us, and sprang from its path before it reached where I stood. The suddenness of the gesture forced me to skid to a stop and spin around to face him again, but Marcus appeared more bored than concerned. "What are you planning to do to me?" I asked.

"Make the remainder of eternity miserable for you," he countered,

"If I have anything to say about it. Somehow, I doubt you're going to be cooperative, even after we kill you."

"Speaking nonsense, are we? You're worse than a priest."

"It will make plenty of sense shortly. As it stands, I'm growing bored with toying." Marcus narrowed his eyes at me and I furrowed my brow, lost in a maze of riddles while attempting to figure out my next move. I felt the ground shift once more. Trusting only my instincts, I raced to close the distance between us and jumped just short of the point where the invisible force cut through the dirt again. Marcus turned as I swiped my blade across his skin, catching the side of his neck before landing on my feet on the other side. Without pausing for breath, I thrust the blade forward, hoping to impale him through his back.

The moment I tried, however, a burst of air threw me backward, tossing me like a rag doll over my wounded mare and onto the road behind her. Tempest let out a pitiful whinny while I groaned, aware that my sword had been knocked from my grip only after the pain subsided enough to make thought possible. Lifting myself onto all fours, I tried to stand and let out a cry of agony when the same violent force which cut through dirt forced me onto my knees and twisted me in an uncomfortable manner. Tears danced in my eyes while sparks of light appeared in my periphery.

"Stupid whelp." The sound of Marcus's voice became difficult to focus on the more I felt whatever spell he'd cast pull at my torso and limbs. Clenching my jaw, I tried to bite back any further noise on my part while listening to the sound of his footfalls close in on me. "You cut me across my face like that'll make any difference," he said.

"All men die somehow," I managed, though my words came out strained. At the same time, the evocation of the memory forced me to relive the other time in my life when I had seen Marcus suffer injury. Seeing the impotent plunge play out much the same at it had the first time, I recalled the amusement in Marcus's eyes before he killed Richard Hardi. His words had been the last my father heard besides my shrill cries of disbelief. 'You missed.' It might have been the amount of pain running through me from head to spine, but something struck me as strange about the retort. Missed what? If the attempt had been so futile, then why did Marcus gloat?

Another twist interrupted the thought momentarily. A bead of sweat formed on my forehead as I peered up to regard Marcus, sensing my expression contort all the more with the attempt to focus on anything other than grief. The sharp teeth which had served to intimidate had retracted back into place, the bleeding wound across his cheek seemingly an afterthought to him. He lifted a finger as though to illustrate this, wiping away some of the blood before he brought the tip to his mouth. Marcus licked it clean and shook his head. "You could always make this easier," he said. "Both on yourself and us."

"And how would you suggest me doing so?"

"Where are the scroll and the medallion?"

I felt the sweat trickle down the side of my face on its way to my neck. My gaze fixed on the breastplate my antagonist wore while I thought of Paolo riding ahead of me, knowing he hadn't yet reached home, let alone my brother's farm. Still, the corner of my mouth curled, as if Jane's cryptic smile had become contagious. Marcus narrowed his eyes at me while the epiphany struck. The breastplate. My father knew where to strike, but had not struck true, had he? He'd missed something vital.

Richard Hardi had missed Marcus's heart.

Swallowing hard, I winced away the pain as much as possible, ignoring the rivulets of perspiration following in the wake of that first bead. Marcus pushed back the folds of his cloak and sheathed his sword while I clenched my eyes shut for a moment, struggling to focus on anything other than the magic being wrought against me. When I opened them again, I glanced from side to side. The gleam of my sword in the moonlight merged with the realization that I needed to latch onto the anger which had fashioned the adult I became one last time.

"You killed my father, you bastard," I said, my gaze turning severe. Marcus met my eyes again, raising an eyebrow, while I gritted my teeth and summoned it all. Years of pent up rage. The lost and confused adolescent I had been. The man he grew into. The feeling of the first time I killed someone and how much I wished from that point forth it had been

Marcus's corpse falling to my feet. For a moment, I didn't give a damn who Henri had been or what this demon standing before me was. He was the one who took Richard Hardi away from me and he was meant to perish.

His eyes widened as the ends of his cloak lit on fire. As the fabric went up in flames, he clamored to take it off and I struggled against his spell much as I had against Lawrence's attempt to choke me. Whoever I was – whatever this birthright I bore entailed – I was something of value to them and not without reason. "Did Jane not warn you about me?" I asked, my grin turning downright cruel. "I told her what I wished to use my magic for and it seems I might get my wish."

My limbs loosened and I rose to a stand while reclaiming autonomy over my body. Marcus threw his crimson cloak onto the dirt while I dashed over to where my sword lay, picking it up and clutching onto the hilt while making the effort to race back toward him. The other man turned to face me in time for me to lift my unencumbered hand, palm facing upward. I narrowed my eyes at his arm, speaking one last time to the element I called a friend. Fire burst into life, forcing Marcus to lift the limb at just the right moment, giving me the only opportunity I knew would be afforded to me. After this, Marcus would be able to overwhelm me and it would be over.

Or, it could end like this.

I aimed for where his breastplate ended and his arm began, striking beneath it and using every measure of my strength to drive the blade into his body. Even when the wound forced him to pause, I gave the sword an extra shove, watching his eyes widen and him bend at the waist, the motions indicative of something other than agony. I didn't know what to expect, and paced backward from him, waiting for what might happen next; aware my efforts might have been in vain.

Marcus peered at me, a look of unadulterated hate in his eyes. If I missed, I told myself, at least I managed to finally have the upper hand in some manner. With the amount of vitriol being cast at me, he would lose his temper enough to kill me and maybe – just maybe – it would delay him from seeking after Paolo and my brother long enough for them to get to safety. Ash began flaking from his face, however, starting as smaller flakes and turning into larger patches which rapidly eroded his form. His fingers fell away and his whole form collapsed to the point of caving in on itself.

Within seconds, Marcus had been reduced to dust, his personal effect dropping to the ground devoid of an inhabitant.

The sight transfixed me for an interminable amount of time. I stared at the mound and heard my heart pounding in my ears; felt my stomach tie into knots while baffled over what I beheld. The sword I had driven through him lay among the other debris and as I picked it up, I studied the blade, expecting to see something other than blood and residue. For the lack of a better response, I strode over to where my satchel had fallen when I was knocked from horseback. Tempest let out a pitiful whine and I frowned at the bleeding wound as I assessed it.

Crouching beside the mare, I petted her mane and sighed. If the past few days had been nonsensical, the evening had turned downright surreal. A startling numbness settled over me despite my concern for the beast, my eyes flicking to the pile that had once been a man, attempting to sort through the thoughts spiraling through my head. It would take me weeks – perhaps longer – to allow the full impact of the evening to hit. Sadly, I didn't have that sort of time and now, I had an injured animal. Glancing around the immediate area, I still found the presence of not one bystander suspicious. Light filtered out from one of the inns, reminiscent of a hearth, and I took a deep breath, thinking it as good of a place as any to look for help.

Tempest grunted when I stood, then laid her head down flat on the dirt once more. "I'll be back for you, girl," I said, not ready to consider yet that putting her out of her misery might be the next task I'd have to complete. Instead, I produced a cloth from my satchel and wiped the sword's blade clean. Slipping the weapon back into its sheath, I strode for the inn and walked inside, working half-heartedly on concocting a story just in case anyone had actually witnessed the confrontation. Surely there had to have been someone. Something still felt off about the air around me, the contest I had just participated in not feeling as complete as it should have.

My chest filled with air as I stepped inside, the breath held as I realized even upon approach that the building sounded far too quiet. The further into the main hall I walked, however, the more this seemed to be an understatement. Flames crackled in the fireplace. Light danced in the lamps positioned elsewhere in the room. The bar looked recently vacated, with plates of half-eaten food on the counter, drinks not yet finished beside those or sitting idle without any evidence of supper. I raised an eyebrow and turned to study the door, the notion that I should leave becoming louder the longer I lingered inside. Taking one step back toward the front, I felt a chill settle in the air.

The door slammed shut and held firm into place. The rush of wind which had closed it bore the earmarks of witchcraft, filling in a completed circle within my thoughts. My pulse sped as a form of dread settled bone deep inside of me. I harnessed the realm of fire; Jane called water her familiar. Marcus seemed to have mastered earth. This left one remaining element. This left one remaining man.

Spinning around in the effort to find another way out, I paled when I saw him standing on the other side of the room, blocking the only other exit from the building.

He regarded me with severity, a slow smirk crossing his lips menacing enough to force a shiver down my back. Talbot lifted a finger to wag it, tilting his head when our eyes met. "Tsk, tsk, tsk," he said, his voice taking on a mocking tone. "Where do you think you're going?" Stalking forward, he took a seat, kicking out one of the other chairs with his foot. A red cloak hung from his shoulders, but no breastplate protected his chest. No weapon had been fastened at his side for him to adjust as he made himself comfortable. As his gaze met mine once more, his next words made my blood ran cold.

"Make yourself comfortable, Christian," he said. "We're going to have a little chat."

CHAPTER EIGHTEEN

To say Talbot appeared nonplussed understated the matter greatly; never before had I seen a man hold himself with such an apathetic air. The way he settled into place indicated he had all the time in the world and yet, when I failed to sit, even the first flickers of hostility from his gaze bore a controlled form of irritation. "Come now and sit," he repeated, his voice even. "I won't ask you again."

I weighed the consequences of disobeying and determined that despite every warning sense within me crying for attention, leaving would be impossible at that moment. Entering the building had already damned me to a discussion and as I lifted the satchel over my head, I wondered how much else I had condemned myself toward. The way I sat across him communicated neither surrender, nor a challenge. He had the upper hand and the game was his to play.

Talbot nodded in recognition and offered a much gentler, more cordial smile to me. "Much better, thank you," he said. Both hands settled on his lap while he crossed one leg over the other. Aside from the crimson cloak, the remainder of his dress indicated someone of noble station, an amulet hanging from around his neck I couldn't be entirely certain wasn't enchanted. The idle thought that he might be just as little a man as his lieutenant crossed my mind. "Doesn't this all run much more smoothly when we cooperate?"

"I doubt I have much choice but to cooperate," I said, the tone of my voice maudlin. Lowering the satchel onto the ground, I assumed a similar posture as Talbot. "What formalities do you feel like discussing?"

He laughed. "These are hardly formalities. I presented a challenge to you and you met it. I thought perhaps we could parlay instead of resorting to the same brutal stand-off you just engaged in with Marcus."

"I'd think you more put off than of the mind to parlay."

"Over Marcus?" Talbot scoffed. "If he was apt to mock the sentimental, you'll find me much more willing to dismiss it. Besides, as you correctly noted, he was too given over to his jealousy. It caused him to underestimate you. A mistake I promise not to replicate."

Nodding, I settled into my chair. My eyes met his, though my mind remained vigilant, looking out for any sign the other man intended to warp my thoughts against me. "Both of you speak in riddles. I only determined he was jealous because of your discussions with him and Lady Cavendish. I admit I don't even know who this Henri is you keep referencing except that you claim he was my father."

"Because he was," Talbot responded, his tone of voice matter-of-fact and the expression on his face laden with amusement. "Richard Hardi was a fabrication, made up by a man in search of a new life. If there's one thing you mortals fool yourself into thinking, it's that you can outrun your past."

"You say the term 'mortal' as though you don't believe yourself one of them," I observed.

"Look into my eyes and tell me that I'm anything like you." He raised an eyebrow at me, sobering once more. "You saw what became of Marcus. Do you think he was an ordinary man?"

I fought against the urge to shudder, remembering the pile of ash. "Both of you look very human."

"A latent condition of what we once were. I stopped being human three centuries ago. Marcus, much more recently. He took the position I'd groomed your father for and to say he was a disappointing substitute fails to grasp how furious I was to lose Henri. Your father was one of my most loyal, most gifted sorcerers."

The anger I had summoned to defeat Marcus seemed nowhere to

be found. A frown tugged at the corners of my mouth, my shoulders heavy and my chest tight. "I fail to see the man I called father in the picture you paint."

"You're wounded. It's reasonable for you to be. I can't imagine what it would feel like to discover a man I idolized once believed in the same cause I saw kill him. A person could lie to you and shelter your feelings, but honestly, it would benefit neither of us for me to do so. You need to see the truth."

"To what end?" I asked, wondering how much of my heart I truly wore on my sleeve.

Talbot slid his hands to grip onto his knee, a small smile returning to his lips. "You hate me," he said. "And yet, you don't know why. Certainly, my followers killed your father and I see the boy within who wants to claw at my face, as though that would restore Henri to life. It's time to grow up, though, Christian. You have no reason to loathe me. What happened to your father is as simple as what would happen to anyone who crossed *your* group of mercenaries."

"And how had he crossed you?"

"Oh, those artifacts he took from me were things I had spent many years searching for. You'll forgive me if I was upset to discover them gone when he ran away from us."

"He stole from you."

"I promise nobody has been fabricating that, least of all me. You seem to have recovered the memory of our brief discussion. And somehow, you know about Lady Cavendish and her discussions with us." His smile broadened wide enough to reveal teeth which matched the daggers Marcus boasted. "Look at you. All grown up and come into your own as a sorcerer. It's strong in your family and you have a chance to cultivate it."

"You'll forgive *me* if I decline the offer after being sequestered by one of your harlots."

Talbot barked out a laugh, lifting a hand to slap his knee. "Oh, if Jane could hear you, her ears would be red right now. These men and women of noble birth get very indignant about their station. I should know. Your father was full of himself when he first met us."

I raised an eyebrow. "What does that mean?"

"Oh, I apologize. I keep referring to him only as Henri, when the full title was Henri d'Avignon. He was the second son of a Count, in a family which had once held strong ties to witchcraft until they curried favor with the Roman Church. His father especially denied his birthright, but Henri stumbled upon his talents unwittingly at an early age." Talbot sighed. "Short sighted mortals, really. They disowned him and granted him only the mercy of being spared an execution."

My tone of voice turned incredulous. "My father was nobility?"

"Born into it, but not with any right toward inheritance when I rescued him. It might have made him more apt to be grateful, but I'd like to think what I offered meant more to him than food and comfort."

"And what was that?"

Talbot lifted a hand, turning his wrist and causing the table in front of us to shift its position. I jumped and he chuckled at my reaction. "Be honest. Christian," he said. "It's the same thing that led you to follow Lady Cavendish down to Plymouth. He wanted to learn his true nature and I provided him the chance."

"I followed her to find your ilk," I retorted. My gaze flicked from him to his hand and back again.

"The lies you tell yourself. You escaped and rode right into a trap, but if you had escaped, what would you have done with yourself? Found work killing people elsewhere? Perhaps settle into an honest living like your father tried to?" Talbot leaned forward in his seat, repositioning his hands to the top of the table. "Let me tell you what his life was like, since your eyes were too young and ignorant to see it. He trapped himself within a personal hell, always wanting to touch the power he held and always less of himself when it didn't fit into his new life. That is the fate that would await you – one of denial and disappointment."

"I might take my chances with it just the same."

"You and I both know you aren't walking out of here alive."

My heart fluttered as the unspoken threat finally made it past his lips. He raised an eyebrow at me and I countered with one of my own. "I thought you considered killing me a waste," I said, attempting to sound more confident than I suddenly felt.

"It would be. But what's keeping you alive right now is at the very heart of our discussion. You have something I want and you are going to hand it over to me," he said.

"How am I to get it if you're not allowing me to walk out of here alive?"

"Because, there are more states of existence than simply alive or dead. What I have for you is a proposition I once extended to Henri, and want to extend to you now."

Talbot encroached further still upon me, and though I felt his gaze drawing me in, I sensed no trickery in his eyes. They both plead with me and commanded me and for a moment, I felt my breaths turn shallow, my eyes get lost in his. "You chose the path of a solitary man," he began. "The rogue who kills for coin, and however you dressed it up to your conscience, you've enjoyed what you've done. What attachment do you have, then, to the mortal world?"

I swallowed past a lump forming in my throat. "My brother. My family. My friends," I said, having enough presence of mind not to list Paolo by name.

"A few personal attachments. Precious little more," he countered, "And all of them so fragile. I could walk out of here after wiping your blood from my hands and break them like twigs." Talbot snapped his fingers as though to prove a point. "That is your first choice. Die like your father had and know I will not relent in my quest to burn everything you love in search of what I want. I do hope I have your attention."

I nodded once, allowing this to suffice as my answer. While Talbot's expression remained serious, he relaxed by a small margin, his demeanor turning pleasant again. "Or," he continued, "You could claim the second choice." Uncrossing his legs, Talbot rose to a stand. Nothing in his posture suggested I should do likewise, so I remained seated in my chair while he strode around where I sat. I sensed him behind me, hearing him crouch and feeling his breath on my neck as he whispered. "Leave this human world behind and cross through the veil to where I am."

My eyes shut, my posture tensing. "Is this the other state of existence to which you were referring?" I asked.

"Another form of eternal life. A much surer proposition than any priest could offer."

"I have never held much stock in the church, sir."

"And neither should you. Ours is the realm of signs and wonders, Christian. You have already made the elements dance, but you have yet to know true dominion over them. These foolish families war over a throne because it's the only power they will ever know, but I control something far more potent. And one by one, I will make them bend the knee to me. This is inevitable. If you are at my right hand, then the people you cherish will be protected. I could strip Henri's brother of his title and place it at your feet, but that would be a pittance compared to what you will have. Dominion over death. And control over the lives of your few human attachments."

My eyes opened slowly, an eyebrow rising in response to the wording of Talbot's proposition. While I heard the part of his offer meant to grip my attention, I couldn't help but to focus on the piece of the puzzle falling into place. I might have never figured out what my father's scroll meant. I might have not considered the medallion I wore around my neck held much other importance other than sentimental attachment. But as I followed the trail of the Luminaries from one noble family to the next, I could only ever harbor the paranoia of something sinister afoot.

Talbot had done more than present a threat veiled in a promise. He had offered me the first glimpse into what I feared when I confessed my suspicions to Jeffrey. I tensed in my chair as I considered the power-hungry and the distracted, members of both warring families of England accepting Talbot's hand and playing right into a trap. Whatever had turned Richard – Henri; whoever my father had been – against the man standing behind me, I had to wonder if I sat in the same position he had.

"Are you certain this offer isn't simply your own judgment being muddled?" I asked, tilting my head to bare more skin to him, observing his fascination with my neck once more. Sinking against the back of my chair, I attempted to make my posture more inviting, inhaling deeply and exhaling in staccato. "You had a weakness for him, didn't you?"

Talbot chuckled. Another gust of breath caressed my throat, his presence looming ever closer. "I heard you mention me stealing a taste of you to Marcus." A hand settled on my other shoulder. "I'll admit his jealousy wasn't entirely unfounded. And my, you are quite the temptation."

"You wish to steal another taste?" I remained still as a statue, my gaze stealing to the hearth across the room. I refused to look away from it.

"Oh, I have yet to take one. I promise you will know when that happens and will find yourself begging for more." His tongue dragged across the back of my neck, causing the wound which had been inflicted there to tingle. I struggled to maintain my focus through it. Flames crackled over wooden logs in the hearth. The walls of the inn had been fashioned in wood, as had the floors, with stone supporting the structure. Fire, I told myself. They had been afraid of fire.

I had to be mad to consider what I was about to do.

Paolo, forgive me. Tell my brother I apologize. I should have listened to him. Always know I love you.

Talbot moaned and I shuddered. The next time his tongue slithered across my skin, I felt something sharp with it, trying desperately not to envision the teeth these inhuman creatures possessed while knowing that was precisely what pricked my flesh. His mouth hovered over my pulse point and it was all I could do not to clench my eyes shut. Instead, I focused long and hard on the bright oranges and yellows blazing not far away from where I sat. "You want me to succumb?" I asked, my voice a whisper.

"I want you to relent to what you know is best," he said. "What we both want. You want your dear ones protected. I want what your father stole."

"And if I don't give it to you, you'll kill them?"

"That is the way this world works, Christian. As a mercenary, you should respect that."

"I do." The lump in my throat bobbed as I swallowed hard. My world had become the colors. Little more. "And if I give you what you want, what becomes of everything else?"

"Does it truly concern you?" Talbot chuckled. His lips pursed, placing a kiss on my throat. "One of these days, my master's plans will be realized through me, and the world will be ours regardless. Better to be in control of your fate and the fate of those you cherish."

"I couldn't agree more."

"Then hold still, my precious boy." I heard the smile in his voice when he spoke again. "I promise to make it a very sweet surrender."

Finally, I allowed my eyes to shut, drawing one last breath in anticipation. "I'm afraid there is nothing sweet about how I intend to surrender."

"I beg your –"

Before he could finish the statement, I lifted both hands and poured all of the focus I could into the mental image I held of the flames. Truth be told, I didn't want to see the agent of my own demise. Not yet, anyway. I channeled the natural bond I had with fire and called to it again and again, fueling the hearth. The oil lamps in their sconces. The cups of ale on the wooden counter that had not been depleted, using it to contribute to the chaotic inferno I intended to create. Talbot stumbled back from me and I exhaled a breath, relenting toward lifting my lids at last to behold how I would perish.

"Stop this at once!" Talbot shouted. "You'll die with me."

"I am well aware of that." Narrowing my eyes, I rose to a stand and paced closer to the hearth. The roar of the fire had grown outside of its box, the lamps already licking flames at the wooden infrastructure of the building. Behind my back, I heard the sound of Talbot chanting an incantation and spun around to face him. I extended one of my hands toward the front door and glared, not bothering to peer at the entrance before causing it to go up in flames. "You said I won't leave here alive," I quipped. "So, we burn together."

Turning around, I set my sights on the back exit, shifting the direction of my hand and knowing that I was about to seal my own fate. It was the only thing that would keep the rest of them safe, I told myself, and yet my heart filled with sorrow as I envisioned my loved ones one last time. The boards of the back door smoldered while the temperature of the room rose. "*Te amo, amico mio,*" I said, intending these to be my last words.

Except that footfalls interrupted me, as did the sudden jerking of my sword from out of its sheath. My focus on the fire broke, but I shifted my attention too late as a sudden, inexplicably horrifying amount of pain surged through me. My mouth fell open, gaze still on the door before my eyes shifted down to the genesis of the agony. I saw metal gleaming in the fire light, protruding from the center of my torso and just above my gut.

Talbot extracted the blade before I could make as much as a whine. I toppled to the floor, unable to bear my own weight while both hands came to rest over the wound. As dark red coated my fingers, I shook and looked upward at the figure of Talbot, while he stepped around me and peered down at where I lay. "You stupid mortals," he said. "Always needing to go about this the difficult way."

He crouched before me and gripped a fistful of my cloak, pulling me up enough to look him in the eyes. I grimaced, resting my weight on my elbow while producing a strangled scream at being moved again. A cold, sadistic smile traced across Talbot's lips. "Well you wanted to be a martyr," he countered. "Did you really think I was just going to surrender to your suicide?" He freed one hand and as he lifted it, the flames I had created started to die down, retreating back into the hearth and lamps which had created them. Talbot shook his head, rueful, while glancing back at me. "Now, both of us know you're going to die like this and your family, then, with you. Are you sure you still want to reject my offer?'

"Go to hell," I managed, my voice strained.

"I'm sorry, what was that again?" Talbot reared back with the blade and plunged it through me again, gripping onto my shirt and cloak tight while the sword drove through my shoulder. I cried out, tears streaming from my eyes I couldn't stop, my vision swimming while I nearly begged for him to stop. It hurt more when he extracted the blade and I didn't know what to pray for; deliverance or death. He laughed, lifting the weapon to his mouth and licking the blood from it. "Won't be much of this left soon," he said. "It'll make turning you difficult if you hold out much longer. Perhaps I'll ask your brother. Or that foreign friend of yours Jane told me about. What do you think?"

"*You leave him the fuck alone,*" I countered. Somehow, I found some hidden reserve left in me. Agony racked me from head to toe, and yet I lifted my hand and pressed it against Talbot's face, singeing the flesh and forcing him to drop the sword. I collapsed onto my side as he fell backward, reaching for the shoulder wound, grabbing a fistful of my cloak with it and feeling the embroidered black rose in my palm. No, I told myself. No, no, no, no... I had to get out of there. I had to warn them all somehow.

"Binding..." I spoke the word aloud just as the thought came to me. Talbot lifted up onto all fours, but I ignored him, gripping the garment tighter while feeling the fabric turn sticky with blood. I gritted my teeth, pulling myself back up onto my elbow. "*Evocatio spiritualis,*" I said. Swallowing hard, I tried to clear my thoughts of all things. Talbot. The pain. The fear racing through me like quicksilver. I murmured the words to the spell I had cast only a short while ago, seeing Jane confined to the bed and trying to use the magic to force myself together again. Tingles raced up my spine. The energy I drew in flowed from hand to cloak and prickled at my skin as I repeated the spell over and over again.

'I bind myself. I bind myself. I bind...'

Until something stopped up the words from forming in my throat and prevented them from being birthed. The sound of shifting footsteps from behind me told me Talbot had come to a stand, but the pain through my chest bore such a bite to it, I could no longer fashion thought. As the weapon withdrew, I fell onto my back, seeing the ceiling above me and darkness encroach upon my periphery. There were no other pleas left for me to offer. No other tricks up my sleeve. The black overtook me and I was powerless to resist.

My pulse stilled inside my ears. The world turned cold before fading out of existence altogether.

Stretched out on a wooden floor – in Tavistock, England – I drew my final breath and perished.

EPILOGUE

I had no idea how long I had been sleeping when my consciousness woke again, but the world had become black and stayed that way. I gasped as if expecting to breathe and shivered, head turning from side to side in an attempt for me to gage my bearings. I saw nothing and gave into the compulsion to scream, knowing I was lying on my back and yet, not able to feel anything beneath me. The sound I produced resonated in a discordant manner before fading abruptly. I fought the urge to panic while aware I should have a pulse thudding in my chest.

"Oh God, where am I?" I asked, ignoring how frightened my voice sounded. "What happened to me?" I lifted my hands, reaching out toward into the darkness without hitting anything solid. Pulling them back, I shook and wished there was something to claw at, but encountered nothing. Brief tendrils of blue light began accompanying my violent flails and when one caught the rough impression of what looked to be a plant, I immediately stopped. I flicked my hand again, spying the item of interest and finally identifying it as a root surrounded by what could only be dirt.

If that was so, than this meant I was underground.

"Bloody hell." Shutting my eyes, I tried to swallow and failed to feel the usual contraction of my throat muscles. Everything felt off somehow, out of sync and at the same time my mind was not yet able to process what I might be experiencing. Was this a dream, I wondered as I paused to stare at the space in front of me.

Regardless of the answer, I realized I had no other alternative than to progress forward.

I hesitated, steeling my nerves, before attempting to figure out what I needed to do next. Go above ground, that much was certain, but each time I reached for something – the root, a clod of dirt – I snatched thin air, which meant I had to form a different tactic. Well, I reasoned to myself, if this was a dream, the normal rules didn't apply. Preempting the decision with a nod, I willed myself away from the rational and into the bizarre, picturing myself simply levitating toward where I might see the sun. As foolish as it left me feeling, within seconds, it began to work.

The laugh I produced sounded just as twisted as the entire experience had become. Passing through the earth, I saw the sky and stopped, righting myself until my feet settled where the ground should be. Once more, I failed to feel anything under me, and at first I crouched and groped like mad for purchase on the grass in an effort to prove my fingers could do something other than pass through objects without interacting. As I did, though, another revelation forced me to pause and take stock of it as well.

While the ground should have been a more verdant hue of green, it was a blander shade, and yet one not without some ethereal quality to it. I thought about the tendrils of blue, turning my gaze toward my hand and seeing a faint light ebb and flow from me as though I had become a living wick and it, the fire on my skin. I still wore the clothes of my employ, and saw the cloak hanging from my shoulders when I turned my head to study the rest of my attire, but the glow gained orange sparks when the first pang of fear ripped through my already shattered psyche.

"What is all of this? Am I dead?" I murmured. A frown tugged at the corners of my mouth, the flecks of orange intermingling all the more with the iridescent blue as my panic grew in intensity. I made the motion of breathing again, forcing myself to look downward again and hone in on the sight of the grass. My feet only needed to settle on it, I told myself. That was all I needed for now. I would figure the rest out when I could just *stand* instead of levitating.

A full flash of red overtook me until I became mad enough to force the soles of my boots down the sparse space I needed them to descend. Once I settled, the sapphire ebbed back into life as my nerves quieted, apt to take the minor victory, just as I promised myself. My gaze lifted to regard the horizon, seeing the moorland stretched out before me with an eastward road running several acres away. Still, the color of the world was wrong in a way which unnerved me.

I knew it was daytime, but the light still seemed faded, much like everything else aside from the colors flickering around my aura. The clouds didn't appear as white. I wrapped both arms around my chest and collapsed onto the ground, in a seated position, wishing I could feel something that indicated I had form or substance to me. There was no nausea, however. No protest in my limbs when I adjusted my position. A soul-piercing scream made it past my lips and yet, it failed to burn my chest or my throat no matter how long and hard I let it out. Currents of vermillion bled through the blue surrounding me and in that moment, I would have sold my soul for the ability to cry. Unable to do even that, I felt the urge to simply surrender to numbness while not knowing if I would even feel that again.

Slumping to my side, I drew my knees up to my chest and hugged them there. The clouds drifted from one part of the horizon to the next and misery mixed with exhaustion as I watched them pass. It was too much to take in that moment – too many things to process – so I decided against it for the time being.

The world faded into black once more. For how long, I could not tell.

To Be Continued...

CONNOR PETERSON

Shadowcast

Book Two

IN ACKNOWLEDGEMENT

And so, we embark on another journey. While writing stories about the vampire Flynn, I've gotten back in the habit of spending each November writing a 50,000 word novel and this is how Deathspell was born. Christian Richardson has been a figure in my mind for a lot longer, but when NaNoWriMo gave me a chance to bring him into the literary world, it filled a fond hope I've had to finally write a historical fantasy. I love history almost as much as I love vampires.

Let me tell you, though, you learn to appreciate history really quickly when you decide to embark on such an undertaking.

In that light, this book is dedicated to two sets of people. For one: The historians who have provided the wealth of knowledge I was able to read both in print and on the Internet. Christian lives during a time period known as the Wars of the Roses and if it wasn't for all of the information readily accessible about period dress, Medieval culture – hell, how to light a candle back before matches – this would have been an anachronistic mess.

The second set is dedicated to the other writers who have undertaken this mad journey called National Novel Writing Month. I've been participating off and on now for almost ten years and have had the chance to meet some truly remarkable local writers through it. It's a blessing and a challenge to share our life experiences, and become better wordsmiths through the effort. Every year, I look forward to seeing you again.

As always, these books are dedicated to my better half as well, who is the reason these harebrained plots and ideas become the cultivated stories they are. I couldn't do it without any of you who stand behind me and give me encouragement. It's a new adventure and I'm excited to bring you all along for the ride.

To brave new worlds!

Connor Peterson
April, 2015

CALLING ALL READERS

You've already done something I appreciate - having this book in your hands. If you could do one thing more, please consider leaving a review on your favorite book platform.

Printed in Great Britain
by Amazon

57276221R00135